T0267823

SPINNING AROUND
The Kylie Playlist

Aboriginal and Torres Strait Islander readers are advised
that this book contains references to people who have died

SPINNING AROUND

The Kylie Playlist

EDITED BY
KIRSTEN KRAUTH AND
ANGELA SAVAGE

FREMANTLE PRESS

The Kylie Playlist

Kylie Q&A

Kirsten Krauth, Angela Savage

How would you go about creating a Kylie playlist? When we were approached with this idea – a playlist of fiction, non-fiction and poetry responding to Kylie's songs – we were excited about the possibilities. Kylie's list of achievements and awards from the past five decades is phenomenal and her star continues to rise.

On top of her impressive music career, she has raised millions for various philanthropic causes and received an honorary Doctorate in Health Sciences for her work in raising awareness of breast cancer. In inducting her into the ARIA Hall of Fame in 2011, then prime minister Julia Gillard described Kylie not only as 'the face of Australia', but as a 'woman of courage and compassion', highlighting her decision to perform and fundraise in Japan in the wake of the devastating earthquake and tsunami earlier that year.

While we were both entrenched 80s pop fans, we found that as we approached some of our favourite Australian writers – and they joined in with gusto – their words and ideas gave new depth to our understanding of Kylie, debunking myths, opening up new worlds. Each discovery about Kylie prompted a flurry of excited texts between us – Have you seen this? Did you know that? – and we thought we'd continue the conversation here.

Angela Savage: I've never met Kylie in person but I think you have, Kirsten? I remember a story you told me about meeting her at Festival Hall.

Kirsten Krauth: Yes, I was about fourteen. I was small but Kylie was tiny, even littler than I'd imagined, diaphanous, all hair. They seemed like blond gods up there on the stage. Kylie. Jason. Craig. It was the early days of *Neighbours* and Kylie was the neatest mechanic ever.

I'd seen her duets with Danni on *Young Talent Time* and watched her in *The Henderson Kids* and now I was at Festival Hall in a dancing competition and the judge was Kylie. I was trying to channel Tania Lacy, doing the 'Locomotion', and I hit that zone you only reach rarely, you know, where your body becomes the music, and then I felt it – the gold sparkle of connecting with Kylie. I looked up and she was watching me.

When Molly Meldrum pointed me out in the crowd, I couldn't believe it. I was relayed by a sea of hands before the bouncers dumped me on the stage.

Kylie held out a signed t-shirt out to me, but before I received the prize, Molly announced that I'd have to dance on my own. I was suddenly very aware of the size of Festival Hall, standing in the place of all those I'd seen before – The Police, INXS, New Order.

I turned around and danced towards the back of the stage but then I looked across to Kylie who smiled back and started to move, too, the kindness shining on her face.

AS: Kindness is one of Kylie's striking qualities. In the course of researching this book, I scoured her resumé without turning up a single trace of scandal – not even prima donna behaviour. I got excited when I found a 1998 clip on YouTube, 'Kylie Minogue Gets Angry at Rude Reporter'. But the headline turned out to be misleading. As someone wrote in the comments, 'So that's what it's like to piss off Kylie. She just smiles harder at you.' I feel like I've grown up with Kylie. Do you?

KK: Yeah. Like many women now in their fifties, I can trace my life through the looks of Kylie. At the time I didn't even know it, but my photo albums have the cookie-cutter stamp of her hair and pose and make-up and outfits. She was reflecting cultural trends too; it was an interchange. The indie Kylie and the femme fatale Kylie and the perm Kylie in the bath blowing bubbles, her face free of the mask.

I wore the white-blonde pixie haircut after Michael Hutchence led Kylie through the crowd at *The Delinquents* launch, the media clamouring, screaming, that Michael had brought out the sexy in her – as if Kylie had no sense of herself or agency at all.

And then Nick Cave the impresario pulling her into his dark murderous world. But I think it was really the other way round – Nick and Michael hitching a ride on Kylie's love train, moving at the speed of light.

AS: I love that image of Kylie's love train! Anyone who has worked with her has nothing but praise for Kylie, using words like 'charming', 'unassuming', 'endearing'. In a recent documentary on legendary record producers Stock Aitken Waterman, who recorded Kylie's first pop hits in the 1980s, Mike Stock describes Kylie as 'the ideal, perfect person. She dances. She sings. She's lovely.'

KK: That doco was so revealing, wasn't it? I had no idea how enormously successful both Kylie and Jason Donovan were in the UK at that time. From that early period, why do you think she became such a gay icon?

AS: I think that loveliness and her evolving sense of style played a big part. Kylie's affinity with the gay community is so deep that the collective noun for Sydney gay men is reputedly a 'Minogue of gays'. I also read that Rufus Wainwright, in listing Kylie among his Top 10 Gay Icons in 2006, described her as 'the gay shorthand for joy.'

KK: She also seems to bring out ambivalence and contradictory feelings in our authors as well ...

AS: That's why I found Dmetri Kakmi's essay 'Slow' so compelling, where he confesses that out of a contrariness born of internalised homophobia, for years he couldn't like Kylie because 'other gays idolise[d her]'. Similarly, in Holden Sheppard's 'Your Disco Needs You', Thomas, fearful of being outed, insists that 'a bloke going to a Kylie Minogue concert is a public declaration of homosexuality'.

Kylie has publicly expressed her gratitude to the gay community for sticking by her through the low points in her career, just as she's stuck by them.

KK: I remember you telling me about your friend who saw her at the Mardi Gras.

AS: Yes, a mate of mine saw Kylie perform at the showgrounds at the 1994 Mardi Gras parade after-party, sitting alongside a friend who was dying of AIDS. After finishing her set with 'Better the Devil You Know', Kylie turned to the 13,000-strong audience and said, 'Thank you for inviting me to your party.' My friend teared up as he recalled this story thirty years on, still moved by the pop icon's humility.

KK: What strikes me is the range of Kylie's career. Along with the hundreds of pop songs in various genres, there are the fashion statements and innovations, the awards, the films and TV appearances, even *Doctor Who*! Kylie's choices have always been bold (German, italic – see Nick Gadd's essay) and she is not afraid to make mistakes. She has a particular talent for comedy and irony. Her work with Kylie Mole and her guest turn as Epponnee-Raelene Charlene Kathleen Darleen Craig on *Kath and Kim* reveal this ability to send herself up to great effect. I really enjoyed watching those clips again.

AS: Me, too—and I love how Alice Pung's 'Put Yourself in My Place' taps into Kylie's sense of humour.

KK: One high point was when Nick Cave encouraged her to take part in The Poetry Olympics in the UK, where she got up on stage in her trackie daks and read out the lyrics to 'I Should Be So Lucky', clearly dedicating certain loving sections to Nick as she turned around to float the words his way. Very funny and empowering in its own way. She also loves collaborating … What's your favourite Kylie collaboration?

AS: There are so many! Along with Jason and Nick, she's done duets with Bono, Robbie Williams, The Wiggles, Kermit the Frog, Pet Shop Boys, Sigala, Shaggy, Flight Facilities, Frank Sinatra, Dua Lipa, and her sister Dannii. My two personal favourites are her duet with Jimmy Little of 'Bury Me Deep In Love', and her performance with John Farnham of The Isley Brothers' 'Shout' at the Tour of Duty concert for the troops in East Timor in 1999.

KK: It also seemed that she was often the person holding everyone else together, the glue, ever professional. Just watch the awkward live performance on MTV Most Wanted of 'Death is Not the End' in 1995, Kylie shepherding Nick and Shane McGowan, two lost tribesmen, towards the light.

AS: You and I have mused on the number of stories and poems in this anthology that touch on themes of reinvention, and also the scope of genres – crime, speculative fiction, romance, even a ghost story – inspired by Kylie's songs. This diversity in the writing isn't surprising, given Kylie's career. But I wonder to what extent her collaborators shaped that career, when I've heard her say, 'I have so many characters lurking in my body, it's frightening!'

KK: I love that line – probably why I find her video clips so entertaining!

AS: You said earlier that you used to watch *Neighbours* in the early days. You know, when Charlene married her beau, Scott, played by Kylie's then-boyfriend Jason Donovan, nearly twenty million viewers in the UK tuned in to watch – more people than the entire population of Australia at the time. In 1988, she became the first person to win four Logie Awards in one year, including the coveted Gold Logie as Australia's Most Popular Television Performer.

KK: Her rise to fame was incredibly quick, but in my memory she wasn't taken very seriously in Australia at the time. She said that Mushroom Records didn't know how to spell 'pop'.

AS: Yes, she enjoyed earlier and greater critical acclaim for her music in Britain than in Australia, where local critics dismissively dubbed her 'the singing budgie'.

KK: There's some fantastic footage of Molly mentioning this and Kylie flapping her wings in response.

AS: She has called out tall poppy syndrome and its influence on her decision to relocate from Melbourne to the UK in 1990. And the barbs clearly hurt: inducted into the ARIA Hall of Fame, Kylie teared up, telling reporters, 'To finally be here and be acknowledged is very nice.' At that stage, she had released eleven albums, sold sixty-three million records and been awarded an OBE. She remains the highest selling solo Australian artist of all time.

She remains the highest selling solo Australian artist of all time. The Princess of Pop.

KK: I did a tour of the Kylie collection at the Arts Centre Melbourne and saw Charlene's King Gee overalls. It's a treasure trove of her costumes, tracing a history of performance and textiles. But I was really there for the hot pants! Small, gold and now too fragile to touch, they've become strangely iconic. They were sitting in a drawer and pulled out for me to inspect, the feeling almost like being in a morgue. Bought at a flea market, they can no longer be exhibited or moved as they are on the edge of disintegration. It's interesting though. I didn't respond really to the clothes displayed, perhaps because they are lifeless without Kylie inhabiting them, spinning around and shimmying on the dance floor.

The amazing thing about working on this book is that when we began it was relatively quiet on the Kylie front. And then 'Padam Padam' came out. As this single soars around the world, I've come to see Kylie as a tour de force in the longevity of her songmaking, her willingness to experiment, her fierce ambition and curation of the world around her. It's taken a long time for this to be fully recognised (five decades), an attempt made to move beyond the façade.

AS: I agree. I have so much respect for Kylie. At an age when most performers are releasing greatest hits compilations and – to paraphrase art critic Robert Hughes – hibernating on the bear fat of their youth, Kylie keeps working on new material and with stunning results.

As we were putting the finishing touches on this anthology, she won the 2024 Grammy Award for best pop dance recording for 'Padam Padam'. She'd won her first Grammy twenty years earlier, for best dance recording for 'Come Into My World'. The Grammy came in the wake of breaking the record for the longest time between appearances on Triple J Radio's Hottest 100: 'Padam Padam' coming in at number forty-eight, twenty-seven years after she last appeared on the list with 'Did It Again'.

In a red-carpet interview on the way to the Grammy Awards ceremony, I was shocked by the power of Kylie's work ethic. Talking about the evolution of her career, she told *Rolling Stone's* Delisa

Shannon, 'I use a surfing analogy a lot – a surfer I am not – but you paddle. You're never going to catch a wave unless you're paddling. And I paddle.'

She's truly an inspiration to creatives everywhere.

Speaking of inspiration, Kirsten, did you ever wear the t-shirt you won in the dance competition?

KK: Sadly, no. It's been sitting at the bottom of my band t-shirt pile for nearly forty years as I've moved around the country. The names – Kylie. Jason. Craig – have faded in red pen the way pop stars and hits blur into obscurity. The t-shirt has a slogan to warn teenagers about the perils of drinking. I think about getting it framed, safe behind glass.

But Kylie, in red, she doesn't fade. Kylie sits astride a car wreck, aflame in billowing red. Small, blonde, smiling, malleable. Always underestimated.

AS: And radiant. Always radiant.

Our heartfelt thanks to all the writers who jumped on board Kylie's love train with us. You, too, are radiant.

And to all the readers, it's time to press play. We recommend listening to the songs as you read each story – and feel free to dance!

I Should Be So Lucky
Angela Savage

My plan to drive from Melbourne to Mildura in a day is foiled by a dead galah. The mounting roadkill is already creeping me out, but the sight of the dead bird's mate fretting over its body tips me over the edge. I have to pull over.

The Corolla's aircon is broken and the seatbelt buckle, iron-hot, threatens to burn through my dress. I nearly scorch my fingertips as I undo the clasp and peel myself from the seat. A light breeze outside is no match for the sun. I spread my touring map on the bonnet to find a new destination. Back in the car, I swig lukewarm water and restart the engine. The radio kicks into life for the first time this side of Wycheproof with 'New Sensation' by INXS.

Moments later, I'm passing through Sea Lake, where a tall, slender young man stands by the war memorial with his thumb out. Shaggy hair and tight jeans, he looks like Michael Hutchence. Melbourne Margie wouldn't dream of picking up a hitchhiker. But Mallee Margie is tired of being timid and figures she could do with the distraction.

Pulling over, I call through the open passenger window, 'I'm only going as far as Ouyen.'

Michael Hutchence shrugs. 'That'll do.' He throws a drab olive duffle bag on to the back seat, slides in next to me and extends his hand. 'Simon.'

'Margie.'

Up close, he's older than I first thought. Late twenties, maybe. He smells of tobacco, dust and cologne. Nice. Not the cheap stuff.

I resume driving. For once, I desist from starting a conversation.

'Where you from?' Simon asks.

'Melbourne.'

'Where you headed?'

'Not sure yet,' I lie.

'I get it.' Simon nods at windscreen. 'Wherever the road takes you, right?'

'Something like that.'

I feel his eyes on me. 'We've got about an hour before we hit Ouyen. If you'd prefer to sit in silence and listen to the radio, I won't bother you. But if you'd like to confess your deepest secrets to someone you'll probably never see again in your life, I'm your man.'

I laugh in spite of myself. He takes it as an invitation.

'A schoolteacher like you—' he begins.

'How do you know I'm a teacher?'

'Apart from the anthology of poetry on the back seat and the amount of stuff on your keyring, you dress like a teacher.'

My cotton frock is yellow with daisies. I finger the button at my neck, wondering if I should take offence. Wondering, too, when I became so straitlaced.

'As I was saying, a schoolteacher like you driving across the Mallee with no destination in mind – who broke your heart, Margie?'

The question is spot-on, catching me off guard.

'His name's John. He's a prick, but it took me a long time to see it.'

More than two years. Ten percent of my life. Wasted.

'What about you? What brings you to the middle of nowhere?'

'Speaking of the middle of nowhere—' he gestures outside, 'have you ever seen Lake Tyrrell? There's a turn-off up ahead. Worth a stop.'

I feel the sharp pang of fear. Simon doesn't seem like the psycho-killer type, but after John, I no longer trust my own judgement.

Perhaps sensing my concern, he adds, 'No worries at all if you'd rather not, Margie.'

There's something in the way he says my name that reassures me. I swing right at the turn-off and follow an unsealed track to what turns out to be more desert than lake. The horizon trembles in the hot, still air. Seagulls wail in the distance. We walk to the edge of a shallow depression encrusted with salt, a repository of tears.

'Victoria's largest and oldest inland salt lake,' Simon says. 'Tyrrell is based on the local Aboriginal word for sky. It's even more impressive when there's water in it.'

'Sounds like you're a teacher, too.'

He laughs. 'I'm just a reader.'

My interest is piqued, but I don't let it show. Instead, I shade my eyes and gaze out over the vast white expanse, feeling the sweat run beneath my schoolmarm's dress.

Back in the car, Simon asks if he can smoke. In response, I push in the lighter on the dashboard and pull out the ashtray.

'Want one?'

Though I haven't smoked in ages, I accept the proffered Winfield Blue.

'You were about to tell me how you ended up in the middle of nowhere,' I say.

'I'm on my way north.' He blows smoke out the window. 'Fruit picking.'

'Where?'

'Leaving it to chance. Mildura. Robinvale. Depends on my luck with rides. A bit far west now for Swan Hill.'

He's like a character from a Steinbeck novel.

'You pick fruit before?'

'For a few years now. Pay's not bad and you meet people from all over. My plan is to meet enough people to travel the world without ever having to stay in hotels.'

'I like hotels.'

'You might want to reconsider Ouyen,' he says. 'Crap motel or rooms above a pub. Great pub, though.'

'I reckon I can rough it.'

We smoke in companionable silence while Angry Anderson sings 'Suddenly'. To think I'd actually cried when they played that song at Charlene and Scott's wedding on *Neighbours*. Listening to it now, the lyrics don't even make sense. But back then, I'd given in to the fantasy: the frosted tips, the white lace, the baby's breath – the whole fairytale.

I glance at the ring finger on my left hand and see the ghost of a band already disappearing beneath the sun and dust of the Mallee.

'Do they do food at the Ouyen pub?' I ask Simon, butting out my cigarette.

'Food, drink, pool. Are you up for it?'

I feel the smile reach my eyes. 'Best offer I've had in ages.'

***

Ouyen's Victoria Hotel is a double-storey red-brick building running the length of the block, broad verandas on both floors. The entrance is a grandiose archway of ceramic pillars and shiny oxblood tiles like the opening to a bloody chamber. A note at reception directs us to ask at the bar for Sharon. A blunt blonde with eyelashes like spider's legs, Sharon assigns me a room without asking for a name and informs me the bathrooms are shared.

Simon makes no move to book a room for himself.

'You're not staying here?' I jingle my key.

'I'll sort something else out.' He leans over the bar. 'Can I leave my bag at reception?'

'At your own risk,' Sharon says.

Simon shrugs. 'Not much worth stealing.'

'You can leave it in my room,' I say and, having pegged him as a freeloader, I add pointedly, 'Pick it up before you leave tonight, okay.'

'Thanks, Margie. Will do.'

I look for irony in his smile, mildly deflated when I find none.

Upstairs, he surprises me by stripping off his grubby blue shirt in the corridor. I glimpse dark nipples, a wisp of chest hair and the outline of ribs before he shimmies into a black INXS t-shirt and hands me the bag. We agree to meet in the bar.

After a cool shower, I slip on my white shirt-dress, leaving the top two buttons undone. Using a scrunchie, I wrangle my damp hair into a high ponytail and dab on some coral lipstick. Halfway down the stairs, I remember we might play pool and button my dress to the neck to hide my cleavage. Country towns and all that.

Simon, standing at the bar, catches my eye and orders drinks. Sipping my beer beneath the impervious gaze of a stuffed Murray River cod, I take stock of the room. Ruddy-faced men in shorts and workboots drink pots of Carlton Draught at uneven clusters of tables. The few women scattered among them perch on barstools like hungry birds. 'The Boys Light Up' is playing on a jukebox. The air smells of spilt beer, stale cigarettes and release.

At the pool table is a behemoth, gut overhanging faded jeans, greasy hair jammed beneath a trucker's cap bearing the Eureka flag. One of those guys whose lumbering gait belies the uncanny dexterity of his game. His doubles companion, Laurel to his Hardy, sports a lush black mullet and a missing incisor that evokes Bon Scott. Their opposition, a pair of young men in matching orange shirts, watch with hands in their pockets as the behemoth smashes his way through the balls on the table.

'You up for a game?' Simon says.

'Sure, but I haven't played in ages.'

'Good thing I'm not competitive then.'

Behemoth pots the black as we approach. I place two twenty-cent pieces on the side rail.

'Chalkboard.' Bon Scott gestures at the wall.

I start to add my name to the list, only getting as far as the 'M' before Simon stops me.

'Use fake names,' he whispers. 'We're in a strange place.'

'Let's make one up for each other then,' I say. Turning the M into 'Michael', I smile and hand him the chalk. 'You look like a Michael.' I glance at the INXS t-shirt. 'But you already know that.'

'And you look like a Kylie,' he says, writing my alias next to his.

'I should be so lucky.'

He laughs. 'I see what you did there.'

'Imagine Michael and Kylie as an item,' I say.

'A woman who dates Jason Donovan would never go out with Michael Hutchence.'

I drain my beer. 'Don't underestimate Kylie.'

***

When I return with fresh drinks, Behemoth and Bon have defeated the boys in orange, who, seemingly undaunted, add their names to the chalkboard again. Michael – as I remind myself to think of him – racks up for our game. We check the rules – no penalty shots on the black, foul and the game is over – and start to play.

Michael pockets a small off the break. He sinks another, narrowly missing a hat-trick.

'What are we on?' Behemoth asks Bon.

'Bigs.'

'Bigs?' Behemoth screws up his face. 'I fuckin' hate bigs.'

He proceeds to sink five bigs in a row but knocks one of ours in on the fifth shot, giving me a two-shot penalty.

I twist the tip of my cue against the blue cube of chalk, adding some to my hand to counter the sweat.

My first shot sends the five just short of the pocket. I glance at Simon, who tilts his chin ever so slightly. I feel the thrill of synergy, leave the five and play the four. When it drops into the side pocket, another frisson. My third shot is pure luck, though I act like I meant it, and follow with another pocket. Simon whistles and my adrenaline levels go through the roof. We're equal with Behemoth and Bon.

My run ends on the next shot, though I leave both our balls well positioned. 'Nice team shot, Kylie,' Michael says as I hand him the cue.

I hold my breath as Bon sinks their two remaining balls, before snookering himself on the black, giving Michael another chance. He proceeds to pocket both remaining smalls but misses what would have been the winning shot. Behemoth swiftly takes the game.

'Macca.' He thrusts out a meaty hand. 'Onya, mate. That's the closest game me and Chook've had for a while.'

'Yeah, nice one, Kylie.' Chook weighs in, shaking my hand with unexpected delicacy. 'Not often a lady gives us a run for our money.'

Michael nods at Macca's near-empty glass. 'Can we shout a round for you winners?'

There's that synergy again: kill 'em with kindness, take the edge off their aggression.

'Not competitive my arse,' I say when he returns with the drinks.

'You can talk, Kylie, you pool shark.'

Margie would've protested, insisting she was merely lucky. But false modesty is not Kylie's style.

'I used to be pretty good back at teachers' college. My girlfriends and I would challenge guys like Macca and Chook, then stack the jukebox with ABBA songs to put them off their game. Worked a charm.'

Michael's nods towards the jukebox. 'Let's see what they've got here.'

There's no ABBA, but there's enough for me to work with. I drop in a gold coin. To lull our opposition into a false sense of security, I start with a few pub standards, before bringing out the big guns: Madonna and Minogue.

Back at the pool table, both teams have two balls remaining.

'I don't know if Macca and Chook are fading, or their opposition is getting better,' Michael says.

He offers me a cigarette. I draw back deeply, making up for lost time.

'Have you peaked yet?' he asks.

'Sorry?'

'You know, that moment where you're just drunk enough and your confidence gives you skills you didn't know you had?'

'Not quite. I'm saving it for the rematch.'

He smiles and touches his glass to mine. 'Cheers.'

I sip my drink, conscious of sweat trickling down my back. But it doesn't bother me. In the heat, beer and haze of smoke, I feel alive.

Despite their comeback, the orange shirts lose before our cigarettes are done and it's my turn to rack up. I'm poised for my opening shot when 'Jailbreak' comes on the jukebox.

'Did you put this on?' Chook asks, his face flushed.

I stand, cautious, cue by my side. 'Yes.'

Chook gives me the thumbs-up. '*Maaate!*'

I nod and play, pocketing a big off the break and following through with another. The remaining balls are clustered and rather than break them up, I edge one towards a centre pocket.

Chook, singing along to AC/DC, smashes the cluster, sinking one of our balls. Michael takes the penalty, pockets two in a row, sets up another two.

If Macca is rattled by our lead, he doesn't show it, potting five in a row to even the score.

Cold Chisel's 'Bow River' starts up on the jukebox. I circle the table, exploring the angles, carpet sticking to the soles of my sandals. I sink one, miss one. Chook pockets their two remaining coloured balls but misses the black. Michael scores and for the second time, we are at match point. Next shot, he sinks the black. Impulsively, I throw my arms around him. He spins me off my feet and we laugh.

For a moment it seems like the whole pub stands still. People at the tables stare at us and even Sharon pauses, mid-swipe, to gauge the scene.

Finally, Macca breaks the ice, backslapping Michael with enough force to send him off-balance. 'Well, I didn't fuckin' see that comin'. Onya, mate.'

He raises his glass to me and drains it. 'Your shout, Chook. Round for the winners, too.'

Chook shakes my hand without meeting my eyes and heads for the bar. Macca decamps to the men's room.

Michael and I touch glasses and drain the last of our beers.

A woman places a spindly hand on mine as she walks past. 'It's about time those two were taken down a peg,' she says, Baileys on her breath. 'Think they're God's bloody gift to pool.'

Chook reappears with the drinks. Macca reappears and racks up with a vengeance. 'Say Goodbye' is playing in the background as he smashes the triangle apart. He's either unlucky or unaccustomed to breaking, as both a big and a small fall into pockets.

'We're on smalls,' he says to Chook, taking a step back and folding his arms.

'I'm pretty sure the big fell first,' Michael whispers.

I nod but let it stand, loath to add to the tension.

Maybe it's my karmic reward for not disputing the break, but I manage to pocket four in a row. I pause to chalk my cue and survey the table. Their six remaining balls block a direct shot on ours but I'm undeterred. Hunters & Collectors give way to Madonna as I hit the white ball against the cushion so that it ricochets onto the purple twelve. To my utter delight, it drops into the side pocket.

Michael whistles. Chook swears. Macca's face turns puce.

I play it cool, steadying myself with a swig of beer and a drag of Michael's cigarette.

'Five in a row, Kylie,' he says. 'Equal to Macca's best.'

I shrug and circle the table again. Best option is to leave the white tucked between the cushion and the blue ten, our last remaining coloured ball. It's risky, but Madonna's telling me not to go for second best. The risk pays off.

Chook attempts to smash the white ball free but grazes the blue. Michael sinks the blue but leaves the black wide of a pocket.

Macca snatches up his cue and barrels towards the table like he's about to slaughter a prime Mallee lamb. He takes aim and shoots, moving clockwise around the table. One. Two. Three. Four. Five. Six. A new personal best.

He's on the black, playing to restore his reputation. He chalks his cue and leans over the green felt, gut bisected by the head rail. He's about to take his shot when 'I Should Be So Lucky' starts up on the jukebox. He straightens up and shakes his head, swigs his beer and tries again. But Kylie Minogue has broken his concentration. The black bounces out of the pocket.

'Cunt.'

The thought that the slur is directed at me rather than the ball sends my heart racing. I take another swig of beer and a deep breath. Silently singing *lucky, lucky, lucky* along with Kylie, I play the shot.

Time stalls as the black ball crawls towards the pocket, teeters on the edge and lands. I listen to it roll down the chute inside the table. Chook stares, open-mouthed. Macca looks fit to explode. The bar seems to hold its collective breath. I feel suddenly sober.

I hold out a hand to Macca. 'We got lucky.'

'Too fuckin' right.' He shakes my hand, punches Michael on the arm and nods at Chook. 'Another round for our lucky friends.'

Dreading the prospect of a rematch, I'm relieved when he takes Chook's stick and his own and snaps them into the cue rack. Once Chook delivers the beers, they're gone.

Michael and I sit down, touch glasses and drink. Sharon brings over a bowl of hot chips and another round of beers, a gift from a regular who – quote, unquote – 'never thought they'd see Macca and Chook lose pool to a sheila.'

When we're done with the chips, I help myself to another cigarette.

'I haven't had this much fun in ages. My ex hated pool.' I inhale with exaggerated pleasure. 'And smoking.'

'He really does sound like a prick. Why did you stay with him so long?'

I exhale in a smoky sigh. 'I thought if I did all the right things, loved him hard enough, he'd change, and we'd live happily ever after. Instead, I got lied to, cheated on and left with a nasty STD.'

'Not—'

'No, not AIDS. A curable one. Thank God.' I shake my head. 'Thing is, the sex was great. I should've left it at that, instead of trying to convince myself it meant something more.'

'Why?'

'I was raised that way.'

'Catholic?'

'How can you tell?'

Michael grins and eyes me squarely. 'So, have you learned from experience, Kylie? Reckon these days you could settle for great sex without trying to turn it into something else?'

'Oh, I think so.' I butt out my cigarette and return his gaze. 'But I won't really know until I put it to the test.'

'Need You Tonight' by INXS is playing on the jukebox. I stand up and take his hand.

***

A shaft of hot yellow light falls on the empty space beside me in the bed. I remember Michael opening the curtain to let the moonlight in, and reach over to drag it shut. The movement makes my head hurt. I close my eyes again and take a moment to see how it feels to be the sort of woman who has a one-night stand.

Hangover notwithstanding, it feels great.

I scan the room for my shirt-dress to throw on for the walk to the bathroom. Hours earlier, past the point where anything about Michael could surprise me, he said, 'I'm going to do something I've wanted to do all night' and proceeded to bite off my top button. He removed it from his mouth and slipped it into the breast pocket of my dress, brushing my nipple with his fingers.

I look under the bed. No white dress. Slipping on the daisy dress instead, I step on a used condom, mercifully knotted. I chuck it in the bin, gather my things and head to the bathroom. I half expect to pass Michael in the corridor, but there's no sign of him and when I get back to the room, I notice his duffle bag is gone. I'm disappointed, though hardly surprised. Still, it would've been nice of him to leave me something other than a used condom.

I retrieve my undies from the foot of the bed where I'd kicked them off. Shaking out the bedsheets unearths another used condom, my bra and Michael's INXS t-shirt. Seems he left me something after all. I discard the daisy dress and put the t-shirt on over a pair of jeans. It smells of smoke and sweat and feels like armour. Checking my bag, I see he's left me half a packet of Winfields and a lighter, too, bless him.

My dress would've fitted him like a shirt. I have a mental image of him wearing it, a little tight across the shoulders but open at the neck, a V of sparse chest hair. The thought makes me smile as I slip the smokes and lighter into my back pocket.

I settle my bill with Sharon, who calls me Kylie. I don't correct her.

Before getting into the car, I remove the house keys and trinkets from my keyring, leaving only an RACV medallion and the car key.

A flock of galahs feeds on the nature strip, untroubled as I slam the boot on my bag. The jeans and t-shirt shield me from the hot car seat and belt buckle. I toss the smokes on the dashboard and fire up the motor.

Beneath a sign thanking me for visiting Ouyen is a man wearing shorts, boots and an Akubra hat with his thumb sticking out. I pull over.

'You headin' to Mildura?' he asks.

I nod and open the door.

'Thanks. Ute broke down. Spare part's in Mildy.'

He closes the door and extends his hand.

'Steve.'

'Hi Steve,' I say. 'I'm Kylie.'

Put Yourself in My Place
Alice Pung

I killed Tori Amos, but her geriatric fans didn't know it was me. This was all mostly their fault anyway. They pitted us against each other. Those oldies, their eyes burning with feral vitality, their ears needing dulcet tunes to block out the *rata-tat-tat* rhythms that had been inflicted on them by life: the sound of gun-taps, the boom of rocket-fire.

Every month at the New Saigon Restaurant and Bar the owners put on 'Superstar Night', a set banquet of eight courses, including lobster, and a bottle of Johnnie Walker. Sixty-five dollars a head, kids ate free. It was supposed to bring our community together. Old men and women, the middle-aged, the young with children and babies: those who'd had their family trees cut off at the root or sprouting new branches, even bearing fruit.

Our community had invested in a huge state-of-the-art, art-of-war sound system and mother of all 1990s karaoke machines. The oldies loved to hear us sing. There was no more surefire way to squeeze the tears out of Old Man Hoc's eyes than a shot of Johnnie Walker and a young woman in a ruched dress on New Saigon's little stage, singing her heart out.

Old Man Hoc was the Chinese patriarch, the benevolent Godfather, the Marlon Brando of the Australian Southeast Asian community. He'd bought the little restaurant that became the classiest establishment this side of town. He was always chuckling at something when he wasn't weeping. His wife was the opposite. She'd gone back to Vietnam to get plastic surgery and now looked exactly like La Toya Jackson. Smiling probably still hurt her.

For that generation, everything hurt. Dominique lost two fingers from the cleaver meant for the roast duck's neck. Mrs Lee had burned feet from dropping a vat of boiling soup at the Pho King restaurant. Most of the women had back pain and eye trouble from early mornings sewing in their garages.

Superstar Night was an evening for the elders to show off their children. Who knew that out of the scrappy remnants of war could emerge something better, something milk-fed and healthy, a generation with all their limbs intact. The progeny not on the stage singing were sitting quietly at their tables, noses wedged in a book, while their mums and dads whinge-bragged about how they only got ninety-seven percent in their last maths test.

My best friend was Tien. Our families always sat on the same table because our dads had suffered the war fighting together. Tien was the smart one. I was good at music and reading and really nothing else. During the Lunar New Year fundraiser for the Quang Duc monastery, when the praises for Tien came particularly thick and fast like arrows into my soft dumb fourteen-year-old heart, Dad got me up on stage to sing 'La Mer', because I had learned it in French. Dad was always good to me like that. Also, he was pissed off at Tien's dad for bragging so much.

I sang the French song, but for some reason on their pirated VHS video the next song up was 'The Loco-Motion', and just as I was about to step off stage, Dad urgently gestured for me to stay on, to emote and locomote, to bring the room into a frenzy of wild railroad-action, to bounce and dance and forget.

From that night on, it no longer mattered how many people patted

Tien on the back for her academic prowess. I had every single one of them paying attention to me.

A few years later, Tien and I had finished high school and parted ways. She'd won a scholarship to study accounting at the city university, and I'd got good enough marks to do an arts degree in a suburban university near a duck lake. I didn't know what I wanted to do, and in our world of factory workers and small business owners, no-one else had a bloody clue what I was doing either. The oldies thought I was studying how to paint.

At New Saigon, I'd become the Southeast Asian Princess of Pop. People always had trouble with my first name, Ky. They'd rhyme it with thigh, even though it was actually pronounced 'Kee'. And my surname, Ly – who knew one syllable could be mangled? *Lie? Lee?* Most called me Keeley, but one teacher in primary school had called me 'Kylie', and it stuck.

My stage name became Ky Ly Minnow. My first name, my surname, followed by something with scales because I was good at piano. I chose Minnow because the Chinese, Vietnamese and Cambodians could pronounce that better than they could 'Minogue', and also in homage to the shark minnow, one of the most common river fish found in the Mekong Delta.

I had a fishy name, but I was anything but. My voice was sweet. I smelt like Impulse Harmony. I had a flat bum and no boobs, but so what. I made a killing those Saturday evenings – five hundred, six hundred dollars, in tips. On nights where there was a huge wedding, I'd get close to eight hundred dollars. There were talks of flying me to Orange County, California, to film a *Paris by Night* video alongside Elvis Phuong.

I did Kylie's whole discography, from the boppy but ubiquitous 'I Should Be So Lucky' to the Gallic 'Je Ne Sais Pas Pourquoi', from 'Hand on Your Heart' – where all could put their hands to their chests and declare their affection – to 'Give Me Just a Little More Time', a late-night siren song to lull sleepy aunts and uncles to part with final tips.

Back in high school, the Australian girls would come up to be friendly and ask me nothing except about my difference. Did I think the canteen did a good enough job making dim sims? Did I like Lucy Liu? No, fuckers, I love Kylie, and we understand her in a way youse never will. We understand the power of that vivacity, that vigour. You may *look* like her, but I am the *embodiment* of her. We are the same height. Same shoe size. Arched brows. Our calves are the same length as our thighs, so when we bend our knees to squat, our feet rest just beneath at our bums. We are a perfectly proportioned petite, not the bobble-head-stumpy-leg variety. I am her Asian sister from another mister.

In Kylie's songs, everyone could join in the chorus, and dance – from your tiny toddler in the godawful tulle dress to the old toothless grannies – pretending to be a choo-choo train. *Ka-mon*, I'd sing, *Do. Do. Do. The loco-moshun with me*, and they'd all get up. They loved me.

When I sang 'I Should Be So Lucky', one or two audience members might be named Lucky (or Freedom or Visa), and so it was like I was singing to them and they'd shove folded notes at me, legal tender, and sometimes they tried in illegal tender places too, until they saw my dad, right at the front, getting ready to smash a VB bottle and rearrange their faces. I was safe, because everyone was watching out for me, the pride of the town.

But then one day, posters began appearing on the windows of our shopping strip: an artsy ink illustration of a woman's face with curly hair, in profile, mouth open in song. *Tolly Amour. Coming soon to New Saigon Restaurant and Bar!*

'You will like her,' Mr Hoc reassured me the next Saturday evening when I came to perform. 'She will go first to warm everyone up, because you still our big superstar!'

But when the woman who called herself Tolly Amour stepped onstage, I saw my nemesis.

She began singing, and her voice was as thin and bright as those massive reels of polyester thread in her mum's overlocker in their garage. The notes she produced garish like the sateen blouses that came from those machines.

Then I heard the song about a little yellow bird that goes flying and gets shot in the wing. Black roses changing their colour. Dancing in graveyards until sunrise. But unlike Tori's depth of feeling and lyrical poetry, it was … well, like Bubblegum Pop. Like Kylie. Like me. She made being torn to pieces sound like something you'd be up for on a Saturday night, with a Bacardi Breezer in the hand. She made 'Cornflake Girl' a song about breakfast cereal preferences.

Instead of Tori's soft natural locks the colour of autumn leaves, Tolly Amour had hair like chilli-dusted packet noodles: rigid auburn curls that cost exorbitant time and money in the 90s. Tori Amos was a classically trained musician. Tolly Amour was a fake. Tori Amos could play two or three instruments at the same time and sing. Tolly Amour couldn't play anything. Tolly Amour was supposed to be at the big city university, studying accounting.

Tolly Armour was my old friend Tien!

And she was massacring Tori's songs – not in a good bloody visceral way – drowning each word to death in a boiling vat of Barbie-pink, high fructose corn syrup. She even skipped a little when she sang 'Happy Phantom'.

And weekend by weekend, that bitch stole more and more of my ground.

Our people couldn't pronounce Tori Amos, but 'Amour' they understood. Tolly also started to sing in French. Instead of the saccharine 'Seasons in the Sun', she sang the darker titled 'Le Moribond'. She sang it worse than Terry Jacks, if such a thing were possible. She stretched the syllables and made the death a thing of weepy pathos.

Her audience, prone to sentimentality, no strangers to deaths in fields and forests and tunnels as tiny as a child's torso, loved it – loved the grandeur she was giving this man's chance to say all the things a soldier couldn't tell his ma or ba or sister. These men, who'd fought in the Vietnam war, who'd survived Cambodia, would openly weep when she sang 'Le Moribond'. She'd always finish with this number.

'Tolly! Tolly! Tolly!' the audience shouted, when in the past it was 'Ky Ly! Ky Ly! Ky Ly!'

My music became darker, but fortunately the previous year, so had Kylie's. 'Put Yourself in My Place', I sang, with the raw envy you could only feel for your former treacherous best friend who, not content with being the brightest and most successful of our cohort, was creeping into my terrain.

I gave Kylie pathos, gravitas, pain. I turned the sequins inside out so you could see the work of the stitching, how careful, how meticulous. 'Confide in Me', I wailed at the audience, but they were lost to me. They hated this new Ky Ly.

Whenever I saw Tolly on a poster it was like someone had shot something icy in my veins with a syringe. Over the months, she got more and more stage time, and I got less. 'Don't worry,' said Mr Hoc, 'she just new, so people want to hear the new songs.'

But let's see her do true Tori like I do true Kylie.

Let's see her do 'Leather'.

Let's hear her do 'Me and a Gun.'

I was just about ready to quit, throw in my act, when *He* appeared.

Black-rimmed glasses. Slick Superman hair. Melty smile. He sang religious versions of The Crickets classics, and called himself Buddy

Holy. He made 'Everyday' sound like the Second Coming, and 'Not Fade Away' like it was about the Holy Ghost. The young Catholic girls in the audience were smitten. Their mums and dads approved. At a time when every Asian man you saw in the news was either a heroin dealer or gangsta, the elders in our community looked upon Buddy Holy as a blessing.

I was supposed to go onstage after him, and I vowed it would be my last show.

I stepped up and did my first Kylie number, 'Where is the Feeling?', one I knew no-one liked much, but that was appropriate to my mood – Kylie in the black-and-white ocean like a drowning and enraged modern Virginia Woolf.

I thought I'd finish off with 'Better the Devil You Know', glaring directly at my old friend.

I whispered the first few lines, but then I really got into it and ended screeching like a banshee, like Sinéad O'Connor did with 'Troy'.

There was complete silence at the end of my swan song.

They all hated it, but of course I already knew this. I expected it, these dumb sentimental old people and these middle-aged families and these aspirational children who all gaped up at me because I was no longer singing sweet balms for their bleeding souls: their trauma, their rage, their resentment, their confusion, their pressure, their loneliness. I wasn't meant to show them any of this; but I was a product of them, *they'd made this mirror.* The mirror had broken and they were seeing their own ugliness. They hated me because they hated themselves, and no amount of sparkle-song could cure this.

I also knew that this was the end for me. No more tips, no more Saturday night fever.

But then a soft deep voice behind me began singing.

A tune about a woman with lips the colour of wild roses.

This was a duet, and my name was Elisa Day, and when Elisa Day turned around, she no longer saw Asian Buddy Holly but a man who'd transformed into a soul with eyes deeper than Nicholas-of-the-Bad-Seeds' surname.

I fell for him, big time.

Unfortunately, so had Tolly.

I kept turning up to New Saigon, not giving a flying fig whether the good peeps liked my music or not.

Unfortunately, so did Tolly.

All we cared about was whether Buddy would duet with us. He did 'Unchained Melody' with Tolly. But he did 'Especially for You' with me.

She loved him for his public confidence of sunny faith and earnest piety. I loved him because he was ironic before the term was hijacked by a generation that didn't understand the significance of Ethan Hawke. Tolly was book-smart, but she probably thought Irony was a new product you sprayed onto clothes before ironing out the creases.

The oldies could see what was going on with the handsome young singer in the polyester suit and the two chanteuses. They smiled indulgently and watched the show unfold. Even Dad cottoned on. One evening he said to me, 'Your voice sweeter than Tien's. You play piano better. Only advantage is she's whiter and not so angry. Powder can fix your face but not your angry. Why you so angry anyway? You know choirboy has hots for you.'

We were on our own little table, off to the side: me, him and Tolly, waiting for our cues to go onstage. Buddy turned to me. 'What I do is a joke,' he said, 'but I've never met a musician like you. You take fizzled-out pop and you make it into something deep. You are evasive and ironic, but you feel things in your songs. Not just love and sorrow, but the harder feelings.'

'Oh, I dunno,' I mumbled.

But from that moment on, Tolly Amour was not a threat to me. Buddy was mine.

After that, he made me listen to his favourite CD, *Tu-Plang*, over and over. 'Too bad there's only one Quan Yeomans,' he mused, 'and I have to end up being part of The Crickets instead.'

'We could form our own band,' I said, 'and call it Expectorator.'

He looked at me blankly.

'It means to spit out.'

'Because ye are neither hot nor cold, thus I shall spit thee out of my mouth!' he thundered.

I looked at him blankly.

'Revelations three: sixteen.'

'Dude, you really know your Bible.'

'Yeah, but only to bash it.'

'You're going to go to hell.'

'You'll join me.'

On stage, in the ardour of our romantic triumph, we could now do the love songs unironically. Our audience lapped it up like sweet manna. Like Karen Carpenter, we were on top of the world. We left poor Tolly Amour on that stage at the tail end of Saturday nights, singing her terrible songs of heartbreak.

But Buddy started to get really ambitious. Every day, he would bug and wheedle and Lady-Macbeth me into leaving our little community and striking it big. 'We're smart as. We're hot. We're funny. We've gotta put ourselves in a situation where we can be discovered.'

'We're not Regurgitator!' I exploded one day. 'We're tribute singers! I'm Kylie Minogue and you're Buddy-fucking-Holly!'

But love was not enough for him. He wanted more. His idea of more frightened me. We were to make caricatures of ourselves, to highlight the minstrelsy we Asian singers were supposed to perform.

'We're gonna act as the ultimate whitewashed duo, as a big screw-you to the music industry and all those stealing our culture!'

He wanted me to kill off Ky Ly Minnow, and make fun of the petite blonde woman who'd made me so much money in the first place. 'Kylie Minogue hasn't made you a single cent!' scoffed Buddy. 'And it's not fair to rob sentimental war vets of their social security dollars every weekend.'

'But we're not robbing them,' I protested. Those old uncles and aunties willingly parted with their money, until my singing no longer pleased them.

But Buddy wasn't listening. 'Now it's time to take money from those who've taken it from us. Can you imagine if we made it big in the USA? We'd be sticking the finger to imperialist buggery ...'

I imagined the Ky Ly Minnow he was imagining – blood-red lips, crazy dyed hair – snarling on the floor and crapping all over the Kylie songs that had once brought such delight to a roomful of faces that looked like mine.

'Do you want to be stuck singing your dumb songs at your cousins' weddings at New Saigon forever?'

I didn't say anything.

Meanwhile, Tolly's mother, Mrs Ho, told me that Tolly was so heartbroken that she'd stopped going to classes. She wasn't eating or sleeping properly. But she kept turning up to New Saigon Superstar Night in a crumpled, gold-sequinned polyester dress, Maybelline mascara running down her cheeks as she sang 'Crucify' and 'Little Earthquakes'. At times, we weren't sure whether it was the microphone feedback or her making those harpooned-whale sounds.

'The community are going to turn on us,' warned Buddy, 'You just watch. You just wait. Let's get out of this town, move to the city and make it big.'

But the community didn't turn against us.

They turned against *her*.

'Get her off my stage, Ho,' hollered Mr Hoc. 'Ho' was not adding insult to injury, as it was her dad's surname. MC Vinnie unplugged the microphone. Tien's father led her by the elbow down the three black steps, back to their table.

Buddy and I clambered onstage, held hands and sang 'Especially for You'. We could see the audience relaxing. Here was their Pop Princess and Golden Boy, to lull them back into their sweet soporific torpor. Here was something they could sway their arms in the air for, something that had the words 'dream', 'wings' and 'tomorrow' in it. I watched them as we sang – the sad, haggard faces of our hardworking elders, the stressed-out, pinched faces of our cousins and the slumped former glory that was Tien.

I loosened my hand from Buddy's grip.

'Together … together …' we sang, but at that very moment, I knew we weren't going to be, Buddy and me. He could sense a shift too, because he didn't grab my hand back.

***

Time moves on, and so have we.

New Saigon closed down when Mr Hoc had a stroke, and became a little arcade place serving bubble tea, Korean fried chicken and light-up, early-gambling-addiction games for children.

I hear that Tolly has her own accounting practice now, a nice husband and two children. Straight out of uni, I got a graduate job with the Department of Education, probably because someone reading the résumés didn't expect that Ms 'Minnow' was Chinese-Australian until she rocked up to the interview. I have been there eighteen years now.

The other day I saw posters for a Tribute band called Durian Durian, with a familiar frontman, hair still as black as ever. Back at home, I watched one of their concerts on YouTube, and knew they stank. They did covers of 80s songs to aging, forty-something women. I suppose I am one too now. It has been half a decade since I last saw him, then a decade, and then two.

I search for Kylie on Spotify, and when I listen to 'Padam Padam' my heart feels the same way it did when I was nineteen, when life was filled with infinite possibilities.

I wonder if Tien feels the same when she listens to the music that moved her in her youth, but I would never dare find her on Facebook and ask. I can't get her out of my head, but she has remained silent all these years, and I don't want to disturb her peace.

I wonder if she knows that New Saigon no longer exists, that perhaps it never did, except in our dreams.

Padam Padam
Chris Flynn

Trust thyself, Emerson said. *Every heart vibrates to that iron string.*

That's what I told myself as I staggered to the waiting helicopter, body bent almost double against the wind that whipped across the tundra, arm raised to shield my face from the down-draught of the rotors, blasting surface snow against my exposed cheek like sandpaper. Even wearing the dark goggles that pinched my temples, I could barely see where I was going. The low Antarctic sun cast a blinding silvery light as it reflected off the ice. To gaze upon it without sunglasses was akin to staring into a supernova, retinas seared with a reminder of brightness that would linger for hours.

Lucky the chopper was red, otherwise I might never have seen it. I clambered into the passenger seat and slammed the door shut behind me. The pilot, who I had met for the first time that morning, was a sullen man called Kavanagh with a hybrid accent that sounded alternately Norwegian and Irish. He sported a lush, red beard and was not amused by the order to convey me to the pack ice, especially given the high winds and brief window of daylight. He had made a point of informing me that he didn't give two shits about my research into the breeding habits of leopard seals and that I was risking his life needlessly.

I stared him down, saying nothing, until eventually he shrugged and told me to wait while he warmed up the engine.

Glad to be in the safety of the cabin, I donned a set of headphones so I could communicate with the man.

'This is going to be rough,' he told me. 'I wouldn't go up today if I wasn't ordered to.'

'You already said,' I replied. 'It's not far. I won't get many opportunities to study them up close like this.'

'If we have to ditch, I'll be mad as hell,' he said.

'How will I tell the difference?' I asked.

To my surprise, he laughed.

'Fair point,' he said. 'All right, here we go. Hold on to something.'

As the helicopter rose from the frozen earth, it was immediately caught in a crosswind and thrown sideways, almost colliding with a nearby jeep. Kavanagh grunted and pulled up, turning the chopper into the stream.

'You nearly hit that,' I told him, pointing to the yellow vehicle.

'Not helping,' he said, wrestling with the controls.

Once we were truly airborne, I relaxed a little. Kavanagh's knuckles were white on the stick, but he held the chopper firmly on course. We headed west. I noticed a couple of scabs on his left hand, from recent cuts.

'You a boxer?' I asked.

He glanced down at his fist curled around the controls and winced. The skin under his right eye wrinkled into tiny creases.

'Not much to do down here except fight and fuck,' he said, eyes darting sideways to gauge my reaction.

I nodded, raising an eyebrow at this forthright admission.

'Those injuries from the former, or the latter?' I asked.

That made him grin.

The smile disappeared as the chopper was buffeted by crosswinds.

'If we don't crash-land, it'll be a miracle,' he said, as the pack ice appeared over the horizon.

'No, it'll be down to your competence,' I told him. 'Besides, how hard can it be to fly one of these things? It looks easy.'

'You want to take the stick?' he asked.

'I wouldn't want to embarrass you by doing it properly,' I told him.

He turned the bird into the wind and spiralled down towards a landing spot marked with a flashing beacon. I tensed in the seat, bracing myself against the roof of the cockpit.

'Should've had a whisky before we set out,' Kavanagh muttered.

'First one's on me tonight, if we don't die,' I told him.

The chopper was almost down when a sudden gust of wind threw us sideways. The cabin tilted at a sickening angle, and I hit my head against the doorframe. Kavanagh jammed the stick forward and dropped the helicopter heavily onto the icy surface. The aircraft slid five metres before coming to a halt. Kavanagh cut the power immediately and the rotor blades began to slow.

'You owe me a drink,' he said, trying to appear calm. If he was anything like me, his heart was hammering a techno beat in his chest.

Padam padam padam padam padam.

'We'll share a bottle,' I told him.

He glanced at his watch. Omega Seamaster. Expensive. Wages were high for a chopper pilot at the arse end of the world. I was a TAG Heuer woman myself.

'You've got forty minutes and then we need to head back,' he said. 'About an hour of daylight remaining, Professor Hooper.'

'It's Doctor,' I told him. 'But I don't like honorifics. Emmyrose.'

I pulled off my glove and extended my cold fingers. Kavanagh grasped my hand in his.

'Hell of a first date,' he said.

***

Due to ironic water restrictions that were lost on no-one, showers on base were limited to two minutes, once a day. I splurged on mine before the party that night. Crouching in a hide observing leopard seals for half an hour that afternoon, even in full gear and with thermal layers covering every conceivable centimetre of skin, had left me frozen. Kavanagh had to run the heater in the chopper at full blast during the flight back, pointedly reminding me of my whisky promise. I got the impression women were in high demand at Antarctic research stations, and that he was staking an early claim for my affections. He was a big, barrel-chested guy. He'd be a lot warmer to wrap my legs around than a hot water bottle.

I bumped into the man in the mess hall. Meals were confusing at Casey. Because of the short days, long nights and shift patterns, the buffet served breakfast, lunch and dinner twenty-four seven. I don't know how the kitchen kept up with demand. While I opted for pasta carbonara, Kavanagh sat down opposite me with a huge plate of dehydrated scrambled eggs and baked beans lashed in hot sauce, which he proceeded to scoop into his gullet.

'It's like watching an albatross gorge itself on plankton,' I told him.

He opened his mouth wide, so I could see the mashed-up food in there.

'Charming,' I said. 'What have you been doing since we got back?'

'Watching repeats of *JAG*,' he said, nodding towards the television screwed to the wall. 'I've already seen this one,' he added. 'The female lieutenant is pregnant and gets blamed for an accident on the flight deck. She won't say who the father is, but it's her CO.'

'Spoiler alert,' I said, trying, and failing, to eat my carbonara in as delicate a manner as possible. The sauce was too watery.

'You got your costume for tonight?' he asked.

There was a dress-up dance party happening at Splinters. Participation was mandatory.

'If I'd known this was the kind of entertainment to expect, I would've packed a gorilla suit,' I told him. 'I'll cobble something together.'

'It's *Neighbours* themed,' he said.

'What does that even mean?' I asked.

'Beats me,' Kavanagh shrugged. 'I'm going as Harold.'

'I can't wait,' I said, wondering how on earth I was going to find an Erinsborough-related outfit among my winter clothes.

As it turned out, a pair of skimpy pyjama shorts, coupled with a checked shirt with the hem hoisted and tied around my midriff in a bow made quite the impression. I felt severely underdressed as I shimmied on the improvised dancefloor, acutely aware that multiple sets of eyes were lingering on my exposed thighs. Having said that, I was praised for embracing the spirit of the occasion. I won third prize.

Kavanagh's costume was a shirt and pants. He cleaned up well, but it was hardly reminiscent of Harold Bishop at the height of his powers.

'This is him after he gets washed out to sea and loses his memory,' Kavanagh explained. 'He winds up here and finds employ as a rugged yet lovable helicopter pilot.'

We took a break to catch up on our drinks. I was already several whisky sours deep. That still seemed to be a lot less than everyone else had imbibed. Party nights at Splinters were legendary orgies of excess.

'Harold Bishop, right?' said a passing woman I had been briefly introduced to as Lily. She was a mechanic, from memory. 'Nice one, Thor.'

'Is that a nickname?' I asked him.

'No,' he said. 'It's a common enough Norwegian name.' He rolled his eyes in exasperation. 'I was born long before Marvel movies ruined everything.'

I wanted to interrogate the man, inquire as to how someone with a Norwegian father and Irish mother wound up working as a helicopter pilot on an Australian Antarctic research base and did he prefer contemporary installation art to classic portraiture; had he ever ridden a horse; did he think New Order was better than Joy Division; had he once spent three hundred euros on food for stray cats in Athens; did he draw an extra box after the list of candidates on his ballot papers, write 'none of the above' next to it and mark his X in that; did he believe the Chihuahua to be the mightiest of hounds, that horror movies deserved more awards, that Maggie Gyllenhaal trumped Jake Gyllenhaal, that postcards were the wisest form of communication with relatives, that sports were more fun to play than to watch, that every human being had a multitude of different people living inside their skin, that like Gaudí's basilica we die incomplete with a thousand unanswered questions on our lips?

Instead, I downed my whisky sour, wrapped my arms around his neck and said, 'I am not the kind of woman who stands on a platform, waiting for a train, Thor Kavanagh. I am a locomotive.'

And then I kissed him.

***

You can tell a lot about whether you're well suited for a relationship if you're able to work together on an odious task without tearing each other to shreds. The nascent, pre-sex, early days of attraction between us were sorely tested when Kavanagh and I were rostered on the same slushy duty shift. I could not bring myself to call him by his given name. He was right. It was too goofy, and the inevitable comparisons to Chris Hemsworth wearing a fat suit in one of those interminable superhero flicks did nothing for Kavanagh's self-esteem.

There were twenty-six expeditioners to cater for in Casey at that time of year, and everyone took turns working in the kitchen, whether they possessed an aptitude for cooking or not. I made an inordinate number of new allies with my no-bake cheesecakes. Kavanagh was all thumbs, making a mess of every dish he touched. He claimed to be more comfortable stripping a carburettor.

I won him over to the cause by explaining that baking was a simple matter of following instructions, exactly like in the manual for the chopper engine. Measure your amounts, get your heat right, stick to the plan. When his first batch of chocolate-chip cookies came out of the oven intact and smelling delicious, his eyes lit up with delight upon biting into one.

'Science! It's just science! I could go on MasterChef,' he said, flicking through a recipe book as he sought other dishes to impress the judges. He pulled me into a bear hug and kissed me on the temple.

'Cool your jets, Gordon Ramsay,' I said. We had a mountain of prep to do before the end of the shift. Peeling potatoes and chopping carrots wasn't the most glamorous work, but it was more Kavanagh's speed. I handed him a peeler. He set to the task with renewed gusto.

***

Temperatures outside had dropped to minus seventy-three degrees, which meant Kavanagh and I were eligible to join the 300 Club. On the stroke of midnight, we would strip naked in front of a cheering crowd of fellow expeditioners and enter the base sauna, which was set to ninety-three degrees Celsius. Then, once suitably boiled, we would go for a stroll outside, wearing nothing but sturdy boots. Two hundred seconds later, we were supposed to re-enter the base and plunge back into the sauna, assuming we were still alive. Our bodies would thus have experienced a temperature change of three hundred degrees Fahrenheit. Alcohol would also play a part in the proceedings.

When the time came, there was no backing out. Kavanagh and I turned up in the gymnasium wearing only bathrobes. I'd downed two brandies while getting changed and felt like I was wearing a suit of armour.

A raucous round of applause went up when we dropped our robes. I performed a brief twirl and ducked into the sauna. Kavanagh perched opposite me, looking for all his manliness like an embarrassed schoolboy.

'I'm really not sure about this,' he said.

'It's an atrocious idea,' I said, pulling my shoulders back. Despite the absurdity of the situation, I wanted him to like what he was seeing.

Faces leered in at us through the window in the door. What was initially an awkward silence turned to a comfortable one as our bodies relaxed in the heat. We had twenty minutes to warm up sufficiently to withstand the conditions outside.

'This is actually quite nice,' I said, after a while. Sweat was rolling down my back in waves.

Kavanagh grinned appreciatively. I liked his crooked smile.

'No more secrets between us now,' he said.

'There might be one more,' I told him, winking.

He laughed and then the door was flung open, and we were dragged out and ushered into a corridor, flanked by inebriated, whooping colleagues. Men and women of science, with PhDs.

'Ready?' Dr Foord said. She was the base medical doctor, and had given us strict advice not to run, under any circumstances, at the risk of permanent lung damage and even death.

'Walk,' she said. 'Despite every instinct to the contrary.'

Kavanagh took my hand in his as the doors opened. The sensation of stepping naked into minus seventy-three degrees was indescribable. Never have I been so aware of the entirety of my human skin in the one instant. The tingle that coursed through my body was so intense, it almost felt like orgasm. Shivers and butterflies. I squeezed Kavanagh's fingers and we set out, eyes wide, on our slow, methodical march towards the metal pole that bore signs pointing to every corner of the globe. Adelaide, Bucharest, Woomera, Jervis Bay, Norwich City, Concordia and Port Melbourne, my home, 3843 kilometres distant.

***

The lack of space in my bunk rendered our time together incredibly intimate. There was no escape from each other's bodies. If one of us wanted to lie flat on their back, the other had to basically stretch out on top of them. Given the weight difference between us, that was often me, clinging to Kavanagh's stocky frame like a limpet on a whale. That's ungenerous. He reminded me more of a leopard seal if they had hairy chests and beards. He would fall asleep like that, untroubled by my full weight pressing down on him as I drained him of warmth. I lay awake for hours after he was out for the count – post-coital men not being great conversational bedfellows – chest pressed against his, listening to the dissonance of our heartbeats.

Padam, padam, padam, mine would thrum.

Puhdum, puhdum, puhdum, came the bass reply.

On the night of the blizzard, I explained bradycardia while he nuzzled my neck, rough fingers stroking the soft skin of my belly, occasionally dipping lower to tease me.

'The heart rate of a leopard seal drops to twenty-five percent of its normal rate during a dive,' I told him. 'They can go as deep as three hundred metres, we think.'

'What's their normal BPM?' he asked.

'*Hydrurga leptonyx*,' I intoned, relishing the prospect of showing off to a lover. 'It means slender-clawed water-worker. Eighty beats per minute, on average. Not dissimilar to us.'

'Depends on what we're doing,' Kavanagh said, running his calloused hand along my inner thigh. I arched my back involuntarily. 'So that goes down to twenty a minute?'

'All cetaceans do it,' I told him. 'To conserve oxygen. The heart of a blue whale only beats twice per minute in the deep. Imagine that.'

PADAM.

PADAM.

'What's the human heart rate get up to during sex?' Kavanagh asked.

'One twenty average if you're on top,' I said. 'One ten on the bottom.'

'I need the exercise more than you,' he said and rolled on top of me.

Later, in the dead of night, he murmured to me as he unfurled my body from his. Something about one of the pins on the tarpaulin coming loose, that the flapping edge could fracture the cockpit glass. A few other sweet nothings. A feeling of affection, of vulnerability, of confession.

It was five a.m. when I woke up and realised he hadn't come back. I lay there for a while. He would be sitting in the mess hall, stuffing his face full of dehydrated eggs with sriracha. All the same, I got dressed and went looking.

The base was quiet, locked down tight because of the storm. Virtually no-one was on shift and those who were had their feet up and chins resting on their chests. I shook someone awake and asked if they had seen Kavanagh. Outside, the blizzard still raged, an inferno of white.

The shift watchman Miles woke the base commander. He came to see me in the mess hall, where I was nursing a cup of instant coffee. He quizzed me as to what Kavanagh had told me he was doing. I heard myself woozily say the words as if I were still dreaming. He and Miles exchanged looks.

'You think he went outside?' Miles said. 'In that?'

'Fuck,' the base commander said, a dour Scotsman called Macready.

'He would've clipped in to the safety line,' he said. 'Gear up. Let's go take a look.' He turned to me. 'He better not be blootered in a corner somewhere, Missy.'

'It's Doctor,' I reminded him. He curled his lip.

Constantly rebuffed by gale-force winds, it took the search team two hours to find Kavanagh. He was sitting upright in a drift, fifty metres from the main building. His carabiner had broken. In the whiteout, he hadn't been able to find his way back to the safety line. It would have been quick. A matter of minutes. Still. He would've died thinking of me, naked and dozing like a satyr.

When they carried his frozen body back into base on a stretcher, I asked if I could see. Dr Foord frowned, but everyone knew what had been going on between us. She pulled back the blanket.

It's never where you expect, is it? That feeling of inexplicable attraction, that fizzle in the blood. The elusive ambience of drowning, of diving deep into the ocean until everything slows, and you become suspended, floating in the darkness, insensate yet aware of everything in the world coursing through your veins as the beat slows and fades.

Padam. Padam. Padam.

I laid my head on Kavanagh's chest and listened.

Give all to love, Emerson said. *Obey thy heart.*

Confide in Me
Nathan Curnow

A pen that looks like a feather, a feather that looks like a knife.
You're on the staircase, Kylie, summoning a confessional poem.

But I'm tired now. Are you tired? I've already said so much,
writing lines year after year as you kept spinning around.

Take me back to Melbourne, 1986 – Nunawading, Surrey Hills.
In the neighbouring suburb there's a boy in love

at Middlefield Primary School. Kylie, your cousin Amanda
scrunched her nose whenever she giggled, a laugh so cute

I noticed every day – her eyes, her smile, her perm.
Now I don't know what the problem is, if it matters who I am,

but I crushed on her as your star rose high
above the Channel Ten studios. What magic happened

down the road to launch your impossible reign
of light, love and disco grit? Our paragon. Our coming of age.

You've been hurt since then, and I have too.
What else can we become? Kids of the eastern suburbs,

that maze of cul-de-sacs. Kylie, you're finally down here,
you've descended the poem's stairs. Tell me a secret,

take my hand, rest your head on my shoulder. There.
I'm ready to keep things quiet, to carry what you need.

I'm the stranger you know. Release it. Lean in to being free.
A line that looks like a magic wand, a wand that looks like a mic.

The strings start up. The beat kicks in. Sing for me, you're mine.

Come into My World
Carrie Tiffany

It was at the end of a row of boxy, dark-brick units. A primary school shared the back fence. The tiny unkempt yard was dotted with soccer balls and basketballs that had faded and deflated and were scattered over the uneven pavers like fallen fruit. The estate agent told me the unit belonged to an old lady who had recently been taken into care. It was a power-of-attorney sale. The money had to be deposited with the nursing home, and would, no doubt, be fully consumed by the time she died.

Inside, the walls were streaked with a single coat of white paint that had been hurriedly applied, but still a drab green tint shone through. The newly polished floorboards were nakedly pale and squeaked underfoot. A cloying smell of acetone was strongest in the small kitchen, which was lined with narrow cabinets, the chipboard flaking at the corners like Weet-Bix. The toilet door was a dirty vinyl curtain that concertinaed on a metal runner that had stubbornly rusted in place. I imagined the old lady living alone, sitting on the toilet, unable to close the door, but with no need for privacy. I imagined her listening to the bells and announcements of the primary school, how they must have organised the day for her – tea and a Scotch Finger at recess, the lunchtime sandwich, a few pages of her library book during afternoon play. Always the hubbub of children shrieking and laughing and crying and fighting, watching the balls accumulate as she looked out of the sitting-room window to the tiny yard, but finally lacking the strength to throw them back.

I mooched about in the garage – too small to be useable – then went around to the front to ask the agent for the contract. He was leaning against the porch cleaning the soles of his pointed shoes with a stick. It was a Wednesday evening. The auction was on Saturday. It was too late to get a building inspection, but the agent said a buyer's advocate, representing another interested party, had arranged one, and the advocate would probably onsell the report to me. He gave me her number and I texted with my request. She replied immediately with her bank details and a request for $800. As soon as the funds were in her account, she would email me a copy of the report. I estimated the report would have cost her $400 to obtain and she'd already billed her buyer for it.

I got back into my car and took some pleasure in negotiating her down to $300, then sending a final text telling her I'd decided not to go ahead with the property. 'Greedy cow,' I said aloud as I turned off my phone and drove away.

***

I was surprised by how much I wanted the unit. I'd been away working payroll assignments on contract, mainly interstate. We were a small team who specialised in major hospitals and health-care networks that were being investigated by the unions for underpaying their staff, so they needed things fixed quickly and quietly and at arm's-length. I was sick of staying in airless hotels and coming home to my rental that wasn't much more than a hotel room itself. It made sense to buy. Another coat of paint, a natty IKEA kitchen, plantings along the back fence to protect me from the school ... I read the contract and started the online application from the bank.

The auction was better attended than I'd expected. Perhaps

thirty people in couples or family groups were standing along the driveway, leaning against the fence in the bright midday sun. The pointy-shoed agent was also the auctioneer. He droned through the preliminaries, introducing each item by saying, 'Ladies and gentlemen ...' The formality of the language and his performance of it seemed arcane, almost liturgical. It reminded me of reading *The Mayor of Casterbridge* at high school and how the boys in the class had laughed when Michael Henchard auctioned his wife and child.

The buyer's advocate was easy to identity in her heels and pencil skirt. The rest of the crowd were probably neighbours, just tyre kicking. There were two younger women conferring with their middle-aged parents. They looked serious and I didn't want to be beaten by the bank of mum and dad. The buyer's advocate opened the bidding low. I allowed the auctioneer to call it twice before I raised my rolled-up brochure. We traded bids in $10,000, then $5,000 dollar increments. I was getting close to my limit when the auctioneer acknowledged a new bidder – one of the fathers. The crowd turned to look at him. He was wearing a baseball cap, his face shadowed and tight beneath the bill. The daughter too was impassive, but the mother, with her arms crossed over her breasts, was agitated, rocking backwards and forwards on the soles of her platform sneakers, her cheeks flushed red as if with exertion. The buyer's advocate bid again, and I bettered her. She scowled at me, and I felt my own greedy surge of pleasure. The auctioneer nodded in my direction and began to call the sale, 'for the first time ... for the second time ...' slapping his own copy of the rolled-up brochure into his hand as if it were a baton or a gavel, for effect. It was then the mother cried out. A kind of animal whimper. When I turned to look at her, she was standing in front of her husband but with her arm raised, palm out at the auctioneer behind her as if he was a car she needed to stop. With the other hand, she gesticulated at her husband, making a long pulling action in front of his throat as if she could physically drag the bid, the money, from him. The daughter swivelled away from them both, moon-eyed, to face the fence. The mother whimpered again, then spoke to her husband in a low growl. He didn't reply. He pouted and looked at his feet, also encased in flashy thick-soled sneakers. The auctioneer cleared his throat, slapped the brochure into his hand again and said, 'Madam, we *are* selling the property,' his tone pleasant enough, but his mouth twisted in a smug, lopsided smile. The mother seemed not to hear him. Her shoulders had slumped forward. She did not turn around. The daughter made no effort to comfort her. The father was already walking away, taking an electronic car key out of the pocket of his large jeans and jabbing it in the direction of a family sedan parked on the street.

There were contracts to sign on the kitchen bench and a bottle of cheap warm champagne from the real estate agency for me. It was too practised to feel like a genuine celebration and there was nobody to congratulate me. For some reason, I didn't want the agent to know that it was my first home and that I planned to live here alone. I was vague with him, hoping he might think I was an investor. I spent a final few minutes alone in the unit. It had been cleaned and painted and all the lights were on, but in the bedroom, I shivered. There were marks on the floor where the wardrobe, the bed and a single nightstand had stood. What had happened to the old lady's furniture? Where were her sheets and towels, her hairbrushes, her reading glasses, her medical stockings? There was a hook on the back of the door where a dressing-gown would have hung – tartan wool but with a missing cord that had been replaced with the belt of a discarded raincoat. And there had been an old-fashioned wind-up alarm clock in here. I could still hear it tick.

***

I took a month's leave to manage the tradesmen and then move in. I would fix the small yard myself, slowly, one section at a time. Because I moved in over the summer and had gone back to work before the school term began, it was another month before I was home to hear a full school day. I was in bed with a heavy cold on a Monday morning when the first bell rang, except it wasn't a bell now, but a short burst of a pop song, 'Come into My World', played over a loudspeaker. The drumming of the children's feet across the concrete playground as they ran into class seemed to enter the music and make it swell with a deeper, more serious rhythm.

I remembered pacing the playground at the last primary school I had attended, Mary Immaculate. I thought that if I kept walking from place to place, it would be less obvious I had no friends. I started at this school in Year 5 after my father had moved away and begun his other family, and my mother was taking the train into the city each day to work in the food hall at the department store. We weren't Catholic, but the school was only two blocks walk away from our new flat. I had my own door key and I timed my departure from the flat so I arrived at the school gates just as the morning bell rang and I could go straight to class.

Mary Immaculate hadn't seemed that different from my old school, except for the uniform and the nuns and going to chapel on Wednesday mornings. There were prayers at assembly, but it wasn't difficult to follow them, and I liked whispering and closing my eyes and touching myself to make the sign of the cross. When we said the *Our Father* I thought of my own departed father and that my mother would have approved of *thy will be done,* and the link between temptation and evil.

The headmistress nun walked with a stick and wore men's glasses. She was our class teacher and some days she wrote our work on the board and went back to her office to sleep at her desk. I don't think she read our workbooks. At the end of each term she gave the top student prize to Bethany Crisp who had a black plastic case full of textas and did elaborate decorative borders around her maths, geography, writing and spelling. A row of white rabbits eating leafy carrots, a row of apple trees with alternating green and red fruit, a row of stars or love hearts ... everything coloured in perfectly, right to the edge of each page. Bethany's mother played the keyboard in the chapel and worked in the canteen and drove the old nuns to their dental appointments. There were also prizes for best service: little zippered bibles covered in white leather. The headmistress nun said they were for being clean and quiet and devoted to the blessed Virgin Mary who was immaculate and preserved free from the stain of original sin. The best-service bibles were given to the children who brought in eggs or fruit and vegetables from their parents' home gardens for the nuns.

On sports day, I claimed a sprained ankle and wore one of my mother's bandages around my leg. My mother was working, but I went along and stood on the oval with the other parents to watch the races. One of the fathers fired a starting pistol in the air. It smelt sweetly sulphurous and gave off a plume of white smoke. When the girls from my class lined up to run, I prayed for Bethany Crisp to lose. She was tall and a good runner. As she crouched over the line waiting for the crack of the pistol I could see the white part along her scalp, how tightly the hair had been pulled into the two pretty, ribboned bunches. At the halfway mark Bethany was easily in the lead. I felt a little breathless as if, just by watching, my body was running too. Then, seemingly without reason, she stumbled and fell. The crowd of parents gasped as Bethany slumped sideways onto the grass. The other girls ran past her; even her friends didn't stop. Then the plastic tape that marked the crowd from the track was pulled taut in front of me. Mrs Crisp had pushed it up over her head as she darted forward towards Bethany. When she reached her daughter, she didn't lean over her in concern, but crouched in a deep squat and picked her up, scooping the heavy child into her arms to hip height, then lurching forward into a run. Mrs Crisp ran. Mrs Crisp, holding her daughter in her arms, ran for the finish line as if there was still time for her to win the race. As she passed me, Mrs Crisp wasn't smiling apologetically or ironically. Her face was ferocious. She looked like soldiers I'd seen in photographs, as they clambered out of the trenches, as they went over the top. Terrified and obstinate. Bethany bumped around awkwardly in her arms, one of her legs had become entangled in her mother's handbag which had slipped down her shoulder and now flew from Bethany's foot. Even as a child, I understood the feeling that passed through the crowd of parents watching from the sidelines. The titter that went up from them. Mrs Crisp had loved too much, she had allowed her mother animal to get free. This was humiliating and somehow unclean.

***

I'm no longer taking the interstate contracts, which means my salary has shrunk, but it's enough to pay the mortgage and I find I no longer want to travel. I'm happy to be at home in my unit behind the school. I carpeted the bedroom, painted it cream, hung linen curtains and framed watercolours of heirloom fruits on each wall. All clean and bright now. Not a mark, not a stain. I've bought my own little clock for the bedroom. I listen to it tick when I wake up in the morning, before the first children have been delivered to the playground by their mothers, before the first bell. The faint tender beat that comes out of the clock seems to fill the room.

When I bought the clock, the shop assistant told me she had one too. She bought hers to calm a new kitten fretting at being separated from its mother.

'It's a good trick,' the shop girl had said as she taped the docket to the box, 'it's the sound, it's like a mother's heartbeat, it makes them think they are not alone.'

Dreams
Jessica White

At the festival, the winter sun is warm, sinking into her forehead as she tilts back her head. She presses her hand against her chest to feel the beat booming. Her friend, who she has known since school, gestures to join her in the crowd but she shakes her head. On the ground she won't be able to feel the music. Instead, she stands in front of the mixing tent. The base of the tent is metal, and as she stands on it, vibrations travel up her calves. She smells grass crushed underfoot, spilled beer, a woman's freshly washed hair drying in the morning sun.

She's grown up in a small country town and music festivals and parties are still new to her. She has moved to a university in a quiet city by the coast, and travels to Sydney every now and then to see her friend. She hasn't been able to make new friends in this place where the flame trees spread like red coral into the sky. She tries to ignore the way the evenings stretch out like a long road, focusing instead on the books she needs to read for class, and the assignments she puts together like a puzzle.

At the festival, the day closes into night, bringing the smell of dew, while neon lights from the stage arc across the sky. She pulls her jumper out of her bag. Looking up, she notices fruit bats flying from the trees, and wonders how they are coping with the light and sound.

At the end of the festival, she catches the slow train back from Sydney. She walks from the station to her college, her legs aching from standing all day, her brain foggy from beer and watching people, but still fizzing with vibrations.

***

In the common room during the week, she reads about the concert in the music section of the newspaper. She can never judge if music is good or not, only if it has a beat that she can dance to. The adjacent article is about Kylie's latest album, the title of which came from a book of poems dedicated to her, *Poems to Break the Harts of Impossible Princesses*, by Billy Childish. Someone had mistakenly passed it on to Nick Cave, who gave it to Kylie, his friend. Was 'hart' a misspelling, she wondered? She pulls her notebook out of her pocket and writes Childish's name into it.

It turns out the British don't like the album much, because it isn't Kylie's usual happy-go-lucky fare. Kylie has written the songs herself, though, for the first time. The album's release has been delayed several times, most recently because of the death of Princess Di.

Her mother had kept copies of the *Australian Women's Weekly* in the lime green cupboards on the veranda at home. She once said that a friend, at a meet-and-greet event for teachers in London, had been in a room with Princess Di. Her mother's friend watched the princess shaking in a room full of strangers, and noticed she had bitten her nails to the quick.

At the end of each year, as school drew to a close, Chiara and her brother would pull out the magazines, pick one each, and make Christmas trees from them.

She came across photos of Princess Di wearing a diamond-encrusted necklace, and remembered the story of Princess Di's shaking. Chiara didn't blame her; she would probably have felt the same.

Her brother, noticing her pause at the page, tapped the necklace and waved. She looked up at him.

'Do you know that diamonds are made from carbon that is compressed under huge pressure?'

She shook her head.

Her brother was a font of facts and sometimes he didn't shut up. She looked down at the page so she wouldn't have to listen to him again, creasing Princess Di in her tiara and sparkling dress into a triangle.

When they'd folded all the pages in the magazine into a triangle, pushing one page against the next, they took their trees out to the lawn and sprayed them with gold paint. The ball rattling inside the spray-paint can was intensely satisfying. She shook it again and again until her brother pulled it off her and told her to stop being annoying.

***

In the library the next day, she enters 'Billy Childish' into the catalogue and is directed to some magazines upstairs. She sits on the floor between the stacks, the carpet rough under her thighs, breathing in the smell of degrading cellulose in old books. She checks the call number and finds the article in an art magazine. Childish, she reads, is an artist, musician and poet. He has some lines by Kurt Schwitters tattooed onto his left buttock. He is dyslexic, but went undiagnosed, and left school at sixteen. He became a stonemason, but it sounded like he did more drawing than cutting of stone, producing some six hundred artworks. He went to art school, got kicked out, then later re-enrolled. She wonders what his poetry is like, and if his use of 'hart' is a deliberate misspelling, a defiance of orthodox English.

She wishes she had a friend from class she could ask, but it takes so much effort just to get through one tutorial that she can't see how to manage it. The mechanics of conversations are baffling to her anyway.

***

On New Year's Eve she and her friend join a throng heading to Fox Studios. The sky is balmy, the sun setting into peach haze. Inside the hall, the light is low. Beside the grandstands, out of the light from the disco balls and strobes, her friend slips half a tablet in her hand and points to her water bottle.

After hours of dancing in high heels, her ankles are aching. She makes her way up the grandstand, finding a spot at the end where she can lean her head against the balustrade. She closes her eyes, resting them from the chopping of light and dark on the dancefloor. She breathes through her nose, smelling sweat, perfume and a chemical tang from the smoke machine. A few minutes later, she opens her eyes to check her surroundings and make sure that no-one is speaking to her. Looking behind, she notices a man lying flat on the seats, a man in the row above bending over and giving him a blow job. She turns away, sees her friend coming up the aisle to join her, and waves.

At the end of the party, they catch a taxi back to her friend's house, and for the first time, from the taxi window, she watches the dawn rise after a night out. She knows other people pull all-nighters all the time, but she goes out so rarely that the pink sky is special.

A few days later, her toenails go black from dancing. A few days after that they turn green, then fall off.

***

When she finishes her third year of uni, Chiara decides to relocate from the city on the coast to Sydney, as she has fewer classes in her final year. Her brother, who has moved into a university college in Randwick, has two friends who need a flatmate. One is studying mechanical engineering and the other is studying medicine. She meets them and they all move into an apartment in Redfern.

She temps during the summer, helping a bank organise their filing system. On Saturday mornings she watches *Video Hits* with her flatmates while bread bakes in the automatic breadmaker. They eat the freshly made bread with too much butter.

They decide to hold a housewarming party, and sit at the kitchen table to workshop themes.

'How about "Your Deepest, Darkest Desires?"' she suggests.

'That's perfect!' says the engineer.

They invite her brother and their college friends. Her brother dons a sheet, spray-paints himself in gold and tells everyone he is God. Two engineers have sourced bras from Vinnies, and slipped light bulbs shaped like domes into the cups. They invite her to press their breasts. When she tries, the bulbs light up. She laughs and wishes she could ask how they made their flashing breasts, but she's too anxious about her voice, and her brother is busy in the corner pretending to bless someone. Instead she places her drink on top of the speakers, watching the vibrations tremble the wine in her glass. If someone asks her, she will tell them that, with her red feather boa, tight black dress and crimson lipstick, she is a femme fatale, but no-one speaks to her. At least, no-one who she notices.

When her flatmates are studying, and her friend is away with her boyfriend, Chiara goes for long walks through the golf course to Centennial Park. Watching women with babies in prams, and couples running together, she feels her loneliness swelling up. Mostly, she can tamp it down, but she's beginning to wonder if she will ever feel a man's gentle hand on the back of her neck. She passes the island in the lake where the ibises cluster. Their reek is powerful today, and she starts to run to find clearer air.

***

When her final year of uni starts, she catches the slow train to the coast a few days a week. She isn't entirely sure of what she's doing at uni, only that she loves books and writing, and it seems good to focus on what she loves. She composes stories and poems and sends them out. Sometimes they are accepted and a cheque for thirty dollars arrives in the mail.

One of her assigned texts for English is Chaucer's *The Book of the Duchess*. As the train passes by the shining sea, through dark forests and darker tunnels, she wrestles with the Middle English. Perhaps if she could hear the words, she would find it easier to understand them on the page. She consults an essay on the poem recommended by her lecturer, and reads the introductory synopsis. The narrator, a poet, hasn't slept for eight years. Praying to Juno or Morpheus, his prayers are answered and, in his dream, he wakes to a room of coloured light pouring onto him. Around him are stained glass windows showing the story of *The Romance of the Rose*. Outside, he hears dogs baying, and on stepping beyond the stories of coloured glass, he finds the emperor Octavian in a hunt for a hart. The men, horses and hounds ride on, and he and a small dog trundle behind. In a clearing, he comes across a black knight, mourning the loss of his lady. As he refers to her as a 'good, fair White', critics have interpreted the story as a reference to Blanche, the wife of John of Gaunt.

When the poet wakes up, he writes down his story in rhyme. Telling stories, her lecturer explains in class later that morning, is a way of healing. Her lecturer reminds them that there is also no story until the dreamer writes it down.

***

At the pub with her friend, she watches the man on the stage playing bass, feeling his song through her muscles and flesh. She taps her feet to the beat, observing how his body barely moves, perhaps because he's intent on his fingerwork. When the singers finish, she can still feel vibrations travelling through the floorboards and into the soles of her feet. The bass player's fingers are moving over his guitar. Then her friend takes her by the wrist and pulls her to the bar.

Waiting for people to finish talking after the music ends is always the most boring part of an evening. Standing on the edge of the group beside her friend, she observes people laughing around her. After an hour, the beers she's had begin to leave her system and tiredness creeps in, slackening her shoulders. She checks her watch, and wonders if it's too early to ask her friend if they can leave.

She notices the thin bass player moving through the crowd. It seems he knows someone in the group that she's standing next to, because he heads their way, waving. He has brown eyes and black hair with a curl to it. His shirt sticks to his narrow chest with sweat. His body language is relaxed, but she notices shadows beneath his eyes.

He looks up and catches her watching. Flushed, she averts her eyes and steps back, out of the circle. She glances sidelong at her friend, who is still talking to the woman next to her, and looks down at her feet again.

She smells him before he touches her arm, clocking the scent of acrid sweat and sweet deodorant. She forces herself to look up, and his eyes seem almost black in the shadows. It's so dark she can't see what he is saying. Sweat prickles in her armpits and at the back of her neck. Her pulse quickens like a hart rushing through a forest. She wants to ask her friend for help but thinks she might appear strange. She sees his body tensing, about to step back. The pressure in her head is so intense she thinks it will crack, but she reaches for her handbag and pulls out her notebook and pen.

She watches his body still, waiting.

I'm deaf, she writes onto a blank page. *I can't hear you.*

She is mortified that the pad is shaking.

Gently, he takes it from her and writes in careful block letters. *WHAT'S YOUR NAME?*

She takes the pen back; it's sweaty. *Chiara.*

A DRINK, CHIARA?

She hesitates, glancing at the bar. There's no direct light near it to help her lipread him. She sees he is writing again.

WE HAVE A WHOLE BOOK TO FILL?

He waves the pad and she smiles. When he takes her hand, she feels the calluses on his fingerpads from playing his guitar. He guides her through the crowd, his thumb stroking the inside of her wrist. The roughness sends her thrumming – a song beneath her skin.

Death is Not the End
Kris Kneen

Back in art school, Henry and his friends used to talk about the apocalypse.

What is your strategy for when the apocalypse comes for us? What will you do?

He'd sit around with all the other art school students and wrestle the possible scenarios out of their imaginations. They were the COVID kids. They still remembered the first lockdowns, the masks, their mothers washing packets of frozen vegetables before packing them into the freezer drawer. They still remembered rows and rows of empty supermarket shelves, a formative memory even though it seemed to them so long ago.

In the apocalypse, who would you eat first?

It was always Henry. The other kids were sure of it. In case of an apocalypse, Henry Bathurst had no place. Henry argued against it, of course, talked about his special skills.

He could document the fall. *Someone needs to document it so that it never happens again. If we don't record history, we never learn from it. We are doomed to repeat our mistakes.* He argued passionately and it was true, Henry was persuasive when he wanted to be. He had argued for his PhD candidacy with hardly any pushback, after all. But when it came to the apocalypse, it was pretty clear that Henry had no practical skills to offer a new colony. He was also a fat young man, heavy and awkward, lots of meat on his bones. If his cohort killed Rachel, they would eat for a day; if they killed Henry, they might be able to stretch it to a week.

Henry's only useful skill was photography, and not just portraiture or landscapes or even journalistic photos. Henry had thrown himself into the art of spirit photography.

At first, Henry didn't know what he was doing. He maintained an old-fashioned darkroom at home when everyone else was working in digital form. He liked the burn of chemicals in his nostrils. He liked the slosh of the fixative rushing over the photographic paper. He loved the way the image started from white, darkening with every passing second till face, clothing, furniture began to emerge fresh from the fog. It was magic and Henry felt a rush every time he watched a photograph developing, a wash of adrenaline like the feeling when you fall in love.

The first spirit was a surprise. Henry was developing a photograph of his mother, watching her long nose find shape, when he noticed something coalescing behind her. As the photograph developed the ghostly form took shape, a baby. It was still a shadow of a creature but you could clearly see the curl of tiny fists, eyes closed, feet caught mid-kick.

When Henry showed the photo to his mother, her eyes widened before brimming with tears. 'It's your sister,' she told him.

Henry didn't have a sister.

'Your sister died when she was only three weeks old. That's her. I'd know her anywhere. That's her face, her little hands, her long neck.'

Henry hadn't ever heard about a dead sister.

He had assumed that the image in the background of his mother's portrait was some odd exposure that had already touched the paper before he exposed it to his mother's face. It didn't make much sense, but it seemed like the only possible explanation.

***

Many years later at university, Henry had been asked to research an historical photographic movement. It was then that he discovered spirit photography. Showmen and charlatans in the late eighteenth century would hold portraiture sessions intending to capture the dead and return them for a moment to the world of the living. This gate between worlds held on photosensitive plates. Ghost lovers who had died, ghost parents, the ghosts of lost children. These photographers were snake-oil salesmen, selling a panacea for grief.

Henry remembered his own mother's tears, her relief when she looked at the photograph. 'She looks at peace, doesn't she? She looks happy.'

His mother kept the photograph in the drawer next to her bed. It was there when she died of leukaemia. Henry found it when he sorted through her things. He kept the photograph, moving it to his own portfolio. When he had to find a focus for his master's project, he took it out again.

It was easy to replicate the ghost effect on other photographs, take the image on a long exposure, introduce the 'ghost'. The photograph would show the translucent image of a figure, fainter if only exposed for a fraction of the time. It was harder to make meaning from the technique. He worked with a local First Nations group to make spirit photographs of First Nations ancestors haunting domestic settings, a kitchen, the lounge room of a family watching TV. The ghostly forms of a massacred family just visible on the steps of City Hall. He didn't think of these photographs as his. He gave them to the people he had worked with and watched as they grew silent. Nodded. One of the men wept. He made photographs for them and as a lucky aside, he was awarded his MA.

Every story is a ghost story, he explained, while arguing for his doctorate. And all the other academics nodded and grunted in agreement before giving him their blessing to continue with his research project.

The second spirit came unexpectedly. Henry had agreed to take photographs for a friend who was having her first novel published. Author photographs, she called them. They looked through images of famous writers, laughing about how they always hid their chins in their hands, or crossed their arms awkwardly over their chests.

Ultimately Henry chose a wall of books as the background, a simple sitting pose, hands relaxed in her lap.

He took two dozen photographs and all of them were serviceable except one. He saw the problem as he was rocking the chemical bath between his hands. The sweet but stern face, neutral expression materialising out of the fog.

And there at her shoulder, a young man, leaning in as if to kiss the author's neck.

Henry thought about keeping the image a secret. He had long harboured a crush on the author and it seemed this image held the story of a previous lover. Henry printed the photo again and again, but in each iteration the ghostly figure remained.

The writer was rocked by the sight of the photo.

'Do you know him?'

She shook her head, but Henry wasn't sure that this was true.

'A double exposure on the negative, perhaps. I don't know, it's happened before.'

The young woman said nothing, put the photos in an envelope with barely a thank-you, and that was their last interaction.

More ghostly figures began to appear in Henry's work. He claimed some of them as his own trick photography. A ghost cat glimpsed behind a study of a vase of dying flowers, a middle-aged woman warming herself in a ray of sunlight in an otherwise empty room, a naked man standing at the edge of a waterfall. He hid these real photos amongst the snake oil, his pretend ghosts. No-one could pick the real from the fake. The ghosts began to turn up so thick and fast that Henry stopped faking his ghosts at all. He approached each new experiment with an open mind and sure enough the ghosts would come marching into view, changing the context of the photographs, breathing new life into scenes so ordinary that they would be otherwise unremarkable.

After graduation and the awarding of the university medal, Henry mounted a major exhibition on his own. These were the days just before the apocalypse. When everything in the world seemed stable and sane.

The exhibition was a huge success. *Dr Henry Bathurst Summons Ghosts*, the paper read. A double-page feature. Henry, looking slightly confused, stared out from the black and white page. *In the hands of expert photographer Henry Bathurst, death is not the end*, wrote a journalist in a glowing review. *Bathurst reminds us of the repercussions of our actions. A photographic exercise in moral philosophy.*

All of the numbered prints in the exhibition sold on the first night and Henry was forced to make a second, limited run of prints to meet demand.

He had them carefully folded in tissue paper and was carrying them to the gallery when he saw the first plane fall.

He stood open-mouthed and watched the slow arc as it left its flight path and plunged steadily towards the ground.

There was the sound of a car crashing somewhere, a few streets away. A siren rang out. People emerged from houses holding their phones up as if offering them to the gods of the sky.

The internet was down. All navigation systems had collapsed. The power cut out before night fell and on that first night, people went missing. Husbands woke up to find their wives weren't in bed. Mothers went to check on vanished babies. Children left teddy bears and dolls in the place where their physical bodies had once been. In frantic searches, whole neighbourhoods joined hands and walked through the state forest, breaking the line only to avoid shaggy bushes and tall gum trees.

By the second day, everyone realised that the apocalypse was well and truly underway.

Without connectivity it was hard to know exactly what had caused it and if it was as widespread as it seemed. There were whisperings of plasma storms, the rise of AI shutting down all power and communications. A rumour spread that some scientist had tasked an artificial intelligence with the goal of saving the planet, the solution being to eradicate a large percentage of humans who were the major strain on the ecosystems. Some people continued to search for the missing. Others sank into the darkness of knowing that nothing would ever be the same again.

***

Henry was involved in one of the first supermarket stampedes. He didn't realise he was not the only person heading to the shop. He used his jumper to pillage a few cans of sardines, beans, tomatoes and bottled water. He had to hold his jumper close to his chest and aim himself with all the force of his hefty body towards the doors, battling grabbing hands and narrowly missing a man brandishing a knife and a garbage can lid like a badly dressed extra in a movie about the fall of the Roman Empire.

Henry turned back to see two women rolling on the floor in the cereal aisle. They had a hunk of each other's hair in their fists, trying to smash the other's head against the cold yellow tiles.

Henry learned about hunger. He learned about cruelty. He learned about selfishness in the weeks that followed. He learned that being fat was something to prize, and he felt sad to see the flesh disappearing off his bones.

Others had stockpiled food and spent their days defending it. Henry had stockpiled chemicals and photographic paper and rolls of film, which seemed pointless at first, but then he was glad he had done this. It was on a forage in search of food when Henry realised he had stumbled into the crash site of that first felled plane.

He wore the camera around his neck out of habit and in a gesture embedded in his arms and his eyes and his breath, he put it up to his face and took a barrage of photographs. Chunks of twisted metal. His camera snapped. A handbag, open and looted of anything that might be useful. Snap. Seats with lumps of something clipped into them, low and tight. Snap. Luggage strewn across charred grass and dirt. Snap. The memory of flames.

At home, he unpacked his scant collection of lemons from a picked-clean community garden, Tic Tacs from someone's burned luggage, a tin of peas from under the linoleum of an abandoned shed. He saw a cat run from one garden to the next and was simultaneously worried and hungry for it.

The few people he passed stared warily at him. He wondered if the killing and the cannibalism had begun.

After a lunch of peas and rice, Henry got to work. He unrolled the film, his hands thrust into a dark bag, something he had already become expert at before the power went out for good, and red lights were no longer a solution for the developing room.

After the negatives were processed, Henry began to feel that familiar excitement. He eased a thick blank page out of the metallic sleeve. He moved to the machine. He had rigged it up with a funnel channelling a blast of bright sunlight down through a tube, ready to explode onto the exposed page. The light travelled through the negative, a process that could only happen in the hour on either side of high noon. A sundial was set outside in the garden and Henry had checked it before setting up, the perfect time for exposure. Taking a breath and holding it was not part of the process, but Henry did it anyway, pulling a lever and counting out the seconds in his head. He released the lever and the spill of light disappeared, the only proof a lingering flash of blue in the shape of a rectangle that still hovered behind his closed eyelids in the darkened room.

The rest was all by feel. Henry took the exposed page and settled it in the first chemical bath, counting, rocking the plastic box, feeling the swish of the liquid. He pushed at the spot where the paper would be with the tongs, making sure it was under the chemicals. At the count, he quickly grabbed and lifted the page with the tongs and slipped it into the fixative bath. The last bath was the wash. He had done this process so many times it felt like breathing, or perhaps eating. He certainly felt like he was being filled up by the ritual of rocking and counting. His hunger dissipated. When the wait was over, Henry hung the page on the line that he had strung up across the room. He felt sated by the process but a little disappointed that he couldn't watch the photo appearing from the white mist. Perhaps he could find some red cellophane in a looted newsagents somewhere and make a small, reddened window to allow him to watch the magic at play.

For now, he was satisfied that the image would be safe and fixed to the page and he turned to the nearest blackout curtain and flung it wide. Light poured in. The photograph rocked back and forth on the line.

Henry opened his mouth. He felt something on his cheeks, the light perhaps, the fingers of an angel stroking his skin. But when he raised his own hand to his cheek it was wet.

Tears.

And Henry let them flow.

He was crying, crying for the world lost to him, for all the years of work that had led him here. Crying for the people who had died suddenly in the first wave of crashes and collapses, the cars overturned, the life support systems that had suddenly ceased to support that life, and yes, the plane that had fallen from the sky, the ghosts, wandering bleary-eyed across his photograph, surprised, confused, looking for their lost lives amongst the twisted metal and seared flesh. He was crying too for those that had gone in the second wave, mystery disappearances, and all the people who had been left to grieve and to wonder, tears without end.

Henry was still crying as he printed the rest of the photographs, a baby falling forward, caught in the very act of succumbing to Newton's second law of motion. A man, slumped in a seat already occupied by half of his own body, chewing on his fingernail in distress. A woman stretching her hands up towards the sky as if to beg the heavens to let her ascend.

Henry stood among the images, which were pinned like dead butterflies to the piece of string. He had never felt more certain of what he must do.

***

Henry wrote the invitations on old photographs, *City Gallery*, he wrote. *Tomorrow*, he wrote. He couldn't sleep that night. He felt the rising anxiety come at him in waves. How would the people receive the work? Until now he had presented the truth as if it were a lie, hiding behind the pretence of a trick, passing spirits off as living souls. What would happen when the charlatan turned out to be a real magician, a reverse Wizard of Oz?

Henry arrived at the gallery at dawn. He hadn't eaten in twenty-four hours and his stomach complained bitterly as he opened the door, locking it firmly behind him.

The images were all framed and hung. The framing shop on Boundary Street remained open. The kitchen at the back of the shop had been ransacked but none of the matt boards or glass frames had been touched.

He divided each of the gallery rooms into a unique space. Blue matt boards in the pet room, ghost dogs and cats still roaming through houses, surrounded by families who had grieved their disappearance, and those who had grieved only after feasting rather well. The room dedicated to the plane crash had frames of crimson, as if each image were still on fire. The third room was framed with yellow matt boards – strangers, neighbours, friends wandering through parks and up the creek and around the state forest, each ghost a story just waiting to be told.

Henry sat in the final room, the grey room, and sipped on water gathered from the last rain. Water was, of course, scarce now. People gathered dew each morning, bottled what little they could glean from the creek. Sometimes the trucks came and there would be a scramble for the precious bottles. More rarely a truck would rumble into town with stacks of food and medicine. There was still some minimal semblance of order, still some food to be had, people pretending this veneer of civility might last, but they were beginning to forget, and fast.

Henry finished his water, then shuffled, tired, hungry, to the front door of the gallery. Voices. A stuttering of light and shade creeping in from under the door. Henry pulled the curtains and they were there, a queue of people, lank, grey, staring-eyed people, stretched down the block and around the corner of the street. Henry had never seen such a crowd outside a gallery. It looked like the impatient mob waiting outside a Kylie Minogue or Taylor Swift concert in days long gone.

Henry took photographs as the people streamed into the gallery. He took photographs of people staring at the photographs. They moved through the exhibition in silence. A quiet bubble of grief seemed to emanate from each room. There were those who howled in the pet room. They all remembered the pure joy of living with a beloved pet. No-one had eaten the family dog yet. No-one suspected a neighbour of killing their cat.

Henry photographed the faces, wet with tears. Noses streaming, eyes red and swollen as they moved into the red room with its horror of burned and rotted flesh. The lost souls wandering through the wreckage, still trying to find their way back to Terminal 2. Some people wept as they saw the souls in the open parklands. Others smiled, laughed out loud. The people in these photographs seemed almost at peace. It was a comfort. The idea that their loved ones were roaming free. Looking at birds, pointing down at stones or up at clouds.

One woman grabbed at Henry's arm, dragged him towards a yellow-bordered photograph. A young man, a wraith, painted in the finest of gossamer threads, stooped to warm his hands at a patch of wildflowers.

'William left on purpose,' she said, 'He was such a tender soul. He saw what we had become, the way we treat each other. And he left.' The woman was weeping openly now. 'He left because he was kind.

See? I didn't think I could forgive him for leaving, but look. That is him,' she said pointing to the shadowy image on the photographic paper. 'All that kindness. See?'

In the grey room, all chatter fell to a hush. People moved from one photograph to the next. House to house to house. They were here. The missing ones. Old Mr Hughes, leaning his ethereal forehead on his own front door, shut to him forever. Mrs Renshaw curled up on her own stoop, just a faded breath of a person, so clearly diseased. A baby like an abandoned doll, sleeping on the cobbled path. A child, caught as a shadow, bouncing a ball against a side wall of a building.

They were gone. It was clear now. They were gone.

One woman fell to her knees, then folded over herself onto the floor. People made way, let her sob as she needed to sob. Craig Renshaw turned and yelled at the gathered crowd, 'Get over yourselves. We're starving here. We're dying. All of us. Dying,' before storming off down the road towards the quarry. People whispered. *Yes, they had suspected him of – couldn't bring themselves to really believe that –* and the next day, when they found Craig Renshaw's body broken at the bottom of the cliffs, no-one seemed surprised. Some of the men laboriously dragged him back to the town. Seemed only fitting after that, the mouth-watering smell that emanated from the empty block behind the church. Seemed right somehow. An honouring.

Henry finished a roll of film and put his camera away. He sat by the wall in the grey room. He knew what he would find when he processed the images. The dead were all around us. He could feel them even now. He felt exhausted.

He had his eyes closed, his head lowered into his hands, when he felt her standing in front of him. She was a young woman, thin, with dark bags under her eyes. He could see the streaks of tears muddying her cheeks. She handed him a bunch of wildflowers and bowed her head a little before retreating. Henry was surprised, then grateful, touched.

Next, a man stepped up and left a bottle of wine at his feet, nodded. Left without a word. Then there was water, a knob of stale bread, a handmade quilt. The old woman who placed it at his feet must have gone all the way home and carried it back, folded neatly. Someone left a collar with a little tinkling bell in his lap and Henry immediately fastened it around his wrist. He felt the rub of something soft and warm against his leg, the trembling of a silent purr, echoing through his body, healing his wearied muscles. He wiped his moist eyes. More gifts, most of them modest, some useful; he was heaped with symbols of gratitude. And he was grateful. Grateful to see a man helping the lady who had brought the quilt back across the road. Grateful to witness a husband and wife wrapping their arms around each other and leaning together for comfort. Grateful to see a stranger reach over and hold another man's arm as he wept silently in a corner.

A woman placed a handful of chanterelles in his hands.

'Thank you,' she said.

'For what?'

'For bringing it all back, the memories. It's brought us back, I think. We were gone, we were dead inside.'

Henry nodded. He was spent. He wasn't sure exactly what he had done here, what the exhibition was even for, what it might have achieved. But he looked at the crowd, thinning now, all the people helping each other back down the road, to their own houses, to their own cold lonely beds, to an uncertain future. Despite what his friends at university had said about him, in case of an apocalypse, Dr Henry Bathurst – charlatan, snake-oil salesman, magician and spirit photographer – would not be the first to be eaten, now.

Shocked
Thuy On

Reading the topography of your face
and I am shocked (shocked)

the blood rush to my own
I should be so lucky

to run my fingers along
your faint blue veins

once again I am shocked (shocked)
the red bright life of you

my hand on your heart
the four chambers of my own

the quiver and pulse
when you shadow near

the thrumming heat of you
such long-lashed flickers

and I am spinning around
shocked (shocked)

wishing I could step back in time
to where all the lovers breathe

to keep the inevitable at bay
so I won't be shocked (shocked)

when we're finally parted
and you stand cold as stalactite.

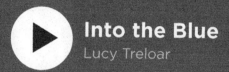

Into the Blue
Lucy Treloar

Francesca arrived out of the blue, same as always.

I was on the beach making sandcastles with my baby Harryo in the late afternoon. She was pressing little stones and shells into their walls and smacking them down so we could start again. The scent of scrubby pines and wormwood rolled down the hills and cliffs. The people walking the waves' edge were golden in the sun. The hard clear light fell on us too. I could see everything; nothing would surprise me.

'Not too hard now, or it'll break,' I said. 'Whoops.'

'Oh. 'Oops.'

'Never mind.'

A cry from above, 'Hey!' It was Francesca striding down the steep cliff path across channels of erosion and loose stones. Nothing slowed her. My heart fluttered up and plummeted and lifted again, remembering other visits.

She slithered across the bank of pebbles above the tideline, swearing lightly to herself – 'fucking stones' – the usual, pausing to call out, 'The ham's arrived.'

I made our old childhood vomit noise. (The ham was our summer culinary ordeal.)

Harryo laughed and jigged – 'Again, 'gain' – and I obliged.

'Not quite as big as the whopper of twenty fifteen it is generally agreed, but it will feed the thousands, I suppose. Poor things. Poor us.' She seemed quite happy at the thought. She was home, yes she was.

I laughed. Francesca plonked down at my side, as beautiful as ever. She has thick, dark hair and brown limbs and clear eyes and straight, fierce brows. Mostly she is hot, which I mention as a fact.

She biffed me on the shoulder by way of greeting, as if we'd seen each other only last week. 'Little G.' A crack opened in her voice, and she rested her head on my shoulder. (Oh god, we were back here again.) 'My heart she is broke.'

Of course it was. I kept quiet when once I would have said, 'Chessie. Oh no. What's the bastard done this time? New bastard? Never mind. *We* love you.'

I know she felt this quiet of mine and sensed some of its meaning. She lifted her head away and sniffed briskly. We were sisters again and would proceed as before – before being three years ago, or possibly four.

'And is this the wunderkind I have been hearing about?' she asked.

'This is Harryo.'

'Harryo,' she said, and Harryo lifted her little head, blinking into the wind, and considered her.

'Do you want to say hello, sweetie?' I asked.

Harryo searched about. She picked up a shell and gave it to Francesca and picked up another shell and put it against the sandcastle wall and looked at Francesca, who took the hint, found an empty spot and pressed her stone in delicately. In this way it was agreed that Francesca was part of our lives.

This is why I love Francesca. She wasn't noisy or gushy. She was quiet. She met Harryo where she was in her immutable Harryo-ness and agreed that she, Francesca, would become her slave for the next while, as it proved to be. It is a gift she has, to see the way to be around people, including me. It has never worked with our mother.

***

The first year Francesca didn't come home for Christmas our mother only said fondly, 'Oh, she was always running away.' And then, to our father, 'Remember her little backpack, and her notes? So sweet.'

And the story would amble on its familiar path, how she'd climb the back fence and run away down the paddock and get blown up the hill.

I saw her do it once, run away I mean.

'She's really going. She really is, Mum,' I shouted.

My mother came and watched with me.

'Go and get her.' I jerked her arm.

But she didn't. If she didn't care enough to get my sister, beautiful Francesca, who did she care about?

At the last moment, at the hill's peak, Francesca stopped and looked into the blue evening beyond this sodden valley. Then she turned so her whole body faced home, her hair streaming back in the wind, and began down the hill, slowly at first, then in a rush, like a seasonal creek coming to life.

My mother said, 'Go and play, sweetie. We don't want to make a fuss.'

I wonder now if Francesca was daring my mother or conducting an experiment to answer the question: Does our mother care?

***

Four years had been ample time for us to talk and wonder about Francesca, which she has always claimed to hate. ('So nosy.') We kept an eye on magazines and the socials. She wasn't 'famous-famous', as she put it, only well known as a screenwriter, a job that meant she knew people who *were* famous-famous. She didn't think anything of them in particular. They were 'just people'.

My cousins held up pictures of film award nights and squinted into the background crowd scenes. 'Is that her?'

'No – at least, I don't think so. Wait—' and I'd take the magazine from them and hold it close. Sometimes she appeared in the arms of people we recognised. Mostly she was smiling.

If it was Christmas, the whole family was at the beach, and if she was not, her absence became a presence of its own. 'Any word from Francesca?' my mother might eventually ask on Christmas Eve. Every few years she would explode into our lives like a heat-seeking missile. She understood the tidal movements of family life. She knew where to find us.

**

Now, Francesca headed around the bay in long strides, sandals dangling from her hand. I drifted up the cliff and gave Harryo a bath.

That night it was just us for dinner. Our mother looked on the scene dotingly; in this moment we made a beautiful picture.

Harryo practised her words: cat, mum mum mum (or um um um), 'nana, meaning banana, though my mother chose to believe she had become Nana. Then 'Chess,' Harryo said, as clear as day.

Francesca said, 'Harryo!' And they beamed at each other.

My mother began clearing the table.

**

The next night there was a big family dinner to welcome Francesca home. Everyone was cooking at their place on the same huge old beach block. Harryo and I went traipsing between houses, picking up the whisk, the big white platter, the green enamel baking tray, the gravy boat, the damask napkins, and delivering them here and there. Harryo stared wide-eyed from my arms.

'Hold on tight,' I said, handing her the whisk.

'Holdin',' Harryo said.

Later, Francesca swept into dinner in a rose satin ball gown of the 1950s – what a sideshow – which made our grandmother reminisce fondly about the night she'd worn it.

'Very nice, sweetie,' our mother said. 'Do be careful. Napkin?' She made a little gesture towards her cleavage and looked hintingly at Francesca's boobs.

'Mum,' Francesca said, but shoved the corner of the napkin down the front of her dress and clasped her hands in front of her like an obedient child. Our mother's face was very bright somehow. Francesca and I assessed her mood: not good. Our eyes met. Francesca made an emoji face of bared-teeth alarm.

And so dinner proceeded, by which I mean carefully, though people mostly seemed unaware. Francesca was charming and self-effacing, trying to minimise her effect. She treated the middle-aged uncles like dear old duffers, which they weathered fairly well, and flattered the aunts wildly – your gorgeous hair, I love that top, and so on – to take their minds off their fading youth.

Finally, when dessert was on the wane, one of the quieter cousins, a sweet kid of fifteen, bravely asked what was going on in Francesca's life.

Francesca said quietly, 'Oh, nothing, nothing at all really, apart from my sad, broken heart. It's why it's so special to be here with you beautiful people. I know I'm home.'

Everyone stopped to look at her, all wanting to save her. This is Francesca's superpower. It's in her eyes, I believe.

'Oh, for pity's sake, Francesca,' our mother said.

It was a relief, a storm broken, a balloon punctured, all the metaphors. Like that, Francesca stopped the performance, worn out. Her head rose above the white napkin like a portrait, as stark as that. She looked at our mother, poised for something. It reminded me of her times running away and staring back across the valley, very still while she made her judgement. Our mother stared and blinked.

'What?' Francesca said. 'What have I done now?'

Our mother began gathering plates in a rush.

'Darling?' our father said.

Francesca quietly began clearing her side of the table.

'Leave them,' our mother said.

Francesca, not taking her eyes from our mother, lowered the plates and left the room. I checked on Harryo – fast asleep – and went to find Francesca. I knew where she'd be.

***

It was quiet at the lookout. A moon was rising over the sea. There she was, back against the clifftop wall, facing the horizon, same as always. How many times had we sat here together?

It was from here that once or twice a cousin had rattled stones down so they hit the roof of a shack nestled at the cliff's base. Gone now. There had been some feeling among the people of the clifftop village – and in our family – that the shack shouldn't be there, and in the end, they had their way. The house was flattened in minutes and left like that. Shards of asbestos still wash up and down in the tides. Francesca would have been fourteen and I eleven.

'But why?' Francesca asked our mother when it was done.

'Because it was illegal. It wasn't their land, they just built on it.'

Francesca became reckless. 'Who cares? You didn't want it.'

'You can't just have people building anywhere. It wasn't even plumbed. It wasn't safe in storms.'

'It was fine. We used to go and visit.'

'You what?'

'Doesn't matter. You destroyed her home to save her from the plumbing and storms. You ruined her life.'

***

I don't know if it was this that shamed my mother's family – though it should have – but a small house on the family block was rented to the woman and her sons, Alex and Bobby, while they 'looked around'.

That cousin of ours didn't like strangers staying there. He began throwing pine cones onto their roof, just sometimes. He said it was the wind that blew them. But one night we went out to watch. There was some excitement in it. We knew it was wrong; that was part of it. It was dusk by then, the light was felted and mottled, like the dye was bleeding from it, and it was summertime so it must have been late.

Alex rushed out of the gloom towards us from the little house. He was tall and fast. We bunched together. Alex stopped, almost within reach, and it seemed like he was about to lunge or strike.

He said, 'You have to stop it. You have to stop. We have nowhere to go.' And he looked at Francesca as if he knew her, I mean really knew her, and said 'Please'. That was the worst part.

I will never forget her face. Or his. Never. Yearning, shame, desperation, rage – and something else. Some trembling energy between them. I understood it very well later.

Our cousin looked from Francesca to Alex and grinned, horribly. He went inside. I went inside. But Francesca didn't.

It was almost the end of summer by then. We left, and when we came back at Easter, Alex and his family were gone.

Francesca aimed her life at flight after that. She worked hard. She went to film school, learned her craft, and it wasn't so many years later that it seemed the world was hers in LA. She became someone we knew from magazines. We made a joke of it, so it didn't seem so sad.

***

Now, I looked at the moon and Francesca's smooth face held into its faint light.

'Hard landing back into family life?' I asked.

She shook her head.

We were quiet.

'I can never make myself small enough for her, can I? I mean, it's just not humanly possible.'

'Tell me about your latest loverboy.'

'Former.' She showed me a picture of a blond, prettyish sort of man on her phone.

'An elven prince, is he?'

Thank god she laughed. 'Another narcissist. We all make mistakes.'

In this way, we recovered.

***

I visited her once in LA. Every part of her life was beautiful: art, home, clothes, food. Every act was done in preparation to be seen and documented. But it must also appear effortless. Effortless took time.

But at the beach over the next few days with Harryo and me, she truly became effortless. She swam. She didn't wash her hair, which turned stiff and began to bleach. She wore no make-up, just sunscreen, and found clothes in the old wooden cupboard: the shorts she'd worn at fourteen, a between-the-war tea frock, a minidress, a long Indian skirt our mother wore as a teenager. She looked like something from the past.

I watched her on the beach one day, head down, scouting for sea glass – a habit. She was on a collision course with a tall man. At the last minute, they looked up and stopped dead. They knew each other and couldn't pretend they didn't. I could see it in their bodies. They moved away up the beach together.

In the evening, Francesca would only say that he was someone she used to know. The same thing happened the next afternoon. From the sharp movements of their heads, it seemed like they were arguing. And then, suddenly, weirdly, they were kissing – wildly.

They rushed towards the cliffs and scrambled up its steep sides. Stones skittered beneath their feet. He heaved her over the last ledge and she almost flew over the lip of the cliff. They'd have to be quick or people walking down the Esplanade might spot them. But there were one or two places that gave shelter, and they looked like they'd be fast.

***

This was how Francesca's summer now divided: Harryo and me in the morning, the man in the afternoon. Family dinner in the evening, and then she went out on an inscrutable walk. Eventually, one afternoon, the man came closer and I saw him.

The strangest thing: I was eleven again, watching them, feeling something without knowing, not understanding the tides of the body, the way they drew these two together. Seeing them like this, close to each other and to me, I saw that this man was Alex.

But he was also the man I had seen walking to the milkbar in the morning with his tiny daughter and a small dog. They were lovely together.

I told Francesca after dinner.

'Shut up, G,' she said. 'Just shut up. You don't know anything.'

***

I checked her room later. The window was open, curtain flying, Francesca gone.

I knew where she'd be.

Her voice came from behind the cliff wall. 'G? Is that you?'

'Yes.'

'Go home.'

'You alright?' My voice quavered.

'I don't need rescuing.'

There was a rustling of grasses, then a deep voice. 'Shit – what was that?'

A tremendous heat filled my chest and rushed up my throat. 'What is wrong with you?'

'Nothing,' Francesca said.

A light came on across the Esplanade, shadowy figures came to a window, the window opened.

I lowered my voice. 'You're not teenagers. You're not star-crossed lovers. You're adults and there's a child involved.' I stamped away.

Back at the house I waited on the veranda. Moths were battering themselves to death against the light above. Two possums glared at me from the rafters. They didn't want my company either.

Eventually, Francesca trailed through the gate and up the stairs and sat at my side on the old wooden bench. Her face was almost blank. 'What if we're meant to be together?' she said.

'Meant?'

'I never forgot him. And then I find him walking on the beach.'

'Oh, right, we're up to magical thinking now. Okay.'

'Fuck off,' she said, but quietly.

One of the possums made that rattling sound they do. 'You piss off,' I said to it, and it subsided. 'It's Alex's daughter. That's who I'm thinking of.' I looked at the moths. A large one had arrived and was blundering around, hitting the light bulb and falling away. 'I should turn the light off.'

'I like kids.'

'Yeah.' The sound of Harryo's thin wail drifted through the screen door. 'Anyway,' I said, and went inside.

***

In the morning I found Francesca standing in front of the open fridge, considering milk.

'Almond or soy?' she said.

I joined her. 'Full cream. Dairy. Always.'

We boomped together in old affection, then leaned against each other, warm against the cold air.

We turned away from the night before, gathering our things and Harryo and heading down to the beach.

We kept an eye on two women exploring the wild garden around the ruins of Alex's childhood home. People like to dig things up for their own gardens. Sometimes they're greedy. I like it in there myself. His mother was a good gardener. The bones of it are still there.

'Remember that night? I asked Francesca.

'Of course. Huge turning point,' she said, looking thoughtful. Perhaps she had some plot churning in her head.

She was restless that afternoon, running around the bay and back through the hills, but came back in much the same state. Unsated.

Our parents were out for some party. We went for a long walk through the evening, taking turns to push Harryo enthroned in the ancient pram. She entertained us with a rendition of 'Humpy Dumpy' that made Francesca laugh.

We got lost in someone's neglected olive hobby farm off a back road and found an apricot tree and picked a few and ate them along the way. With little growling animal noises, Harryo ground and mashed hers with the serrations of her newly hatched teeth. The juice ran down her chin and neck into her white top. Oh well.

It would remind me of something later, when it had been washed and the stains removed as best they could be, and I didn't know what. I was curious about that. I felt something coming.

The sea had turned pink – almost oily in the late light. We walked slowly down the Esplanade past the rich houses and the poor shacks where old leatherish fishermen sat blinking into the sunset, chugging their beers, chatting and coughing companionably. We nodded and they raised their stubbies to youth or whatever it was that we represented – their glory days or just neighbourliness. 'Nice night for it, ladies' and so on. From long habit we called out 'How 'bout the sunset?'

Harryo fell asleep and an apricot fell from her hand and rolled ahead of us. 'Oh,' Francesca said, and when we caught up with it gave it a boot to send it ahead again.

A small holiday crowd had gathered at the lookout above our path – all sorts, very peaceful – and watched the sunset. Beauty is beauty and all, but my attention flagged and I looked about.

Alex was there, over near the cliff wall where he and Francesca had been the night before. A blonde woman leaned into his side. She held a little baby against her front, its head nestled into her neck. In front of them a small child, wispy dark hair blowing about in the breeze, balanced along the sea wall.

Francesca was utterly still. I inched forward to block her view. She pulled me back and watched. Francesca wouldn't care about making a noise, but for now she had herself in check. Still, she was as brimful as she'd been as a runaway child. I don't know if the woman knew. She shook her head a little so her hair shimmered against her back.

The sun fell like a red-hot penny into the water. Francesca gripped my arm and held tight, staring into the light.

'Stop it, idiot,' I said. 'You'll go blind.'

'Blind,' she hissed. 'I've been blind for years. Don't tell me to stop. I should never have left.'

The crowd, thinning now, looked curiously at Francesca. She has a sort of density of presence that makes people watchful. The woman looked back and put her arm around Alex and let her hand slide down to his bum. Oh, she knew.

'Might as well go ahead and wee on him,' Francesca said. 'Mark her scent.'

Alex's head tipped back as if from a blow, but he righted himself and took the woman's hand and drew her away, calling the little girl – Moppet or Poppet or something.

Harryo sucked her fingers. Life is more elemental when you're a baby; your oral fixations are less complicated. Alex gave one last glance at Francesca. His wife somehow bore him away as if he had no will, though she staggered under her burdens: husband, child, baby. He could have broken free. In some part of himself he must have decided.

Francesca half turned from the sight, folding her arms across her front, tightly, holding herself together, her mouth a grimace. She shut her eyes against the woman crossing the road with her children and Alex.

I watched the woman. Let him go, I thought. But she wouldn't concede, not now, and I had to admire her strength. The decision would have happened privately, earlier in the day. This was just a piece of theatre. It was there all through her: pride, belief, security, love, her children. Alex was part of that. About him and his feelings I have no idea. A family is a kind of house. It can persist despite evident weakness or collapse despite apparent strength.

But Francesca . . .

'She's nearly asleep,' I said, leaning over the pram.

'Wait,' Francesca said. 'Wait here with me a minute. Hold my hand.'

I held it tight. 'Why?'

'To stop me throwing rocks through her windows.'

I pictured her running wildly in the deepening dark, like some strange creature that had emerged from phantasmagoric light to terrify us all.

***

Later, I wondered whether she came home for love, to see if this time someone might chase after her and bring her back.

When she got in her car next morning, I just watched. I would not plead, though I would cry later; I always did.

The car window hummed down.

'Well, seeya Chessie,' I said.

'Yeah, seeya G.' She twinkled her fingers lightly. There was a pause. She drummed her fingers against the car door, her mouth set as she faced forward, her eyes rather bright.

Suddenly, Harryo patted my cheek and leaned over. 'Chess, Chess, Chess,' she called, and stretched out her arms, her starfish hands, and I followed her lean and she patted Francesca's cheek and leaned down, curving over my arm like a warm cat, and gave Francesca one of her unformed kisses.

Your Disco Needs You
Holden Sheppard

The worst part about today's tutorial isn't that I rock up thirty minutes late, or that I'm pissed as a newt from cheap pints of Swanny D at the uni tav, but that Fredéric Dupont isn't in class today.

I also missed the memo about an in-class assessment. Our lecturer has been replaced by an exam invigilator who looks like Bonnie Tyler crossed with Skeletor, and everyone's head-down over their desks scribbling frantically.

Bonnie Skeletyler looks *pissed*. She hands me the assessment, tells me not to disturb everyone and that I won't get any extra time.

I slump into a chair. My head's spinning. I write my name and student number but every time I try to focus on the test paper, my brain spaces out. Fuck it, the test's only worth ten percent. I'd rather fail this unit again than force my brain to fart out coherent sentences. Never force a fart, as the wisdom goes.

It's not like Fred to wag. Guess I'm not gonna see him today after all.

I feel a cold pang in my torso. There's a sad stalactite solidifying in my solar plexus.

I *really* wanted to see him.

Well, damn. I've spent weeks convincing myself me and Fred are just having fun: a uni bromance, fuck buddies, whatever you call it. I told him I'm ultimately straight – that I don't do feelings when it comes to dudes.

Guess I'm full of shit.

'Stop that tapping,' Bonnie Skeletyler snaps at me.

I didn't even notice I'd been vigorously hitting my 'Stolen From Rodney Murray Building Co' pen into the hole in the corner of the desk.

I'm sure it means something Freudian that I don't wanna know about.

It's not until Skeletyler calls 'pens down' and everyone looks up that I realise I don't recognise anyone in the room.

I glance at the blank test paper in front of me, which is for a marketing analytics unit I already completed last semester.

'You boofhead,' I mutter, kicking my desk.

I wasn't just late. I wandered into the wrong classroom and didn't even know it.

***

I get out into the corridor at the same time as my usual class – next door – finishes.

I'm lurking outside, smoking a cigarette and pretending to check something on my phone, when Frédéric Dupont emerges from the building and into the sunlight.

I can't help but grin every time I see him. No homo, but Fred is objectively an extremely good-looking guy. Even if I was completely straight – which it would appear the ship has sailed on – I would still be like, bro should be a model. His chocolatey skin is smooth and blemish-free. He always wears tight-fitting, designer-label t-shirts that hug his toned body and he seems totally unfazed that in Australia most guys don't wear Armani to their Bachelor of Commerce lectures. His black hair always looks shiny and lacquered. I swear the bloke walks into a room and looks like he stepped off a perfectly illuminated runway every time, like his face has an in-built ring light.

I'm both attracted to him and jealous, cos next to him I look like a big drunk bogan potato.

'Thomas!' Fred calls when he spots me. He always pronounces my name the French way. *Tom-ahh.* I kinda like it.

'How's it goin', mate?' I say casually, immediately noticing the blue-and-white print on his t-shirt. At first I think it's a Greek goddess in Mykonos, but the words say *Kylie – Aphrodite.*

I instinctively take a step back from him.

'Where were you today?' Fred asks. 'I know you like being late, but this is a new record.'

I don't want to tell him I was so drunk I went to the wrong class. There's a point at which an adorable level of buffoonery crosses into an embarrassing level of possible brain damage, and today I seem to have seesawed across that fulcrum.

'Just felt like wagging,' I lie, all cool and aloof. 'Been drinking at the tav with Harry and those guys.' I take a drag of Benson & Hedges Smooth. 'Did I miss anything interesting?'

Fred smirks. 'There was a bit of a hoopla.'

He uses the word 'hoopla' way too often and pronounces it in this weirdly endearing French way, but I never want to tell him in case he stops doing it.

'Stroppy Horse Girl started ranting about homophobic conservatives again,' Fred goes on. We've made up nicknames for almost everyone in our class, rather than learning their actual names. 'And then Harry Potter on Steroids snapped back at her and said she was so open-minded all her brains had fallen out.'

I snort and nearly choke on my cigarette smoke. 'Holy shit. Now I wish I'd been there. What did Goth Daenerys Targaryen say?'

'Oh, she was on Stroppy Horse Girl's side, obviously. Asked Professor Rice to boot Steroid Potter from class for being offensive, but she didn't.'

I ash my smoke. 'I'm willing to bet he wasn't even being offensive.'

Fred's smirk falters. 'Look. She's annoying but she had a point. He was actually being a douche about gay people.'

'What did he say?'

'I didn't hear it all. Something about gay guys being too sensitive and something stereotypical about us all being into Britney Spears and stuff. He was being a tool.'

'Bro, you're literally wearing a Kylie Minogue shirt as you tell me this.'

Fred's eyes flash. 'I'm proud of the music I like,' he says quickly. 'It's about the tone. He wasn't just saying it – he was using it as an insult.'

I shrug. 'Wanna grab a drink at the tav or what?'

Fred crosses his arms. 'I have another class now, remember? Which is a shame, because … I have something cool to surprise you with.'

'What's the surprise?'

Fred looks me up and down, making a slow judgement call. 'Not now. I'm in too much of a rush. Are we going to hang out again tonight?'

I swallow. *Hang out.* Those words I'd taken literally, without recognising they were morphing into a euphemism for *date.*

The angel and devil on my shoulders start a bitter tug of war. I want nothing more than to hang out with him. I want nothing less than to admit what this is.

'Yeah, orright,' I say, ashing my cigarette into the garden bed.

Fred's face lights up, and my heart glows back, a warm fireplace in my chest. I love seeing him smile. He's told me before how lonely he's found it, being an international student here. And you can see it on his face when he goes through the campus. There's this sadness to him, like he'd hoped to find so much more in Perth. I kinda know the feeling, moving here from Geraldton and thinking I was starting this big new city life, and then realising it's all pretty much the same.

Maybe that's why we get along, deep down. We both thought the shiny new thing would fix us and it didn't.

'*Super*,' he says, with the French pronunciation. 'Where are we going?'

I figured 'hang out' meant I'd just kill time at the uni tav from now until he finished his next class, but it seems like he's expecting me to up my game.

'You wanna grab a feed or something?'

'A meal could be nice.'

'A feed,' I correct him. 'We could hit Fast Eddy's.'

Fred's face falls. 'Again?'

'I like it there,' I say.

'It's like the diner version of a dive bar.'

'So what? I like dive bars.'

Fred's lips twitch open, like he's about to fight further, but then he visibly calms himself. 'Okay. Fast Eddy's it is. I can tell you about my surprise there.'

***

Fast Eddy's is the only greasy spoon in Perth open twenty-four seven. It's divey retro style with 1950s memorabilia hung all over the walls: bent metal number plates for cars that have long since been turned to scrap; tin road signs from an Australia that no longer exists.

When I first moved to Perth, me and my mates would go clubbing on Friday nights, hit up the Brass Monkey and Mustang Bar and

Paramount, before staggering into Fast Eddys for an oil-drenched, three a.m. Cop-the-Lot burger to soak up the roiling sump of bourbon in our guts.

When me and Fred first started hanging out, I'd wait until my housemates passed out each evening, then sneak to pick Fred up from his share house and drive to Fast Eddys for a midnight feed. Smashing a steakburger among the night owls was always weirdly chill. Like, everyone had some reason for being at that diner so late, so nobody was throwing suspicious looks or asking questions.

Tonight, me and Fred take our usual window seat, facing onto Murray Street and half-watching the drunks stumble past in the dark.

'So, you're sticking with the Kylie Minogue t-shirt, ay?' I ask, after we've ordered.

Fred glances at his *Aphrodite* shirt with a slight smirk. 'Well, yes. I have my reasons.' He pulls a lilac-coloured envelope from his pocket; the corners are bent. 'Surprise!'

I grin. 'You didn't have to get me a present!' I pretend to rattle the envelope. 'Oooh. Sounds like cash.'

Fred smiles. 'It's not money. Just open it.'

I tear the envelope, fully expecting a couple of crisp pineapples to tumble out and make me richer.

Instead, there's two tickets inside:

Kylie Minogue
Kiss Me Once Tour
Saturday 14 March 2015
RAC Arena

A strange, laser-fast exchange takes place as I look up.

Fred is beaming until he sees my screwed-up face of *what-the-fuck-is-this-shit*. In an instant, his face crumples, the joy knocked out of it like I've slapped him; and simultaneously, I work hard to contort my face into a gracious semi-smile – but it's too late, and the damage is done.

'You don't like it?' Fred asks, tears springing to his eyes.

I scramble to find words that won't make me seem like a dick. 'What – what the hell made you think I *would* like it?'

Dick words not avoided.

Fred swallows and draws his slender arms up around his chest, like a shield. 'I figured – well – Kylie is an Australian icon, n'est-ce pas? Aussies love her. Especially gay Aussies. I thought you'd be excited.'

'But you know the kind of music I'm into,' I say, tugging on the chest of my black oversized Disturbed t-shirt with the demonic The Guy emerging from hellfire.

'People can like more than one genre, you know,' Fred says. 'It is physically possible to like heavy metal and dance pop. You see things in such a black-and-white way. It's stupid.'

'It's not stupid. It's just what I like.'

'So you don't like Kylie Minogue?'

'I don't dislike her or anything. I think she's good-looking. I liked that song she did with Robbie Williams. She was funny on *Kath & Kim*. I'm just saying, like, you gotta be a proper fan of someone to pay money to go see them live.'

'It's a gift. All you need to do is come with me.'

'And all you need to do is understand I don't wanna fucken go!' I snap.

We sit in a strange, ringing silence for much too long. Our distorted reflections in the window are hunched, facing apart from each other.

'It's just a concert,' Fred says.

'Maybe in France it's just a concert,' I reply.

He doesn't get that in Australia, in the circles I grew up in, a bloke going to a Kylie Minogue concert is a public declaration of homosexuality.

'No need to be a jerk about it,' Fred says eventually, his hurt morphing into anger. 'If you don't want to come, that's fine.'

'Why not ask your friend Marlena? Or even Ricardo – isn't he gay, too?'

'Everyone I know in this city isn't available that night,' Fred says, his tone growing sullen.

'Look, I don't mean to be a dick ...' I start.

Fred slides the tickets back across the wooden table and out of sight.

'Forget I said anything,' he says, plastering on a smile.

I don't know if it comes with being French, or coming from a higher-class family than me, but he knows how to switch on the charm and do the polite thing. I wish I knew how to charm people. I got too much mongrel in me, and it always gets me in trouble.

'Food's here,' Fred says, looking up at the waitress.

Once we get some grub into us, the conversation pivots back to what we usually talk about. Tarantino movies and music and video games, while he has his maple pancakes and American milkshake – he's got a real sweet tooth – and I smash my steakburger and beer.

When we get into Fred's hatchback, a loud electro Kylie song starts playing on the stereo.

'Jesus Christ, she's everywhere,' I mutter, trying to make light of it.

Fred gives a wince he probably hoped would look like a smile. 'I wouldn't have expected you to be a "Timebomb" fan,' he says. 'Bet you'd like this one, though.'

He skips songs until he lands on a track with a familiar guitar hook I've heard on the radio for years.

'Wait – this is Kylie?' I say. 'I thought it was Garbage.'

'You don't have to insult her,' Fred says.

'No, no – I like the song – I mean, I thought it was the band, Garbage. I've spent my whole life thinking it was their song. What's it called?'

"Did It Again," Fred tells me. He raises an eyebrow. 'Maybe you'll be pleasantly surprised if you do come out with me to the concert ...'

'I TOLD YOU I'M NOT FUCKEN READY TO COME OUT.'

Fred stares at me in mute horror, and I immediately feel crook in the guts that I lost my shit at him like that.

'Fred,' I say quietly. 'I'm sorry, I didn't mean—'

'I didn't say anything about *coming out*,' Fred says. 'I told you from the start I don't want to pressure you to do anything you're not ready for. This is just a concert.'

'Okay, well, you know what, this is something I'm not ready for,' I fire back. 'And it's not just a concert, okay? I might as well walk down the street waving a rainbow flag. I might as well change my name on Instagram to MASSIVE FUCKEN HOMO.'

'But that's so ridic—'

'I'm telling you that's how it is. With my mates, with my family, with every bloke I know. You wanna make me go to this concert, you're making me out myself. I don't wanna do it.'

'Good, because I don't want to invite you anymore,' Fred says, tears in his eyes.

My heart breaks. 'Fred, please don't cry – come on ...'

'No, fuck you, Thomas. All my friends told me not to fall for a straight boy because it would be a whole lot of bullshit I don't need, and I said no, you were different. Guess I was wrong.'

'You *were* wrong!' I counter, mounting a poor but honest defence. 'I'm *not* different, Fred. I am the same as every curious straight guy. I am confused and paranoid and hung up on nobody ever fucken finding out about me, okay? You've given me too much credit.'

Fred scowls. 'You act like a jerk then you tell me it's my fault?' His voice is sub-zero.

'I didn't mean to—'

'Get out of my car, Thomas. You can find your own way home.'

I swallow. I don't doubt that he's right, or that it's what I deserve.

I get out of the car and slam the door.

Fred drives away with an angry throb of electro music blaring from his windows.

I flag a taxi, and on the drive to my share house, I stare out the window at the lights of Perth and think about how fucked I am.

If I go to the concert, I feel like I'll be outing myself.

If I don't, I let a stupid fight about a pop singer end what was probably the best thing to ever happen to me.

Either way, I'll let Kylie Minogue define my life, and there's nothing gayer than that.

***

Fred and I don't speak on Friday.

On Saturday, I DM him to ask how he is. He leaves me on read.

Probably fair.

***

I live in Como with two of my Gero mates, and tonight we've got another mate coming over for drinks. By five o'clock on Saturday arvo, we've already gone through a full slab of Emu Export and the night hasn't even started.

It's my ideal Saturday hangout. Beers around the pool table. Games of darts and beer pong. Footy pre-game show on in the background while Cold Chisel blares from the stereo.

But I can't stop thinking about Fred.

I scroll through Insta while waiting for my turn at pool. Fred's posted a new selfie giving the peace sign in his Kylie t-shirt:

> So excited to see the legendary Miss Kylie Minogue in concert tonight! She's one of the reasons I thought Australia would be so cool to move to. Hope she plays Les Sex – my favourite from the new album!

I feel something like ice re-form in my stomach again.

I scroll back through his old photos.

A photo outside the Bell Tower: Here I am, Perth – can't wait to make this place my new home!

A photo at Charles de Gaulle airport: A new adventure in my life is about to begin!

A photo beside a river in his hometown of Rouen: I've been accepted to university in Perth, Australia! J'espère que mon anglais est assez bien mdr! Can't wait to see les kangourous and maybe meet a hot Aussie boy! :P

With each caption, the cold stalactite in my stomach grows sharper, piercing my flesh from the inside out.

'Oi, Tommo, you've got two shots, Dewar sunk the white ball,' Marshy says, handing me the freshly chalked-up pool cue.

I hesitate. I'm gonna be drinking with these guys every weekend for a long time to come.

But I only have one chance to fix my mistake.

'Marshy, take my shots for me,' I say, putting my bush chook down. 'I completely forgot I'm meeting a uni mate at a gig tonight.'

'A gig?' Marshy splutters.

'Yeah. An alt-rock band. Kinda like Garbage.'

***

I meet Fred outside RAC Arena, greeting him with a fistbump as crowds of women and gays swarm the entrance.

'Good thing you dressed up for the occasion,' Fred says, with a smirk.

I was too many beers in to think about wearing nice clothes. I'm in my oversized firetruck-red Five Finger Death Punch jersey with the big skull and the Maltese cross, a grubby Fox snapback on my head covering my scruffy hair.

'I'm here, right?' I say, ashing my cigarette. 'That's what matters?'

Fred's face softens. 'I'm happy you changed your mind. But why did you?'

I search for a casual, aloof answer and there isn't one. Nor do I have anything deep.

'I just wanted you to have a good night,' I admit. 'And I knew it would make you happy if we went to this together.'

Fred's face glows. 'I would never out you. You know that.'

'I just thought ... you know what, it doesn't matter. Let's hit the bar and have a good night.'

We head into the arena, where the iconic Kylie Minogue appears on stage in a red corset, to a roar from thousands of fans amid a deafening buzz of electro music.

Fred grabs my shoulder, jumping up and down in elation. 'It's

"Les Sex"! First up! My favourite song from the album!'

I smile back at him. Goddammit, I love seeing this man happy.

Kylie smashes through a bunch of songs I don't recognise until she gets to 'Spinning Around', which I let myself do a mild foot-shuffle to.

The next song starts with this bombastic, almost military-style drum that immediately gets my attention. Male backup singers chant the song's title – 'Your Disco Needs You' – in unison.

It's gotta be the campest song I've ever heard – complete with an a cappella section in French that Fred shouts along to verbatim – but what comes at the end blows my mind. Kylie starts singing this insanely high-pitched wail, and something in her voice cuts deep into my chest, a laser pointed directly at my heart.

I don't understand pop music and I don't understand Kylie Minogue, but this wail, this coloratura of light, it transcends language, it forms a wordless plea that all humans can understand. It is pain. It is loneliness. Kylie sings higher and higher, crescendoing notes that sound like opera. It is a pleading to be seen and understood: a lonely soul calling out for a mate, promising to go anywhere it needs to, as long as they can be together.

Kylie rides the high note to hell, the music stops, the stage goes black, and the entire arena – including me – erupts.

'How incredible was that!' Fred screams in my ear.

'It was,' I admit. 'It really was.'

After the concert, sweaty and exhausted, we stumble onto Wellington Street.

'I'm starving,' Fred says, brushing confetti off his shoulder. 'Want to go to Fast Eddys?'

'Always,' I say. 'Do you want to, though? I thought you weren't a big fan.'

Fred shrugs. 'If you like it, I'll go. Compromise makes these things work, right?'

These things. The thing we aren't saying we are. The thing we are becoming.

'Glad you feel that way,' I say, checking that Milligan Street is deserted enough for me to sneak a quick grasp of his hand. 'Cos what goes around comes around.'

Fred squeezes my hand back with a quizzical look. 'Wait – what does that mean?'

'Disturbed just announced a new album and they'll be touring it,' I say. 'You'll come with me, right? Fair's fair.'

Fred's mouth flattens into a line of disgust. 'But they scream all their lyrics. It sounds like their lungs are trying to explode out their mouth! And those guitars. It's just noise!'

'Frédéric Dupont, I went to your disco, now you gotta come to mine,' I say. 'Your mosh pit needs you.'

Dancing
Miriam Sved

In the Venn diagram of Hyke and Promo's personalities, the thin sliver of what they would both admit to enjoying was mostly just drag.

They went to drag shows all the time, back when they were at uni together. Even then though, at the sticky-carpeted pub where they always went to see the shows, they weren't really into it in the same way. Hyke (usually called Joanne or Jo), an unrepentant Butlerian, respected the enactment of performative gender. Promo (Kevin on his birth certificate, but he'd tried and mostly succeeded in making Promo happen for real) loved it the way he loved McDonald's Happy Meals and 90s party drugs and YouTube videos about ordinary women bedazzling the shit out of already ugly clothes – with a wide-eyed delight in which Hyke knew there was a deep, smuggled core of irony.

'Why do you *like* him?' Hyke's partner Kat said, only once, under intense duress. It was just after their second child was born. They hadn't seen much of him for a few years, for obvious reasons, but that day Promo had come over for a rare interaction with all of them. He'd called Hyke Dad, declined to hold baby Amelia because of her muscular incompetence, said postpartum Kat looked wonderfully spongy, and called three-and-a-half-year-old Reuben a cunt.

'I don't think Reub even heard,' Hyke said, staring down at the baby who was stretched long-ways on her lap. Reuben, who'd been quietly dismantling one of his trucks in the play corner, said, 'Cunt cunt cunt cunt cunt.'

Kat took a visibly slow breath while Hyke focused all her attention on the baby.

'Why. Do. You. Like him?'

Hyke rolled her eyes – as if she was in on the joke – and jiggled Amelia on her lap, maybe a little aggressively. The baby's emotional perversity was extreme. She had cried throughout Promo's visit; now, when some noise cover might have been helpful, she was resolutely peaceful.

'Cunt?' Reuben said into the silence, on a speculative upward inflection.

'Don't say that word, sweetie,' Hyke said, hoping Reuben would default to his central imperative – all attention is good attention – and keep saying it in his solemn chipmunk voice. But she could feel Kat's focus, unwavering. Kat was clocking two to three hours' sleep a night and had precious little adult interaction; she wasn't in a place of letting go.

'Seriously,' she said. 'I mean, I think you think everything he does is some kind of contrarian performance piece, but who is it even *for* at this stage? Have you considered that it's *not* a performance? Have you considered that he might just actually be a—' She grimaced theatrically.

'Cunt,' Reuben said.

Hyke had not considered that. Why not? It was hard to explain to Kat, at least in the current arena of their lives – a war zone with the two of them battling for scarce resources. Things that had been precious would become crushed frivolities if she tried to give them form.

Like the look on Promo's face when he hoisted himself out of

Maccallum Pool, where they'd gone skinny-dipping one balmy summer night with the lights of the whole city spread before them. Promo called it magic land, no trace of irony.

Or listening to a long and involved fairytale he made up on the fly to get her through her first and last experience of LSD. Hyke would never remember it properly but it involved hackneyed components – a dragon, a hidden cache of treasure – that Promo managed to assemble into something so new and surprising and entertaining that Hyke could forget she was having a bad trip. Kat would probably pierce the skein of this memory by suggesting, with tired forbearance, that the magic had been a product of the trip itself, and Hyke wouldn't be able to counter the logic although she'd know it wasn't true.

The magic was Promo. Always, since the first time they met at their uni gay group, or queer group, or LGB group – this was the 90s in a place channelling the 80s so there were no other letters – and they'd fallen into immediate opposition over the group's nomenclature, which was the only thing ever discussed in the group. Hyke championed QC – Queers on Campus – and Promo fought for RBG – Rich Bored Gays. He wasn't Promo then, that came later at the campus bar, where he called her a humourless dyke and she called him a problematic homosexual, and they cleaved to the names and to each other in response to the hum of educated outrage it evoked from the others.

Hyke and Promo, self-identifying as a reviled institution, held firm through the irony deficits of undergrad, and the cash deficits of postgrad and the attention deficits of early adulthood – graduate jobs (NGOs for Hyke, corporates for Promo) and early relationships and Hyke's defection into the landed gentry (a run-down terrace in Marrickville). Ultimately it was the sleep deficits of early parenthood that broke them, although Hyke wasn't sure if this was clear to anyone but her: how the ravages of those years, especially on her relationship with Kat, demanded compensatory sacrifices.

She and Kat were in their late thirties by then and they were maturely fortified by a covenant, ratified daily, to not fight dirty. They tried to appreciate each other, even if only as combatants in the trenches. They went in for the second one knowing all the things the first had taken out of the other; knowing, as well, each other's sore spots, the thin patches where any contact was likely to break the skin. Kat knew never to complain about Hyke's mother, but to let Hyke complain about her with free-flowing savagery. She knew that no domestic irritant was as painful to Hyke as any kind of grain product crusted to the bottom of a bowl, and that Hyke could be prodded out of sleep with good grace at any time of the night – to feed a baby, to pace with a baby, to worry about whether a baby's fontanelle should have closed over by now – but that when she fell asleep during the day, she was unable to come around and adopt the façade of a loving parent for a long time.

Kat, by contrast, was pretty much saintly. She worked from home and did the lion's share of the childcare and housework, and she had very few trigger points compared to Hyke's array. What she had – what sometimes seemed like her one blaring inflammation – was Promo.

It had never worked between the two of them, in any of the permutations with which Hyke had tried to acclimate them to each other – going out at night (Kat hated Promo's clubs), going to the movies (Promo was slyly contemptuous of the films and of Kat's opinion of the films), going out in a big group (they triangulated their mutual irritation through whoever else they were talking to).

All that was before kids, when they had no idea how wealthy they were in time and energy. When Hyke could spend hours – days – worrying about how to make her partner and her best friend like each other. After kids, that was over. Especially after Amelia's birth, which coincided, coincidentally or not, with the emergence of Reuben's issues. There was no more time and no more energy to spare. Extraordinary sacrifices had to be made.

After the cunting visit – the only time Promo had met her daughter – they barely saw each other for years. There was only the tenuous connecting line of social media, always difficult to interpret through Promo's ambiguous irony filter. There'd be nothing for weeks, then a photo-essay about the Lacanian significance of various styles of hipster beards, or about the traffic signage in his suburb. Hyke often interacted with this content, feeling that their shared history was worth the disproportionate amount of time it took her to come up with the right emoji response to an octagonal sign of a stick figure cartwheeling over an unfenced cliff-edge (😵). But she felt a complicated stab when Promo hearted the sweetly sanitised family shots that Kat tended to post and tag her in (the four of them out at the park on a sunny day, a laughing tumble of a family selfie, no hint of the poonami that the baby was about to unleash or of Reuben's accompanying meltdown). She didn't trust the little red hearts Promo often bestowed on these images. Or rather, she trusted that she saw through to their dark mocking core.

Then the pandemic. Reuben was in school, and somehow the fact that he'd been reading since he was three didn't make him an easier home learner. Amelia wasn't sleeping anywhere near through the night. Hyke and Kat were both working from home now, at the small table in the dining room where Reuben was 'at school', the lucky one sometimes getting to retreat to the bedroom to take a meeting.

Other people had it so much worse. Hyke kept telling herself how lucky she was, but at some stage something in her went dormant. It was easier after that – she was more patient with Reuben, with all of them. She could still do her work and function outwardly, and the good thing about being so busy every minute of the close-breathing days and interminable nights was that she never had to consider what it was that had stopped moving within her. She could keep going and going and no-one would know the difference.

She forgot about Promo though. It took weeks – maybe longer than that, she wasn't sure about time anymore – to realise he'd gone silent. She went searching for signs of life down the online holes, Facebook and Twitter and Insta. Nothing, not for months.

It had become unthinkable to call him out of the blue: the strangeness of that would be an acknowledgement of all the months and years when it hadn't happened. So she texted and emailed, trying to keep it light, trying not to show fear.

In the endless time of silence afterwards – hours or days or weeks – she felt so densely packed with thoughts of Promo that they seeped out of her and she told Kat about the messages and the waiting. Kat was sympathetic and worried to an appropriate degree.

Then: *Heeey, Humourless Dyke. It's so good to hear from you. I'm thinking of writing a complete compendium of dogs in order of their gayness. How are you??*

The text made her groan with relief and then lie down on the bed, although it was still the workday that now overlapped with getting the kids bathed and fed.

Instead of working or parenting, she texted Promo back, and they had an exchange about whether greyhounds were gayer than staffies were gayer than oodles (anything, they decided, was gayer than oodles), as if nothing had happened.

Also as if nothing had happened, the government had started letting people out. Out-out, no restrictions. You could go to restaurants and movies, you could go *dancing*. All of which seemed so unreal and unlikely – like something from a movie about the future or the deep past – that, at first, Hyke thought it was part of Promo's shtick when he told her he was going out to a drag show. Tonight! Their old place! She should come! When she realised he wasn't joking, Hyke felt a ripple of pure panic that jolted her off the bed and out to the living room, where she had to finish her day's work and help get the kids through dinner and bath and bedtime. She sent Promo a laughing emoji, although she didn't know what she was laughing at or what he would think she was laughing at.

While the kids were eating, Kat asked about Promo. She called him Kevin. Hyke wished she hadn't said anything about him, now that she knew he was okay. He had been a no-go topic for so long that she couldn't remember the specifics of the embargo, but some of it was contained in the way Kat's eyes stayed on the top of Amelia's head when she said his name. Hyke tried to keep it light the same way (a completely different way) she had with Promo. She told Kat he was fine. Told her, as well, about the drag show, trying to give the words the weight of absurdity with which they'd struck her (imagine going to a pub now, imagine *dancing*).

Kat didn't take it like she expected. She didn't take it badly, but she didn't take it lightly. She looked up from their daughter's downy head and her eyes were sharp-focus.

'He asked you to go out, and you said no?'

Hyke was standing guard over the food on Reuben's dinner plate, making sure none of the different food groups touched each other. 'No, well, I didn't exactly say no. I just didn't … he probably wasn't even serious.'

Kat kept looking at her.

'What? What?'

She sighed. Kat's sighs contained multitudes. 'Babe, he's been alone a long time. And I don't just mean the lockdown.'

'What does that mean?'

'I always thought it was sad how he never puts down any roots. He just skims across the surface. Someone like that, being forced to just, like, sit with themselves for months and months. Well, when you said he'd gone quiet I was pretty worried. And now he's asking you to see him tonight? Reaching out to you.'

Hyke focused on Reuben's dinner, on a rogue pea that had made a break towards the potatoes. It wouldn't be wrong in relation to anyone else, but Promo *reaching out*. He didn't reach out. He didn't *check in*, or *catch up*, or *connect*. You wouldn't ask Promo *R U OK?* and he wouldn't ask you.

Hyke made a clumsy swipe at a pea that wasn't even outside its territory and her fork grazed the plate with a skin-glitching noise. Reuben put his hands to the sides of his head.

'Sorry, kiddo, sorry.' She put the fork down carefully and stroked the air around her son's shoulders without touching him.

'You think this is some kind of cry for help? That he's...' She mouthed the word *suicidal* in the air above the kids' heads.

Kat gave another of her with-the-lot sighs. 'Well, I don't think he's *happy*. Do you?'

Was Promo happy? It just wasn't the sort of question you'd apply to him. It would roll straight off. He'd say, *Who needs to be happy, I'm gay*.

'He's pretty gay,' she said, almost to herself.

'What?'

'Nothing. I guess I'm going out.'

***

It is wonderful and somehow unnerving that their old pub is still there, open for business. Like visiting a dead relative in a dream. It seems altered in a subtle but jarring way: everything cleaner, airier, simultaneously less dingy and less sparkly. At least the carpet's still sticky.

Hyke is unnerved, as well, by the bodies. It isn't actually packed – she can see space between the people. But still, all those bodies; it's anthropologically bizarre, and the strangeness is compounded when she sees Promo's face through the crowd.

'Humourless Dyke,' he shouts. A temporal slippage; decades are gone.

He makes his way through the people and comes at her in an awkward hug.

'Come on, let's go get our spot then I'll go to the bar.'

Hyke wants to stand and keep looking at him. His face is a surprise. It's so unchanged, and she'd forgotten the redolent power of it (the rippled illumination of an open-air pool at night). And that grim conversation with Kat had planted an expectation of something else. Some leeching or adultification.

But he turns and starts making his way through the crowd and all Hyke can do is follow, trying not to touch anyone.

They are going to a spot by the stage where they always used to stand, where they will stand tonight to absorb particles of other people's sweat and spit and viral air. Hyke can't figure out what to do with her own face, especially when Promo turns around to check she's still following, then beams as though it's a delightful surprise to find she is. The deep familiarity of his shape, his movements (Promo running ahead of her through city streets, on a night when they'd just stolen a construction company sign he liked the look of).

He sashays his hips as they get to the stage and the opening bars of a country song blare out. An immaculately made-up queen comes on, a shimmering jumpsuited cowgirl.

Promo whoops. Hyke remembers another drag show, maybe the last one they went to, Promo saying the queen was *closer to real pussy than you're ever gonna get.* It makes her laugh. The cowgirl, she notices with a shot of confused longing, has a tight, gorgeous arse. Promo shouts and puts his hands out towards the stage as a twang of synthesised guitars cuts the air and the crowd solidifies, a current of human energy connecting the room and hitting Hyke in the chest. Promo puts an arm over her shoulder, his face lit up from below. In the moving prism of that light there is one moment when he looks very old, the familiar planes of his face lost in harsh lines and shadows; in the next moment the impression is gone, he's young and shining again. The cowgirl is bootscooting and lip-syncing to a song Hyke doesn't know, a song about going out dancing, a high chirrupy voice that's both deeply familiar and out of context, a voice from across time like a promise made in childhood, a dream of flying, a never-stopping now. Hyke is sure everyone else feels it too. She looks up into Promo's beaming face and cries out, hoots, jumps with the crowd, an arm around Promo's back, her sweat mingling with his.

Now a dance partner appears on stage beside the cowgirl – a tall topless man in black jeans and a cowboy hat, abs rippling cartoon-ishly. In the flow of the song the cowgirl runs a finger down his chest and starts to dance with him, thrusting hips, head thrown back, the crowd going nuts for it. Suddenly the stage is flooded with men, all topless in huge hats. With their smooth-oiled skin the impression is organic, a forest, the cowgirl dancing between the trees with her sparkling jumpsuit lit up against their trunks, the music stalling in a repetitive refrain.

Then another figure, this one black clad from head to toe, a hooded reaper. He pulls the cowgirl out of the trees and pulls her into himself, her sparkles smothered in the folds of his cloak, her face a pantomime horror, a fade to dark. When the song ends, everyone around Hyke is still shouting joy. Promo gives an ear-ringing whistle. She looks up into his face and sees him old and young, the life in him, ravaged and ravenous. She reaches for his hand but pulls back at the last second, not wanting him to look at her. She can imagine what he'd say – *Hey, there's no crying in baseball.* But she might see terror there. The bars of the next song start to swell. She swipes the hot tears away so that they meld with the sweat and unnameable substances on the floor.

Spinning Around

Ellen van Neerven

I feel most queer when pushed
against a straight space.
I spin, I spin, I spin
360 the doubt, roll with the beat.
It was 2000. We all were finding
a dream to stick. I wanted a sister.
To be a sprinter. 200 metres,
mosquitos and hot pink.
Rollerblades at the disco. I fell
into the gaps of my uniform.
What happens to young people
too afraid to lift their arms
above their heads? Do they
become adults with stiff shoulders?
I stopped dancing
and tried hiding.
Years later I emerge. I'm here!
And I know why. Free-dancing to
gather the silence and noise. Sweat
like glitter on my chest. I'm twirling.
Dizzy with fireworks. Whirling.

    I spin, I spin, I spin

In Your Eyes
Grace Chan

Our three hundred and fifteenth boyfriend is exactly our type: vulnerable narcissism disguised as meekness, a mellifluous tenor voice, and a brain with an unusually high proportion of fatty tissue. His soft mouth twitches incessantly, as though practising his next words. The way he gazes at us – eyes luminous with tentative hope, searching for his reflection – fills us with anticipation.

He seems less and less interested in the movie as it progresses. He brushes a lock of our hair across his narrow nostrils, which bracket one another like quotation marks. We lie on our back on his queen-sized futon, gazing up at the sun-streaked images moving across the ceiling. He'd been so excited to set up his new projector, to show us this artsy thriller about a group of writers who go on retreat in a remote cabin. We had felt his excitement like the warm fizz of a lemonade left in the sun.

The boyfriend's granny flat is familiar to us now. The square window gives a view of the red-brick façade of his parents' house, and the huddled brown shapes of the Dandenong Ranges. On our left, his laptop perches on an antique writing desk, framed by a potted monstera and an air purifier shaped like an enormous bubble wand. This is where he teaches English to executives and students in Asia. On our right, the kitchenette is cluttered with coffee-making paraphernalia, last night's takeaway boxes still greasy with Taiwanese fried chicken, and a plate of something fresh from the oven that his mother brought across just an hour earlier.

Late afternoon sunlight pours through the window, distorting the movie and blanketing our legs with warmth. We watch a young woman in a red swimsuit lope across the ceiling, her brown hair swinging at the small of her back. A young man emerges from the cabin and cradles her slender neck in one hand. It is difficult to tell if the gesture is romantic or aggressive. We feel relaxed and slow. We imagine this is what it might feel like to sleep.

The boyfriend grows restless, drawing his knees up to his chest, swivelling them from side to side to stretch the muscles in his back. When he rolls off the futon and unfolds to his full height, his fair hair sticks up in all directions from his head like a lion's mane. He examines his mother's treats, breaks a muffin apart and holds a chunk to our mouth. We let him place it on our tongue, push the sticky bolus to the back of our mouth. Desiccated starchiness with a whiff of citrus. Smiling, we force the lump down. Even after being here for so long, we find ourselves unable to acclimatise to their cuisine, which is marshy with occasional salty or saccharine flotsam.

The boyfriend leans over us, his head obscuring our view of the young woman now succumbing to a blistering rash. Licking his lips nervously, he says, 'Hey, were you in Theo's Fine Foods this morning?'

We bring our attention to him. 'Where?'

'Oh, it's the gourmet supermarket on High Street. You know, where the yuppies buy twenty-dollar granola and refill their glass bottles with kombucha on tap.'

We return his expectant grin with a mirrored one, and then turn it into a frown. 'Nope. Never been there. Why?'

'Huh. I would've bet my little finger it was you. Same height, same walk. I actually called out your name.'

'What happened?'

'Oh, you – she – pretended not to hear me. She walked very quickly into the next aisle. It was quite embarrassing. You sure you weren't there and just, you know, forgot? She even had your hair – shiny and black and tied up in a ponytail.'

'A lot of people have black hair in a ponytail.'

He looks immediately chastised. 'Sorry, I hope you don't take that the wrong way. You know I don't mean it in a racist way. You must have a doppelgänger. I hear everyone has one, out there somewhere.'

We lay our head on his shoulder as a gesture of forgiveness, which he curls around.

'How freaky,' we chuckle, and watch until reassurance smooths over his face.

***

During the second half of the increasingly implausible movie, as the red-brick house turns into a silhouette against the sunset, we make out with boyfriend on the futon. His hands sneak under our crisp, lavender cropped t-shirt; we swat him away playfully. As he turns to the solemn task of drawing spirals in our ear with his tongue, we reach out to the other of us who roams the adjacent district.

All of us know the unspoken rules. We return to Her for the monthly rituals. We never spill secrets. And we avoid overlap: partly to avoid confusing the locals, but mostly out of respect for one another's work. Nevertheless, despite our best intentions, minor boundary crossings happen from time to time. We harbour no hard feelings.

We reach out along the existing connection and call our shared names. The other of us calls in response. The other of us is holding hands with our three hundred and ninth boyfriend, gliding around an ice-skating rink. Movement swooshes through us, pop music pulses in our ears, and disco lights swarm our vision. We know that the other likes to draw out their liaisons, despite knowing that they are all doomed. The other also enjoys the specific brand of dried pineapple stocked at Theo's Fine Foods – savours the tart, chewy morsels between their molars until they are ground to dust. We compose a gentle suggestion: *We have heard that the wholefoods deli near Ferntree Gully Station has an exceptional range of preserved fruit.*

***

When he steps into the shower, we sprawl on the futon, swamped with homesickness. So far from the lake, we can hardly sense Her. Our vision grows clotted with black soil and moonlit water, and our nose swells with the tinny musk of home. Our skin tingles with the remembered brush of our kin – we are not singular, not alone, never alone.

Stomach churning, we step out of the granny flat and walk to the bottom of the garden. The sun has slipped below the horizon, and a line of eucalypts sways in the breeze, washing us over with indigo shadows. The trees and the earth bring the clean smells of decay and renewal.

The wind dries the patches of saliva on our ears and neck, touching us with a cold finger. We push our bare brown toes into the brown dirt. Strange toes, strange bodies. A line of ants traverses the hillock of our right foot, aiming for a crumb of muffin stuck to the crest. Our gaze follows the trail to a sandy mound at the base of a tree. Tiny creatures swarm the nest, pouring in and out of the entrance hole with frenetic energy.

The door slides open behind us. We turn to see the shape of him, limned in the kitchenette's light – beige chinos, cotton t-shirt. Dressed to go out. He calls in that sweet tenor: 'What do you want to do tonight?'

160

We glance at the murky, starless sky, and then at the silver station wagon sitting in the driveway. We think about the lake, flat as a pool of tar and brimming with hidden places. Our stomach has stopped churning. It seems like a good night for a drive.

***

Boyfriend is exuberant. He pushes his canvas sneaker onto the accelerator, hardly slowing down for bends in the road, which is out of character for him. But we shouldn't be surprised. He's thrilled by our sly spontaneity, by the fine-toothed brush of danger, by the possibility of coupling messily in the back seat. They all get this way.

The highway snakes east into the hills, a narrow black river unbroken by streetlights. Occasionally a car travelling in the opposite direction roars past, sweeping its headlights across our faces. Boyfriend talks at length as he drives – about his students, about his family. His pleasant voice reverberates around the shell of the station wagon. We slump in the car seat, our limbs loose and unencumbered beneath our thin clothes. We look out of the passenger side window. Dark bushland spreads like an oil slick to the horizon, where the city lights coalesce into a thin yellow smear. We will miss his voice.

'I've only been teaching her for two months, but she's progressed more than some students do in a year. She's enjoyable to teach, if you know what I mean. Eager, quick, hardworking. But I worry about her. She seems more and more subdued – so much so that I wonder if she's depressed. I asked her about her situation. She said she's studying economics at Wuhan University of Technology, lives with her boyfriend. Maybe he isn't treating her well. He expects her to manage the household, do all the cooking. A bit of a chauvinist. I did suggest she talk to someone, maybe a university counsellor, if they have those. Or her family doctor. But I didn't want to say too much. I'm just her tutor, you know? I don't want to be nosy. But I do worry.'

He glances over at us, and we indeed discern a worried expression on his face, although we're not entirely sure if he's demonstrating to us how worried he is about his student, or seeking reassurance that we're paying attention to him, or concerned that he's saying the wrong thing. We put a hand on his wrist and tell him that it's in his nature to be caring. The crease in the middle of his forehead disappears and his mouth softens. The view of the city has also vanished. The earth rises up on either side of the road like steep riverbanks, crested by tangled trees.

'I was meaning to say – I hope you didn't find my mum too intrusive today. She can be a little over-involved, but she means well. She wants to get to know you better. That's why she asks so many questions. Did you like her muffins? Oh, I'm glad. I'll let her know. She can be a little fragile. My dad and I have always had to look out for her, you know? I remember when I was a kid, my dad used to tell me not to cry in front of her, not to talk back at her, that sort of thing. Because it would be too much for her to handle. There was one time I got terribly bullied at school – punched in the stomach, rubbish smeared all over me – and I couldn't even tell her. For a whole week, I would wait until she fell asleep before I let myself bawl in my room. It was awful.' He casts another searching expression upon us. 'Hey, do I turn left up ahead?'

We pretend to check our phone for directions, but we don't need them. We know this place well – the rock-strewn gullies, the tangled scrub, the channels where water rushes and flows underground. We tell him yes, turn left, and follow the road until the asphalt turns to dirt.

***

We turn left and follow the road until the asphalt turns to dirt, and then we follow that road further down, to where the earth falls away beneath the wheels of the station wagon with a dull flutter like wings beating. The trees knit their branches overhead, obscuring the dim phosphorescence of the sky. The car rolls with its own momentum, bouncing over the irregular surface, until tree roots reach out their massive arms to embrace us. We stop in a tumble of rotting leaves.

His eyes are bright with panic, but we lean across the handbrake and leave a residue of relaxant on his lower lip. We tell him to get out of the car. He obeys. He stands tall and still in the leaf litter. His heavy breaths and the gurgling of his digestive tract are loud in the quiet forest. As we walk around the car towards him, he watches us trustfully, his pupils vast and round.

Each of us performs the capture differently. There are as many ways as there are bodies of us – a manifestation of our subtle variances despite our obvious similarities. The capture is, after all, the culmination of our labours, and an artistic expression of our skill.

This body captures swiftly, with compassion. There are several places on the human body where the arterial circulation runs close to the skin – the places where you can feel a strong pulse. Jugular in the neck, radial in the wrist, femoral in the groin.

We go for the groin. Unhinging our jaw, we drain his blood in nineteen seconds, our throat distending painfully with each gulp. As soon as this is done, we flood his veins with the preservation fluid stored in our thoracic sac. His features distend in a grimace of horror; his skin acquires an ashen blue undertone.

In general, we prefer a relatively painless method such as this, even though it is more complicated. There are, however, several of us – more pragmatically inclined who simply inject the capture with a venom that paralyses skeletal muscles yet allows the diaphragm to continue working, the heart to continue pumping, and consciousness to persist. This postpones necrotic decay, but unfailingly triggers an acute stress response in the capture. Cortisol, unfortunately, renders the meat tough and astringent.

Kneeling in the dirt, we fold the floppy limbs across the torso and carefully wrap the entire body in layers of fine, flexible webbing ejected from our loins. The ferrous slime in our mouth, the achy swell of our stomach, the damp odour of the forest and tickle of tiny creatures scuttering across our bare feet render us feverish with nostalgia and longing. We can feel more strongly the presence of the others, and we can feel Her.

We drag the enmeshed corpse down the slope, carving a long groove in the yielding earth. We close our eyes, drawn towards the seeping noises of the lake. Down here, we are multiple and mutually known. Down here, where water runs through filagree roots and webbed mycelium, we will deliver our capture to the others. As we count the months, we will fill his capacious cavities with tiny eggs, gleaming silver with promise. His flesh will ferment to perfection. We will break bone to reveal glistening brain and silky marrow. We can already see the way Her eyes will shine with pleasure.

Made of Glass
Emma Viskic

I hear the news on the way home from dropping the big boys at school. My mind's on the rattle in the engine and the overdue electricity bill, and the teacher's snippy 'Here at last, Mrs Jenkins', and wondering if I should have corrected the 'Mrs' now the divorce is final, so it takes a while for the reporter's words to sink in. Dr Dempsey's dead? *Our* Dr Dempsey?

I turn up the radio so I can hear over the twins squabbling in the back seat, catch the scant details. The doctor was found dead in his driveway early this morning, a possible head wound the suspected cause. The reporter doesn't say the word 'murder' but it hangs between the words 'police' and 'in attendance.'

It can't be true. I mean, Dr Dempsey was a stubborn old crank, but he made house calls to croupy babies and had attended half the town's births. Who'd want to hurt a man like that?

It's not until Liam asks if we'll get a new doctor now, that I realise the boys have fallen silent and are listening.

I flip the radio to a random music program and say in my brightest voice, 'Who wants a back-seat dance?'

***

I drop the twins at kindy and drive straight to craft group. I was going to skip it today to have some alone time in my greenhouse, but news like this morning's requires the emotional support of women. Plus, Betts should be there with information from her cop husband.

The group meets in an old pitched-roof weatherboard in town. Officially the Community Centre but known as Drunk Hall because of the way it slumps towards the neighbouring pub like it's sleeping off a big night. It's warm inside, despite the chill day. The Arnott's Family Assorteds are set out on the trestle and the urn is on, its steam fogging up the glass-covered portrait of the Queen. Most of the craft group's here. Nine or ten women, including my sister Jill. They're sitting in a circle at the far end of the room, their voices animated as they discuss the killing. Jill's the only one not joining in. Even from here, it's obvious she's been crying. Shit, I hadn't thought about Jill. The doctor's death will have hit her hard.

There's a brief lull as everyone turns to see who's arrived. Their disappointed expressions give me a clammy-skinned flashback to high school, but I know it's not personal – like me, they'll be waiting for Betts and her inside knowledge.

I cross to them and squeeze myself into the too-small bucket seat next to my sister. She's puffy-eyed and blotchy, her usually perfect make-up smeared. It takes a lot to make Jill look this bad, but Dr Dempsey's seen her through all the fertility treatments and failed attempts to conceive.

'What am I going to do?' she asks me.

'It'll be all right.' I try to put my arms around her bony shoulders, but she shrugs me off.

'I'm sure another doc could help you, love,' someone says, and they all chime in with their misguided attempts to comfort her.

'God. I wouldn't expect any of *you* to understand.' Jill yanks the sewing from her quilted craft bag and begins work, jabbing the needle like a blade.

The rest of the group share a glance with me, then get back to rehashing the news while they work. I reluctantly haul the sewing from my shoulder bag. I'm more at home with a rake than a needle, and the soft dolls we're making for the upcoming fete are the stuff of nightmares. Mine is, anyway. The rest are looking like huggable little bubs, but I'm still at the sausage stage, stuffing wads of wool into fabric casements. Still, these women are the few in town who seem to realise that divorce isn't contagious, and that it's 1982 not 1952. They've even welcomed young Cassie into the group, and not many would do that.

I'm making a hash of attaching the legs to the torso, looking at the door every few minutes, when Betts finally arrives. She's wearing a long, embroidered skirt and matching blouse, with a silk scarf knotted at her throat. She swishes towards us, dark hair bobbing. The baggy black dress I thought looked passable this morning suddenly feels like a tent.

She ignores our questions until she's settled in a chair. Gives it another beat before she says, 'Well, they've flown the baby to the children's hospital.'

Everyone looks as confused as me, so I say it out loud, 'Um, what baby?'

'Oh, I thought you knew. Maybe I shouldn't ...' A Mona Lisa smile flirts with her lips.

'Just bloody tell us, Betts,' Jill says.

Betts flushes. There's an awkward pause, then she fills us in. 'They found a baby in Dr Dempsey's car. A little newborn boy. They think Dr Dempsey discovered the mother trying to leave it and, well, she attacked him and ran.'

We stare at her.

'Is the bub okay?' young Cassie asks.

'I don't think so.' Betts's voice wavers for the first time. 'He was there all night.'

No-one moves. The hall is quiet enough to hear the wind moaning in the electric wires outside.

There was frost on the grass this morning. The boys ran around stomping it flat until I yelled at them to get in the car.

I turn to comfort Jill but she's looking at Betts, her face stark white.

'Do the police suspect anyone yet?' she asks.

'Yeah,' Betts says. 'Every woman in town.'

***

The butcher's is crowded the next afternoon. Worse than the usual pension-day crush – half the town seems to be crammed inside the white-tiled walls. I was hoping to repot my orchids this afternoon, but I've got four ravenous boys and no dinner, so I wait, breathing in the mingled scents of bleach and blood and the old dears' mothballed coats as they order their single chop and speculate about the killer.

Mrs Jennings is in front of me, her voice nearly as loud as her fluoro lollipop-lady uniform. I'm nearly at the counter when she casts a glance at me and says, 'Yep, it'll be a single mum, mark my words.'

Single mum or not, I've got a reputation to uphold, so I don't deck her. Instead, I give her my sweetest smile and say, 'Someone doing it tough, you mean?'

She sniffs. Under the fluorescent lights, her yellow coat casts a jaundiced tinge across her face. 'Well, I wouldn't call that reason to abandon your child.'

Nicco the butcher looks up from the counter, where he's patiently selecting chops for the customer ahead of me. There's no sign of his usual genial smile.

'Worse than abandon,' he says. 'The baby died an hour ago.'

Only two days in the world, not even the beginning of a life.

'That woman's a monster,' someone says behind me. 'They should lock her up for good.'

'Lock her up? They should string her up.' The words come out of my mouth but it sounds like someone else's voice. Hard, unyielding.

A murmur of agreement ripples through the shop and Mrs Jennings nods approvingly at me. 'You're right about that at least.'

***

Detectives arrive from the city and take over Drunk Hall. The draughty foyer is set up like a doctor's waiting room with chairs set around the walls. Betts was right about the pool of suspects. The room is filled with women of childbearing age, including my sister. She'd have to be low on the list. It's not just the fertility stuff; Jill's so thin it's hard to know where she keeps her internal organs. I used to have a waist like that. Darryl could span it with his hands. Back before I'd had four kids, that is, and Darryl started putting his hands all over the waitress at the Cosy Cuppa.

I take a spare seat next to Cassie who's trying to rock her cranky one-year-old to sleep while sneaking longing glances at the teenagers sitting opposite. Three girls in school uniforms who might once have been her classmates, they pretend they can't see her as they giggle and chat, loudly establish that *jeez, no, they're not being interviewed, just their mothers.* None of the adults are talking.

I've got all the boys with me and it's nearly dinnertime, so they're at their whining, squabbling worst. They look like cherubs compared to Shirley Sherman's, though. Her four are literally bouncing off the walls, daring each other to run full tilt at the wood panelling and attempt backflips. Shirley flips slowly through a copy of *Cosmo*, seemingly oblivious to their yells or the glares Jill's giving her. No-one can measure up to the mother Jill is in her mind but I'm on her side with this one.

When Shirley's called in for her interview, she yells for the kids to follow, gives the youngest a swift clip across the head when he's not fast enough to respond. There's a short silence once she's wrangled them inside, then Jill says loudly, 'Well it wouldn't surprise me if it was her, that's for sure.'

'Totally,' someone calls from across the room. I never gossip, but the others join in.

'Did you see their hair? Nits.'

'No way. How could she have hidden the pregnancy?'

'Remember that woman a few years back? It was on 60 *Minutes*.'

'Oh yeah. Had all those kids and no-one knew.'

Beside me, Cassie is staring at the floor, her face bright red. Poor Cassie, a mother at sixteen, because she was five months pregnant before anyone realised, including herself.

'Careful,' I say to the room, 'let's not start anything.'

But the women have spoken – Shirley Sherman is guilty.

***

That night, the first rock is thrown.

***

Everyone's talking about it at kinder drop-off. Despite the icy wind, the mums hang around by the gate, coats buttoned, faces warm with colour. The rock smashed through Shirley's bedroom window and, depending on who's telling the story, barely missed hitting Shirley's boyfriend/someone else's boyfriend/someone else's husband. The one thing everyone agrees on is the baby booties.

'Blue ones,' one of the mums tells me. 'Tied to the rock.' Her eyes are alight. 'I knew it was Shirley.'

'Just because someone threw a rock doesn't mean she's guilty,' I say.

'No smoke without fire. Don't you reckon?' Her gaze drops from my face to my beltless dress the same way the cops' did yesterday. The two detectives were nothing but polite, but I could feel them assessing my bulk, thinking, 'Yep, she could've hidden a baby in there, no worries.'

'I guess so,' I say. 'Those kids of hers are so dirty. They gave mine nits.'

I mean, it's not gossip if it's true.

***

A handful of women are called for a second interview. No idea why I'm lumped in with the unwed mothers when I'm a legitimate divorcee. It's ridiculous to expect me to have a night-time alibi. Who do they think's looking after the kids? Not their bloody father, that's for sure.

Jill's reading to the boys when I get home. She gives me a smug smile as I gape at them. I was expecting mayhem given their approaching bedtime, but they're snuggled against her on the couch in their PJs, smelling like shampoo and talc. The house is tidy, too. Jesus.

The idea slides into my brain. Maybe not an unwanted baby, but a wanted one? An illegal adoption gone wrong, Dr Dempsey the go-between. As a kid, Jill defended her toys with nail-scratching ferocity. I could imagine her lashing out if the doctor had threatened to renege on the deal or demanded more money.

If she's the killer, everyone will think I knew.

'Everything okay with the P-O-L-I-C-E?' she asks.

'Yeah, I think they're closing in on someone.'

I watch carefully, but she looks genuinely relieved.

***

Cassie quietly offers to host the next craft session. It's the first time she's invited anyone to her home. The whole place smells like pine antiseptic and is so clean it hurts. It's more of a granny flat than a house, with a cramped living area and kitchenette, but it's bright and cheerful, with second-hand toys and dozens of splodgy finger paintings taped to the walls.

It's only a month until the fete and we're way behind. We're supposed to be doing the dolls' hair today, long strands of twelve-ply that will bring life to the dolls' blank faces, but half the group's missing. News has leaked from the hospital, via a nurse's neighbour, that Shirley had her tubes tied after the last kid so the role of suspect is wide open. The six of us present work in silence, casting sideways glances as we jab long needles into the dolls' heads and yank the strands through. Only Betts seems impervious to the tension. Must be nice being a cop's wife – no second interview for her.

Cassie's up and down and up and down in between sewing. Bringing unwanted cups of tea and mopping stray crumbs. It's a relief when the postie blows his whistle, and she takes her excited little one out to collect the mail.

'Bless her heart,' Betts says. 'She's trying so hard.' Betts is wearing another ridiculous embroidered skirt and blouse today. A three-month exchange to Paris in year eleven and she's still putting on the artsy bohemian act.

There's a cry from the front yard. We drop our work and run for the front door, crowding to get through.

Cassie's standing by the letterbox, clutching her son to her chest. Lying on the cracked concrete by her feet is a sheet of paper with a single word printed in large red letters: *Murderer*.

'It wasn't me,' Cassie sobs. 'I'm a good mum. Really, I am.'

I pull her into my arms. 'I know, sweetheart.'

Second pregnancies show earlier than first ones; I'm sure I would have noticed if she'd had another child. Pretty sure.

***

That night I'm wrenched from sleep by a loud bang, the tinkle of falling glass. I'm up and out of bed, moving as quickly as I can without waking the boys. I do the rounds of the house twice before I think of my little greenhouse. I grab the torch from the top of the fridge and run.

Three of its windows are shattered. Shards of glass wink like fairy lights as I shine the torch inside. They're caught in the fern fronds and tomato seedlings, the hearts of my precious orchids. A rock the size of my fist lies in the wreckage, a blue bootie tied around it.

It's an effort to move, but I get my gumboots and dustpan and try to clean up. I can't do it. The tiny splinters have burrowed into every pot and seedling tray. They're part of the soil now.

***

The detectives leave. According to Betts, the case is still open, but no-one's been detained over the deaths or the broken windows, the graffitied 'murderer' scrawled across Shirley's and Cassie's front fences.

Betts gives us the run-down without her usual dramatics. She's been a lot quieter since she got a rock through her kitchen window a week ago, even taken to wearing normal clothes. She looks a lot smaller in trackie daks.

***

Two days before the fete, the craft group joins the other stallholders to clean Drunk Hall. Instead of the usual chatter, the only sounds are of sweeping and clanging buckets. It was my suggestion to come, but I'm beginning to think we should just cancel the whole thing. The place feels dirty, no matter how much we polish.

Beside me, Betts is scrubbing at a mark on the wall like it's personally attacked her. At least the other mums are still friendly with her – none of them will even look at me.

One of the kindy mums rushes in when we're nearly finished. 'Did you hear about Cassie? She's up and left. Packed her stuff and lit out in the middle of the night with her kid.' The long silence is broken by Betts. 'Well, I guess we know who's guilty, then.'

The news sweeps through the room like drought-breaking rain, bringing sighs and excited chatter.

My sister's the only one frowning. She turns to me. 'Do you really think it could've been Cassie? I know she's young, but she's so gentle with that baby of hers.'

Little mousey Cassie with her scrubbed-clean house and child's eagerness to please. It is hard to imagine her killing a man and facing us the next morning as though nothing had happened. But around the hall, women are discussing her guilt, apparently confident in their convictions. Friends, neighbours, colleagues. They smile as they catch my gaze, give me the raised-eyebrow nods of allies.

'Absolutely,' I tell Jill. 'Not a doubt in my mind.'

Everything Is Beautiful
Julie Koh

It was raining the day I arrived in Tsuyazaki. I had taken a bus there from Fukuma Station, sitting in front of a guy who'd leant forward and struck up a conversation. We were the only ones on the bus besides the driver. The guy's name was Craig Money. I had to get him to repeat it because it was foreign and hard to pronounce. Craig was in his thirties and said he was half-Japanese: his father was a local sailor, and his mother an English teacher from Paignton. To be honest, he smelled like a moulding dishcloth. I asked him what he did in this town, and he replied that he liked to ride the local buses all day and night. I thought that was odd but didn't probe further. After all, here *I* was, a middle-aged woman travelling around Kyushu with no real aim, due to grief over the passing of my father.

'If you're looking for something interesting to do,' Craig said, 'there's a new guy in town who's an ikebana master. They say he can see ghosts too. He works out of a cafe called "Ekadbo space". The name uses English letters. If you read "Ekadbo" forwards, you can see the word "kado", or "way of flowers". Read it backwards and it says "obake", for ghost.'

I thanked him for the tip.

The bus drove along the coastline. Pine trees and rain streaked past my window. The grey sea stood still in the distance. The route terminated at Tsuyazaki Bridge. I got off the bus and turned to ask Craig where he was heading next. He'd already vanished.

I found a place to stay, then went down to the water for a walk along the seawall. The rain had stopped. The streetlights were now on, but there weren't many of them, so I had to watch where I was stepping. No-one was around except for the occasional car passing along the main road out of town. I ended up perching on the wall, gazing down at the waves crashing against it. I'd thought sitting by the beach at night would be more romantic than it actually was. Instead, I felt a bit scared, alone in the dark. All I could think about was how easy it might be to fall in and hit my head on the concrete blocks in the water below.

If this had happened while my father was alive, he would have said I deserved it – that I had a natural lack of foresight, meaning my misfortunes were largely my own fault.

The sky was overcast, but the town was buzzing. The music festival had begun. A school band marched past me, and I followed it for a while, acquainting myself with the narrow streets and the old wooden merchant houses.

Two performances were happening at the same time in adjacent buildings. In the former indigo-dyeing house, a saxophone quartet was playing anime covers. Next door, in the sake brewery, a large group plucked their shamisens. I sat outside on the steps of a miniature shrine sandwiched between the two buildings, listening to both performances simultaneously.

A pair of chatty women – both in berets, one pink and one blue – were standing nearby, discussing what they wanted to do next.

'How about that cafe where the guy can see ghosts?' said the one in the blue beret. 'I heard it opened in the summer. Should we go?'

'Oh, Ekadbo?' I said.

The other one nodded. 'It's very close.'

I went with them.

The cafe was located in a merchant house that had a brass bell hanging over the entrance. Up the front was a retail area selling an assortment of t-shirts, leather cardholders, jewellery and indigo scarves. An avant-garde chandelier hung from the ceiling, adorned with dried flowers and driftwood. The cafe seemed to be up the back.

I heard the ghost man before I saw him. He had started speaking to the two women in a soft voice and was holding up a small yellow pepper for them to admire. I'd assumed he'd be old, but he was about forty, with shoulder-length hair and a side part. He was wearing a white shirt and black pants, and introduced himself to the women as Mr Kenichi Eguchi.

'Why don't we go upstairs?' he said. 'I use the second floor to share stories about ghosts.'

We followed him. On the way up, one of the women whispered to the other that he looked like Nino from the boy band Arashi. The other vehemently shook her head.

The second floor was a tatami room. Mr Eguchi invited the woman in the blue beret to open the cupboard there. She looked a little scared and pushed her friend to do it instead.

The pink-hatted woman was reluctant but gave in. She slid the door open. The blue beret let out a yelp and nearly barrelled right out of the room. Standing inside the cupboard was an ichimatsu doll the size of a three-year-old. The doll had a blunt fringe and thick, straight hair which fell just below her shoulders. She wore a red kimono and white tabi. A shorter doll sat in front of her, with two smaller ones at her feet. The way they were all positioned was reminiscent of a floral arrangement.

Mr Eguchi said that the tallest doll was full of bad things. It was the kind of doll that people might buy for a girl of around three – a sort of twin that would field all the misadventure that would otherwise befall the girl.

'If you put a plastic bag over this doll's head,' he added, 'you can see the condensation from her breath.'

According to Mr Eguchi, the shorter doll didn't have a spirit in it. It once belonged to a severely troubled woman. Some of her energy had rubbed off on the doll.

'When my wife and I first opened the cafe,' he said, 'the sensors went off one night on the floor where we were sitting. We rushed over to see if there had been a break-in, and found children's footprints had appeared along one wall.'

He pointed them out. I went over and looked. Footprints in the dust, the size that a three-year-old might make.

The woman in the pink beret raised an eyebrow. She was probably thinking that he'd dragged some poor toddler through the dust to make the footprints. Her friend, though, was fully into it, and asked Mr Eguchi about the time he realised he could see spirits.

'I can't remember,' he said. 'But I'm sure I got the ability because my father sold antiques for a living. I was always around old things. The tallest doll used to be in my father's shop, before he passed away.'

We had been standing for some time, so Mr Eguchi invited us to make ourselves comfortable. He sat seiza-style, while I sat awkwardly with my legs to the side. The blue beret, her speech becoming more rapid and intense, asked if ghosts were trapped in our reality because of unfinished business. Mr Eguchi said that it was only in some cases.

'There are different types of ghosts. Some don't have consciousness and don't notice me – those ones are harmless. I've seen them stuck in the scene of an accident or suicide, on loop. Or they stand or walk absentmindedly within a very limited area, emotionless and zombie-like. Others don't realise they're dead and they're acting like they're carrying out an ingrained daily routine. They might wait at castle ruins as if they're protecting the castle. Or they might commute to school or wander around the office just like when they were alive. They'll pass through walls because they're in their own world, full of different buildings and layouts. If they lived two hundred years ago, that's the world they inhabit, and they go around wearing the clothes they died in. These ghosts aren't living in our reality. It's a sort of liminal space between here and heaven or hell. Maybe they're ghosts or maybe they're something like memories.'

'I guess everyone should be well dressed all the time,' I said. 'Just in case we die accidentally and no-one finds us and gives us a proper funeral. We could spend eternity in the same terrible clothes!'

No-one responded. Maybe the thought of dying like that made them uncomfortable.

Mr Eguchi continued. 'Other special ghosts also exist in our reality. They have consciousness, and can be dangerous. Some are curious, and they come up to me. Others have a definite purpose or preoccupation, with no intention of doing anything else. Or they might have a grudge or unresolved feelings, and can interfere in the world – they might even be more like a demon than a person.'

I looked at the tallest doll. Her eyes seemed to be boring into me. I wondered if she had unresolved feelings, having been created to bear the suffering of others. When I tuned back into the discussion, Mr Eguchi was explaining that humans and ghosts looked the same to him.

'But when you're walking around,' said the blue beret, 'how do you tell the difference? Do you only work out that someone's human if you can reach out and touch them?'

'It doesn't really matter to me if it's a spirit or a person,' Mr Eguchi said. 'I don't try to distinguish between them. It's about context too. If, say, I see something in the middle of Minamihata Dam, and it's night-time, it's probably a spirit. But if they're doing something that could be dangerous to themselves, I'll try to make my presence known. If they notice me, I'll know they're human.

'I try to keep my gift switched off most of the time by concentrating on living things. Not humans, but nature, like flowers. Though when my mind drifts, that's when I see spirits. Sometimes I'll move out of a person's way on the street or stop the car to let someone walk across the road. And my wife will say, "What are you doing? There's no-one there!" It freaks her out.'

He spoke to us about his paranormal experiences at great length, never shifting from the seiza position. He said he'd once seen a monster. It was female, five metres tall, and green. Her arms came out from the lower part of her body. Her eyes looked like those of a goat, but the pupils were T-shaped.

He was remarkably calm while telling these stories. His energy was almost monk-like. Maybe he'd have to be calm, after all the things he'd seen.

As he spoke, I kept glancing at the tallest doll. I noticed the blue beret was doing the same, as if she was frightened it would leave her sight. The conversation finally ended when the woman in the pink beret got up and said it was time for them to catch the train to Onomichi.

I visited the cafe frequently after that. I didn't really have money to spend, but I loitered in the shop pretending to be interested in buying a purse or a scarf while Mr Eguchi talked to customers. He would tell them about how his father was a master of ikebana who had introduced him to the ritualistic art form at the age of three. How he had gone into hairdressing and then the fashion industry. How, when his father died, he resumed ikebana, becoming a master of the Sogetsu style.

He would serve drinks to his customers and improvise flower arrangements based on their vibes. He'd get into a flow state while doing this, and would sometimes choose big expensive blooms. When this happened, his wife would scold him, because the arrangements ended up costing more than the customer paid.

For one woman, Mr Eguchi pulled together a pink gerbera, a cockscomb, eucalyptus leaves, UFO green peppers, and twisted branches of dragon's claw willow. I guess she was a weirdo.

The woman's husband dropped in at the end of the session. He'd brought Mr Eguchi a box of yokan.

'These are delicious, from Oita,' he said. 'Did my wife tell you that she dragged me there the other week to see the higanbana in bloom?'

'Such a beautiful flower,' said Mr Eguchi. '"Higan" means the level of enlightenment that is one step before nirvana. And there are so many other names for the plant. The Buddhist name is "manjushage". And in English, people call it "red spider lily". The scientific name is "*Lycoris radiata*". I read somewhere that Lycoris was the pseudonym of a beautiful actress from ancient Rome. It seems she inspired the poet Virgil to name the sea nymph Lycorias after her – a nymph that lived below a riverbed. In Korea, the flower represents, among other things, "one-way love". The flower blooms and then it's gone, and only after it's gone will the leaves come out. The flower symbolises the female, and the leaves are the male, so they never meet.

'The problem with higanbana is that there's poison in the root.

Farmers plant it around their farms to kill moles. So people know a lot about the poisonous part, and as a result don't like the plant. But its meaning was originally so lovely. It can bring people to nirvana.'

'But don't they sprout around cemeteries?' said the man. 'My mother told me they grow in hell.'

The woman looked embarrassed. Mr Eguchi smiled and said nothing more. When the couple left, he passed the box of yokan to his wife, who took it into the kitchen. He wasn't a fan.

I suppose I gradually became an apprentice of sorts, since Mr Eguchi let me watch everything he did in the cafe. He often ran the place alone while his wife was off working her other job.

Between customers, we kept each other company in silence. He made sculptural arrangements for the store without speaking. He liked using driftwood with his flowers, which he'd collected from the nearby beach.

In my own mind, I secretly began referring to him by his first name, Kenichi, and enjoyed memorising and repeating the lines he used on visitors. Sentences like, 'Flowers are unique miracles of nature' and 'I want people of all ages to come into contact with the charm of flowers'. My favourite one was: 'As the founder of Sogetsu once said, flowers become human in ikebana.'

Sometimes while he was talking to other people, I'd go upstairs alone and sit looking at the doll.

I speculated on how old she was. Sure, she looked about three, but was she really forty? Sixty? Seventy? Had she always longed for a real father? For how many years had she watched Kenichi in his father's store? Had she somehow drawn him back to her? Why did he keep her so close to him? Surely her presence wasn't healthy – maybe she could cause him some serious harm.

When I was done speculating, I'd go back downstairs. I'd stay until Kenichi shut up shop. On the occasions that his wife was there, the two would walk across the street and get into Kenichi's beloved car, which was sleek and fancy. Then they would set off without me – zooming south along the shoreline out of town.

At one point, the wife brought their pet cat to the store in a special carry bag. They had scheduled a visit to the local animal hospital. The cat was a Himalayan, with blue eyes and voluminous grey-white fur. It looked a little bit like one I'd seen before, but I couldn't remember where.

'What a fluffy kitty you are,' I murmured.

'Pokoponmaru,' Kenichi said, gathering it up in his arms and scratching it under the chin. 'Look at your amazing beard!'

It struck me that he knew the cat's name but had never asked for mine. The cat leapt out of his arms and streaked around the store. It seemed to be looking for somewhere to hide. I couldn't help but follow it around as it darted here and there. I felt like I was in a trance.

'I've never seen such a lazy cat move so fast,' I heard Kenichi say.

I only stopped chasing the animal when Kenichi's wife sidled out of the kitchen, wiping her hands on her apron. I overheard her whispering to him, 'I still don't like this woman hanging around. It can't be good. Do we need to call someone?'

'I feel sorry for her,' he said. 'I'll manage it.'

I sat on one of the cafe chairs as Kenichi tried to coax the cat back into its carry bag. Why did he pity me? All I wanted was for him to see me – only me.

If he were ever to portray me in a floral arrangement, what would he choose? Something exotic? Maybe I would just be a pile of grey driftwood, chewed out by insects, eroded by water. Maybe the only reason for my existence was to bring out the beauty of flowers.

Before I knew it, Halloween was fast approaching. I went around to the cafe and found Kenichi dressed in a white gown and a wig of long black hair that hung down to his waist. It completely concealed his face. He was gently teasing his wife by dangling one hand out in front of him. His hand was daubed white and the nails were painted bruise purple. The polish went outside the lines, onto the skin around his nails. Kenichi's wife was wearing fox ears and a tail.

It was bright outside. I accompanied the two of them to the tourist information centre, where little kids and adults from the town had gathered. They wore black sheets, white sheets, cat ears and witch's hats, and carried plastic jack-o'-lanterns. One guy sported a clown mask with an axe driven into the skull. I followed the group as they walked down to the shoreline and paraded along it. The kids avoided Kenichi – his ghost costume was too much like the real deal. The group went trick-or-treating, stopping off at places including Ekadbo. Kenichi's wife gave candy to the kids while he took photos. Then the group went to pray at an important local shrine.

Kenichi had been looking forward to an event he'd organised for later, on Ekadbo's second floor. A ghost hunter was going to come and tell paranormal stories. But in the lead-up to the event, when it was quiet in the cafe, Kenichi pulled off his wig and left it on the front counter. He appeared sad, even desolate.

'I have to lie down,' he said. He had turned pale.

'Do you have a fever?' I asked. He didn't seem to know. His wife came over, concerned. He reassured her that he was okay – just a little nauseous and dizzy. All he needed was a nap before the event.

He went upstairs. His wife cleared some plates from one of the tables, and took them into the kitchen. I sneaked up to see him.

He was completely knocked out, lying on the tatami. I crouched and lay down next to him, facing in the same direction. I touched his hip with one finger, and let it rest there. He was shivering. I ran a hand along his side, lightly, tracing the curve of his body up to his shoulder. I began to stroke his hair, to put my lips to his neck. I inhaled his scent.

'Papa,' I said. 'Wake up.'

He didn't stir.

I moved the rest of my body against his and clutched him to me.

Then I felt hot air against the back of my neck – tiny, panting, disgusting breaths. Chills ran through me. The air filled with the patter of miniature feet. I stayed still. Tiny fingertips caressed my waist, crawled up my side. A tiny body pushed itself against mine.

I rolled over and faced the doll.

The despicable creature opened her mouth wide, from ear to ear, and bared ten rows of miniature teeth. She lunged forward.

I jumped on top of her and twisted her head. I knew she was made of clay, but it felt like flesh. I twisted that head around and around until I tore it off completely. The bad things inside her rushed out in a black cloud, screeching.

I smashed her body against the wall until the chest shattered and the limbs broke off. As I did this, I had a passing thought that what I really needed was a bokuto.

I picked up the head again and was about to bash the face in when I noticed Kenichi was kneeling, watching me. He was trembling. Sweat had soaked through his gown and was running down his face.

I looked around me. The body parts were no longer scattered over the tatami. The head was no longer in my hands.

Then I saw the open cupboard. The doll was standing exactly where she had always been – pristine and beautiful – looking out at me with an inscrutable smile.

The storytelling event went ahead. Kenichi let me stay. I supposed he wanted a break but didn't have the energy to make me leave.

He remained in the corner and let the ghost hunter run the show. Afterwards, Kenichi told his wife he wasn't well enough to drive home and that they should crash at the guesthouse down the street.

I waited in the cafe of the guesthouse for Kenichi to come down.

He did not seem well rested. When his wife went off to Ekadbo, he remained, looking vacant and ill, sitting opposite me at a big table. A bunch of people from the town soon joined us. They had come for their weekly newspaper-reading workshop. One of them was the man who had given Kenichi the box of yokan. He had turned up at the cafe with another box of the stuff. The guesthouse owner sliced up the yokan and put it on the table to share.

Each of the participants in the workshop had brought a newspaper, and they spent time cutting out articles. They then took turns going around the table talking about the articles they'd chosen. Kenichi and I listened in. One man read out an agony-aunt column in which a woman confessed that she was tired of looking after her elderly aunt, who had dementia. The aunt would often go missing for hours on end, wandering through the neighbourhood.

Another man, in a ponytail and overalls, held up one of his articles. 'They still haven't found this woman. The florist from those mountains.'

Everyone at the table knew the story, except for me and Kenichi. They were shocked that he hadn't heard the news. He told them he'd been preoccupied.

The police were searching for the woman, who had been missing for weeks. The decapitated heads of her father and younger sister had been discovered in a rowboat floating in a river near their home. The rest of their bodies hadn't yet been found.

'The woman and her sister ran a flower shop,' said the man with the ponytail. 'Their father had been a florist who passed his expertise on to his daughters and played them off against each other. Apparently he told the older one that she had no natural talent. That she'd never be as good at floristry as her sister, and would have to ride her sister's coat-tails for the rest of her life. When she was young, he used to lock her in a cupboard and sometimes beat her with a bokuto.'

One of the women scrutinised the photo in the article. 'She doesn't look like a killer.'

She passed the article to Kenichi, who looked closely at it. Then he looked at me, and looked at the article again. Did he think I resembled that woman? She was incredibly plain.

'Are you all right, Mr Eguchi?' the man with the ponytail said.

'I'm fine, thank you.' Kenichi reached over to the middle of the table and used a pick to select a slice of yokan. He placed the slice in his mouth and began to chew. The workshop went on.

Afterwards I followed him to Ekadbo. His wife was there alone. She came to the entrance. He spoke quietly to her, then shut the door in my face.

I sat on the seawall beside the dark road that led out of town. I inspected each set of headlights as they approached and sped past. Finally, I made out Kenichi's car – I could tell from the intense brightness of its lights. He was, as expected, driving his wife home.

I stepped out onto the road and faced the car. He would see me, and he would stop.

But Kenichi didn't slow down. He accelerated.

In a flash, I remembered the river. The heads of my father and sister, nestled perfectly in an enormous mass of red spider lilies. How I'd pushed the boat out then walked all night along the river. And the grey cat that crossed my path.

'What a fluffy kitty you are,' I'd said. 'What are you doing in a place like this?'

It had darted off towards the riverbank and leapt off the edge. I went up to where it had jumped. The cat was nowhere to be seen. I leaned out.

It was then that I lost my footing. I felt my head strike something, and I was suddenly under water, everything pitch-black.

The headlights were now upon me. The car passed right through my body. I turned and watched it shrink into the distance.

I wondered who could be driving at that speed at this time of night.

The car disappeared from view. I noticed a pretty young woman standing by the side of the road. I went over to her. Her eyes were vacant. She couldn't see me. She was clearly human and alive, but she seemed like an empty vessel, with nothing going on in her mind. Then, her face still blank, she let out a monstrous, hollow wail.

While she made that strange sound, I had an urge to take over her body. But then I had a sudden feeling that I'd done so before.

It was time to find someone else to inhabit. I left the howling thing and began to drift along the shoreline towards the next town, my feet above the water, a trail of red spider lilies sinking behind me.

Slow
Dmetri Kakmi

I

Before I discovered writing, my primary modes of expression were fashion and dance. I still love clothes as much as I revel in music that rouses the body to an orgiastic frenzy of movement that lasts for hours, leaving me ecstatic and hanging out for more.

Growing up in 1970s Melbourne, I dreamed of being anything other than my 'woggy' self. And so, I used clothes to turn myself into an ideal. Problem was, my fashion sense was out of kilter with the times and I ended up looking like a character from *The Addams Family*. If I had not been kidnapped by disco queens, I would have been a goth.

From 1979 onwards, I started turning up at gay nightclubs in my black, distressed, asymmetrical designer outfits and danced all night to Patrick Cowley's Hi-NRG anthems, looking like a misfit amid the Village People clones. No wonder I never got laid. But it was music video, then coming into its own, that truly captured my imagination with images of singers striking impossibly glamorous poses in outlandish fashions. I thought I had died and gone to Heaven – the nightclub in London, not where God lives.

Every Sunday, I settled in front of the television with my little sister to watch *Countdown*. Here was a world beyond my traditional Greek upbringing. I was not a rock'n'roll man. Mine was the province of disco and electro-inspired New Wave – the forefathers of house and techno. In quick succession, from the late 1970s to the mid-1980s, I went from The Pointer Sisters, Sylvester and Boney M to Grace Jones, Pet Shop Boys, Visage, Eurythmics, Kraftwerk, Laurie Anderson and any number of crazy Blitz Kids coming out of London. Most were one-hit wonders, but how bright they burned on the dancefloor firmament before they were replaced by someone equally brief and dazzling.

Music video was the late twentieth century's primary mode of artistic expression, exceeding that of painting, which seemed moribund and navel-gazing. If you wanted to take the temperature of the times, you looked to music and fashion, not the art gallery. All you had to do was check out Boy George, Leigh Bowery, and Prince to see that. Grace Jones towered over all of them. From the 1980s onwards, she merged powerful visuals with reggae-inspired electronic music to turn herself into an ambulatory artwork that has stood the test of time.

Feeling uncomfortable with the way masculinity and femininity were defined, I was drawn to gender-benders who projected a fearless sense of self through style and music. Blonde cookie-cutter babes like Kylie Minogue, who hit the stage with 'The Locomotion' in 1987, did not feature in my universe. The final released version of the song was standard Stock Aitken Waterman, and Kylie looked as if she had stepped off the set of *Neighbours* into an under-sixteens disco. She was too naff and I did not understand her appeal. If anything, I preferred Kylie's sister Dannii with sexed-up Euro-dance hits, like 'Put the Needle on It'.

Fast forward to 2011. It was late at night, I was sitting up in bed, sleepless, cruising YouTube, when my eye was snagged by an image of a man in speedos. I clicked on it, watched the video two or three times in a row, and then wailed: 'Argh, my inner gay is coming out!'

The video was 'Slow'. The singer Kylie Minogue. And I was ravished.

When I mentioned this to a friend, she said: 'You're a contrarian. You probably didn't like her because she's a gay icon.'

My friend was right. The well-aimed remark made me see that I harboured internalised homophobia. Other gays idolise Kylie. Therefore, I can't like her. Many gay men play this game with themselves on the way to finding out who they are and where they belong in the varied substrata in gay (sub)cultures. It is a way of raising above the fray. I am not like other homos; I am better or different. I don't subscribe to stereotypes. But, of course, I did. Worshipping Grace Jones is about as gay as you get.

'Slow' made me realise that Kylie had changed. She had refined her conception of self. She had become stylish and sophisticated, creating beautiful images and compelling songs.

Once I confronted my inner contrarian, I could admit to liking 'Confide in Me' and 'Can't Get You Out of My Head'. And I love 'Where the Wild Roses Grow', the duet with Nick Cave. The video, with references to John Everett Millais' painting, *Ophelia*, is poetry. It also shows Kylie's versatility and the respect she has garnered from other artists in the music industry.

II

Three things stood out about 'Slow':
    the video,
    then the music/vocals,
    followed by *the dress*.

Aside from being an obvious selling tool, music video is the way a performer projects a private fantasy of self onto the public consciousness. In 'Slow', Kylie was a smoky temptress. In 'Come into

My World' she became the carefree urban chameleon. Video is an effective way to cast a spell and to bewitch spectators; to draw them into a make-believe world and hold them there.

An effective video makes space for the viewer to enter the image and become part of the dream, not only as an observer, but an active participant. Through an interplay of empathic imagination and a willingness to lose yourself in glamour, you become your idol and, for a time, assume the persona.

This is vital because the effective music video and accompanying pop song must speak to the viewer/listener's hidden yearnings. I am thinking of songs that did this for me in the 80s: 'Love My Way' by Psychedelic Furs and 'Tainted Love' by Soft Cell spoke to gay men about same-sex attraction in ways that called for urgent expression, despite social opprobrium. The Grace Jones cover version of 'Walking in the Rain' by Australians Vanda and Young became my personal anthem when I realised my favourite androgyne was telling me to revel in my outcast state.

What did 'Slow' bring out in me?

A lot.

First, it made me think of 1980s offerings, like 'Sweet Dreams (Are Made of This)' by Eurythmics and 'We Are Glass' by Gary Numan. Simple concepts, elegantly executed for maximum effect. Except, of course, there is nothing simple about 'Slow'.

'The Singing Budgie' has always been about enjoying the moment, in a nice, clean, fun sort of way. To a large extent, that is the secret of Kylie's success: no matter what is happening in the world, she remains a beacon of light. I firmly believe that if a gay guy dies and heads off into the tunnel, Kylie will be waiting for him at the other end, ready for a dance.

Despite acreage of flesh on display, via revealing costumes and semi-naked dancing boys in live performances, no-one would call Kylie raunchy – the way her dark-haired sister Dannii can be. I have always thought of Kylie and Dannii as different sides of the same coin, like goody-two-shoes Samantha and her wicked cousin Serena in the 1960s TV series *Bewitched* – good and bad, light and dark, sanitised and sexy. Extending the comparison into the sociopolitical realm, we see that, like Samantha and Serena, Kylie's 'goodness' has been rewarded with career longevity while Dannii's 'badness' consigned her to playing second fiddle to her sister, despite impressive vocal talent.

Kylie would never sing 'Put the Needle on It'. If she did, she would make it sound sweet and innocent. Despite being in her fifties, she comes across as a fresh-off-the-boat ingenue. There is nothing threatening or confronting about the image she projects. Even after the lightly risqué lyrics of 'Padam Padam', Kylie remains coyly, kittenishly sexy without being about sex per se, the way my other favourites, Lil' Kim and Azealia Banks, most definitely are. I cannot imagine Kylie gleefully lowering herself on a microphone the way Lil' Kim did in an early video, or lasciviously twerking the way Azealia Banks does in the video for 'Anna Wintour'.

Perhaps that explains why I do not think of myself as a Kylie fan. She is safe and I like performers with an electric charge. Yet 'Slow' turned my head. Through a series of calculated tableaux, it elevated the girl from Camberwell to the realm of incandescent female beauty, placing her firmly among the premier Australian pop stars.

III

Directed by Baillie Walsh, the video was filmed at the Piscina Municipal de Montjuïc, in Barcelona, and it shamelessly targets Kylie's primary audience.

Wait for it.

Gay men.

Shot with Walsh's usual finesse and technical precision over two days, it begins with the camera panning across a teeming urban landscape, shimmering in a heat haze, as a man prepares to dive from a diving board. His speedos are a shade darker than the blue sky. In silence, he raises his arms and begins to gracefully plunge into a swimming pool far below. Shades of blue will dominate throughout to reflect *the dress* and the mellow mood.

It is only when the man is in the air, the city spread behind him, that sound effects intrude. The mournful whistle of the wind accentuates the diver's isolation and the dramatic moment of man against the elements. He plummets with a splash into sparkling water and vanishes under the surface. The camera pans to the edge of the pool. The babble of talk is heard as the man pops out of the water (miraculously dry) and steps over a series of mostly male Spaniards, spread out beneath him, like a smorgasbord of sizzling flesh.

Forty-two seconds into the video, the diver steps over the baby-blue beach towel on which the star indolently lies and the gentle burble of electro-synth music begins. Kylie wears a body-hugging minidress that draws the eye. Looking down from high above, she looks like a sex siren artistically arranged for a 1960s girly calendar. The breathy, insistent vocals usher in a series of postures, hip thrusts and movements from the bathers lying around her. Choreographed by Michael Rooney (actor Mickey Rooney's son), who also worked on 'Can't Get You Out of My Head', the effect is an elaborate Busby Berkeley–like spectacle that places Kylie at the centre of a vortex of desire. Everyone in the frame circles around her and is drawn to the nucleus. The overhead shots are intercut with close-ups of Kylie's face as she strikes a series of poses calculated to ravish and beguile.

As the song pulsates to a close, Kylie pulls a lavender veil across her face, mysterious and remote as the Delphic Oracle.

Red lips, blue eyes: end.

Kylie does not touch the dancers. They do not touch her. Though a lot of surreptitious fondling is going on around her, Kylie remains an island unto herself, remote, isolated, untouchable. Though she sparks it off, she does not take part in the orgy that spreads like an incendiary fire. This is the realm of the untouchable goddess. You may look, but you cannot touch. To touch is to shatter the dream of romantic love and unattainable desire.

It worked on me.

In four minutes, a performer who had existed in my periphery stepped forward with force, evoking everyone from Ingres' odalisques to Brigitte Bardot and Marlene Dietrich. Along the way, she created a short film that is a work of art, a sublime merger of sound, colour, dance and image. Moreover, the messy blonde hair, the luscious lips, the creamy skin, the seductive writhing, act as the perfect canvas for a stunning Balenciaga dress.

IV

'Slow' was the opening track on the 2003 album *Body Language* – the first of three singles and, in my view, the best. Released the same year as the US invasion of Iraq, 'Slow' has become emblematic of that military disaster, in the same way that 'Can't Get You Out of My Head', released two years earlier, reminds me of the 9/11 attacks on New York City.

The song was written by Kylie, British songwriter and producer Dan Carey, and Icelandic songwriter and singer Emiliana Torrini, and produced by Carey, Torrini and Sunnyroads.

Musically, 'Slow' utilises a minimal style of production, described as an 'electro-pop/disco fusion with percolating crackle-and-pop beats to sugary vocal overdubs' by Sal Cinquemani in *Slant Magazine*. For 'sugary' I use 'breathy'. For much of the time, woven through and around the gentle baseline, the song is suffused with almost subliminal sighs, whispers and airy expulsions that pull you in and push you out, like a dance of desire between two individuals who cannot make up their minds whether they want to get together or not. 'Slow' is a siren song. Come here, Kylie is saying. Step back, take your time. It will happen when it happens. If it happens. And even if it does not happen, the journey is worth it.

The vocal delivery is classic Kylie. It puts to good use her quivering, wispy soprano to create a perfect, carefully modulated, seductive delivery in which every pause is calculated for maximum effect. My ears immediately perked up when I heard the German minimalist influence, burbling away in the baseline. Popularised by the Cologne-based label Kompakt, it is characterised by a stripped-back aesthetic that uses repetition and an understated progression that can be traced to early Detroit-based house and techno producers, like Kenny Larkin and Robert Hood.

The overall effect is trance-like (the state of mind as well as the musical form) and hypnotic – a real seduction, and as close to perfection as pop music gets. The languor of hot, breezeless days seeps into every note. The indolence manifests in the bodies splayed around the singer, giving rise to gyrating, sybaritic movements. When the dancers manage to rouse themselves during the chorus, they barely rise above their beach towels, managing only to thrust hips or arch backs in a series of movements that culminate in some of the male dancers suggestively sliding down skimpy swimsuits.

It is the perfect song to play while having sex, as potent as Donna

Summer and Giorgio Moroder's 'I Feel Love'. No wonder it charted high around the globe and critics went mad with plaudits when they heard it. Kylie cites 'Slow' as a peak moment in a long career, as well she should.

V

On the Turkish island where I was born, we were too poor for high fashion. There was only functional clothing to protect your body from the elements. My mother either made my clothes or I inherited my cousin Nick's hand-me-downs.

My nascent education in the art of clothes-making came from across the other side of town, where my father's sister lived. Aunt Paraskevi was a seamstress. Given her name means 'preparation', I like to think she paved the way for me and fashion to get together at some stage. Greek and Turkish women came to her for new outfits. She was probably prevailed upon to make clothes for me and my sister as well. The front room of her house was always filled with young women, chattering and learning the trade. As a boy, I sat on the floor inside their enchanted circle and watched as they worked magic with fabric, thread and needle. Silver thimbles flashed. Sharp scissors snipped, and slivers of coloured thread rained down. Seated in the middle of it all, I was captivated by the way these joyful nymphs turned a bolt of fabric into a shirt, dress or suit that transformed a humble wearer into a bird of paradise.

But I did not want to make clothes. I wanted to strut around in them.

My family emigrated to Australia when I was ten years old. When I was twenty-two, I enrolled in a modelling course with Helene Abicair and briefly worked as a catwalk model. It was my way of building self-esteem and overcoming crippling shyness. It worked like a tonic. I was tall and thin and the agency sold me as the 'exotic' European type. In no time I was prancing around with the best of them, getting crazy haircuts and spending the little money I had on designer clothes. Turned out the agency did not want weird haircuts; they wanted the non-descript look, which probably explains why they stopped booking me for shows.

When buying clothes, I initially looked to Giorgio Armani. When he proved too conservative for my tastes, I turned to Katharine Hamnett, Vivienne Westwood and Yohji Yamamoto. I was still trying to find myself through clothes, my eye seduced by the way designers used texture, fabric and detail to create garments that were unique and unusual. I lived in my then unfashionable baggy black cargo pants from Katharine Hamnett and oversized white Westwood t-shirt with *Destroy* written across it. Both pieces hung on my body and redefined my skinny silhouette in ways that suited the androgynous aesthetic I wanted to project. The great Japanese designers and legendary European couturiers are still my heroes. The works of Alexander McQueen and Rei Kawakubo send me into paroxysms of delight in ways that very little literature does.

Oscar Wilde claimed that only superficial people think looks don't matter. I concur. A sense of style is important. It is the first thing people notice and it is the impression they take away. Clothes can make you visible and they can make you invisible; clothes can even make you feel better about yourself by imprinting onto the skin a look that emboldens and invigorates. It works the other way around, too. Clothes can demonstrate how you feel on the inside, and how you see yourself in the mind's eye.

Fashion designers are visionaries working in concert with and, simultaneously, against the body. Like sculptors with clay, they reimagine and reshape the body – its shape and its contours – pushing flesh to the limit in an effort to create a sense of beauty and style for the wearer. Beautifully designed clothes are a fantasy of becoming, of reaching higher than we might dare. It is a Promethean act of self-creation and I think that is the reason some gay men are drawn to fashion and extreme costume-making, such as we see in legendary Leigh Bowery. In a world that seeks to define us, we use clothes to tell the world who we are and what we can be. Nobody understands this better than honorary gay man, Grace Jones, who used everyone from Armani and Issey Miyake to legendary Japanese costume maker Eiko Ishioka to turn herself into a work of art.

In her own way, Kylie does something similar in 'Slow'.

Except, Kylie *frames* the dress, rather than *becomes* the dress. Her personality is not strong enough to subsume the outfit and make it part of her. She can only use it to create a temporary persona, which will be doffed in time to take on yet another. In that sense Kylie is more like Madonna than Grace Jones.

The dress came from the 2003 Spring/Summer Balenciaga collection. It sprang from the mind of Nicolas Ghesquière, the then creative director. Ghesquière had taken over at the helm of the famed luxury house in 1997 when he was only twenty-five – a remarkable achievement that showed incredible trust in his abilities to rejuvenate a faltering house. He did not disappoint.

For this collection, Ghesquière was inspired by his childhood love of scuba diving; he was a sporty child. The dresses are a viscose silk substitute, disguised as neoprene, the stuff from which scuba diving suits are made. That is why they hold their shape and cling to the body, displaying every curve. Ghesquière's youthfulness and exuberance showed in the way he ignored founder Cristóbal Balenciaga's signature forgiving silhouette and went full out for sheer minidresses that acted like a second skin, tight and erotic, yet oddly restrained, with soft lines.

I gasped the first time I saw the dress on Kylie.

'What is she wearing?'

It was such a luxurious, sexy piece of drapery, wrapped tight around her curves in alternating bands of midnight black and aqua blue, the neckline plunging almost to the navel. My first impression was of a wondrous present waiting to be unwrapped, layer by enticing layer.

Initially, I thought the outfit was transparent, befitting the poolside. Like Marilyn Monroe's famed see-through dress, I thought I saw more than I was seeing. Then I realised there was a body-hugging sheath beneath the alternating shades of ruching – a gathered overlay of fabric strips pleated to create a rippling effect. Ghesquière used ruching to great effect throughout the collection – possibly his most memorable for Balenciaga – but the Kylie dress was the best iteration. She wore it better than the model on the catwalk. The dress almost disappeared against the model's olive complexion and light-brown hair. Whereas it leaped to the fore when displayed against Kylie's peaches-and-cream skin and blonde hair.

To my surprise, I thought, 'I'd wear that, if I wore women's clothes.'

What was going on? Was Kylie bringing forth my inner drag queen, too?

VI

Despite seeing myself as an androgyne, I have no desire to wear women's clothes. I am totally comfortable balancing the feminine in a masculine body.

So why did I suddenly want to wear a dress?

I saw myself on the catwalk, legs elegantly crisscrossing each other as I walked the length of the room. I felt the silky fabric against my skin; I ran my hands along the rough textured ruching as it gave way to sleekness beneath; I felt the plunging neckline liberate my cloistered chest. The years melted as I shed the masculine carapace and luxuriated in the kind of freedom and playfulness society allots only to women. I was young again, a dazzling model on a catwalk.

And perhaps that is, in part, why drag queens and transvestites appropriate female garb. To shed inhibitions and to liberate the male form.

The dress in 'Slow' opened my mind to the fantasy of fashion. Like music and dance, fashion lifts us out of the everyday and drops us into a spectacular vision of daydreaming. Even though it is temporary, it is real, potent and seductive. It carries us away. It breaks down barriers and it allows us to escape.

For the first decade of my life in Australia, I wanted to be blond and blue-eyed, like the Anglo boys in primary school. I was not. I was swarthy, brown-eyed and brown-haired. Given the way kids treated me, I thought I was ugly. I would never be handsome or accepted. But Kylie's pristine whiteness, her corn-yellow hair and green-blue eyes, combined with the Balenciaga dress, acted as a talisman that allowed me to become another person, and even another gender. Revealing that a sense of self is malleable and in flux.

Internally, we are plastic, constantly changing and evolving towards an unknown point.

Internally, we hold a world of promise and potential – the promise and potential in Kylie's eyes.

Especially for You
Adam Ouston

In 1988, following a twenty-year study conducted on 106 foreign tourists presenting themselves to the Santa Maria Nuova Hospital in Florence, chief psychiatrist of the clinic's Mental Health Service, Dr Graziella Magherini, having produced a complete catalogue of their ailments, stood back and looked at them as a whole, as might a painter admiring a mural or ceiling fresco, and noticed that it brought to mind a passage she'd read many years before, in which the French author, Stendhal (aka Marie-Henri Beyle), fresh from Napoleonic duty, on Wednesday 22 January 1817, took a day trip to Florence, entered the Basilica di Santa Croce, where, kneeling, surrounded by frescoes by Giotto di Bondone and the lustrous paintings of Baldassare Franceschini, within touching distance of the tombs of Niccolo Machiavelli, Galileo Galilei and Michelangelo Buonarroti, was entirely overcome by emotion, which, as he then stumbled from the porch of the Santa Croce, aroused sudden and acute sensations in the body – racing heart, dizziness – as well as the feeling that life was, or would be very soon, slipping away.

1.

Aitken and Waterman: Which bit's the fucking chorus?

Kylie and Jason: The *TOGETHER* bit.

Aitken and Waterman: But the fucking song's called 'Especially for You'. Everyone will think it's called *Together*.

Kylie and Jason: It opens with *Especially for you* ...

Aitken and Waterman: Who fucking cares. That's not what sticks in your head. It's the *Together* bit that sticks.

Kylie and Jason's Managers (in chorus): They're your lyrics. You think we should change it?

Aitken and Waterman: Change what?

Kylie and Jason's Managers (in chorus): The chorus?

Aitken and Waterman: No.

Kylie and Jason: The title?

Aitken and Waterman: It's a fucking Hallmark card. The name's too good to change but it has nothing to do with the hook. The fucking thing has two choruses and that will confuse people. What a fucking nightmare. It's already October. Scott and fucking Charlene get married in a month.

Kylie and Jason: We got married a year ago.

Aitken and Waterman: That was in 1987, and in fucking Australia.

Kylie and Jason: Yeah, and?

Aitken and Waterman, and Kylie and Jason's Managers: No-one fucking cares about Australia.

Aitken and Waterman: We're only here so we can finish this fucking song, and then we're back to London.

Kylie and Jason's Managers: Over twenty million people in the UK will be tuning in to see Scott and Charlene get married. The song has to be out when that happens. You two are still a couple, right?

Kylie: Hm-mm. **and Jason:** Yes.

Aitken and Waterman: We're going to have to fix this mix in London. If it's even fixable. What a fucking nightmare.

Kylie: We'll stay here all night until it's right.

Jason: We will?

Kylie: You can go. I'm staying. Actually, don't go.

Jason: We will!

Aitken and Waterman: You can't tell which one's the hook.

Kylie and Jason: Can't you have two hooks?

Aitken and Waterman: Messy. Confusing.

Kylie and Jason's Managers: People don't like it. Then they can't find it in the shop. We have the studies. You have to give them something simple to recite and remember, otherwise it's just money down the gurgler.

Aitken and Waterman: Not to mention a shitty fucking pop song. People are going to think it's called 'Together'.

Kylie to Jason: We need to talk.

2.

Quickly thumbing her way back through Stendhal's *Rome, Naples et Florence*, Dr Magherini located the passage in question, and although her veins were fizzing with the humidity and rush of discovery, a condition she should one day also look into, and heart beating in tandem with the poet at a distance of almost a century-and-a-half, she was not quite as overcome as the author himself, though that's not to say she wasn't thrilled – if indeed we can call the diagnosis and description of diseases and syndromes *thrilling* – nevertheless, she was struck by the parallels between Stendhal's account of mental and physical malady and the accounts of those tourists who'd travelled to Italy from all over the world only to be brought to her rooms – many of them literally stretchered straight in – from sites of cultural significance, mostly museums and art galleries, in particular those pieces considered great works of art and structures considered great works of architecture, because it was not the case that these people were being rushed into her care in swarms of ecstasy and blissful union with a higher power, like some sort of visitation from on high, far from it: what these people were complaining of was the complete opposite – dizziness, heart palpitations, hallucinations, disorientation, depersonalisation, diaphoresis, asthenia, profound exhaustion and anxiety; hell, in short, and not so much the Dantean sort where one is besieged by murderers, swindlers and a three-headed devil, but rather a more contemporary inner hell in which everything becomes threatening, life slips away, all joy – at least for the moment, perhaps longer – is extinguished and such was the force of the likeness, Magherini decided to call it Stendhal Syndrome, which of course has its detractors and non-believers – 'codswallop' according to the more hard-nosed critics – the most staunch being the medical profession itself, which refuses to recognise it in the *Diagnostic and Statistical Manual of Mental Disorders*, therefore placing it firmly in the same category as Stockholm Syndrome, Paris Syndrome, and Jerusalem Syndrome and the same ballpark of other pseudoscientific diagnoses such as female hysteria, homosexuality, and 'sluggish' schizophrenia, the latter used by authoritarian countries when locking up dissenters who expressed no observable symptoms of the disorder but were deemed ripe for symptoms appearing sooner or later.

3.

Subjects were required to rate how memorable the song was on a scale of one to five, one being 'I completely forget' and five being 'I can't get it out of my head'. They were then asked to write down which parts of the song they actually remembered. Only fifty-four percent of those who heard the song could predict the title of the song without having been given any prior knowledge. Eighty-six percent reported feeling more invested in the song when they knew the two people singing the duet were dating each other. When prompted to describe those feelings, respondents used words like, 'warm,' 'intimate', 'love', 'dreamy' and 'hopeful'. Sixty-seven percent of subjects reported being made to feel sad, with the primary reason being because their love lives paled in comparison to the ones presented by the song. Other negative emotions included jealousy, envy, anger, vengefulness, bitterness and depression. These negative emotions did not negatively impact their connection with the song. In fact, those who expressed negative emotions tended to score higher on retention and desire to hear the song repeatedly. These subjects indicated they would likely play the song for friends and family and even co-workers. Three respondents reported feelings of deep self-loathing and the desire to harm themselves or even end their own lives. They were eventually allowed to leave and referred to the appropriate mental health professionals. On the night following the focus group sessions, one participant – not one of the three listed above – leapt from the seventeenth-storey balcony of their inner-city apartment building. It was decided there was no direct correlation between their activities that day and their final activity that night, although it was noted by authorities that the word *together* appeared nine times in the note they left behind. Seventy-one percent of subjects indicated they would purchase the single or an album featuring the song as a gift for a significant other. Forty-two percent would also buy it for a parent. Twenty-one percent for a friend. And nine percent for a colleague. Ninety-two percent said the single would make a great birthday gift. Only three percent of respondents reported any erotic feelings associated with the song, with an overwhelming majority using the phrase 'Ken and Barbie' to describe the artists, alluding to the fair hair and absence of genitalia. Subjects reported that the couple's 'cleanliness' allowed them to listen more openly and give more liberally. When provided with glossy pornographic magazines and a series of the artists' headshots, most subjects were unable to find a suitable body type, position or contortion in the former to match the latter. Many reported feeling a sense of taboo reminiscent of incest, which in some cases was reportedly arousing but, in most cases, not. Several respondents were observed masturbating, though up to half of this cohort were using the supplied adult material as opposed to images of the artists. It is important to note that this response was triggered only in those subjects in terminal paresis (GPI), which accounted for less than twenty percent of all respondents. When prompted to provide explanations, their reasoning was that it forestalled thoughts of death. Doctors indicated that we should not read anything into their behaviour, as erotic response was a common symptom of their condition. Seventy-seven percent of all respondents wanted to see the artists married in real life, with the word 'fairytale' appearing in the responses of eighty-nine percent of subjects. Eighty-four percent of subjects described themselves as heterosexual. The song appealed mostly to heterosexual women, followed by homosexual men, followed by heterosexual men, followed by homosexual women. Fifteen respondents did not disclose their sexuality; this cohort displayed excellent lyric retention and scored highest in predicting the name of the song. Thirty-nine percent of subjects listed the artists as Scott and Charlene.

4.

While Magherini chooses Stendhal especially for the handle of her disorder, she might well choose Sigmund Freud, who reported severe feelings of alienation and depersonalisation when visiting the Acropolis in Athens, or Carl Jung who, in his autobiography *Memories, Dreams, Reflections*, details his desire to go to Rome in 1949 – when he was already an old man – something he'd had on his bucket list for a long time and had baulked on seeing it through for fear of the emotional impact of encountering the very heart of European culture, but on entering the offices of his travel agent in Zurich to buy a ticket he passed out and, when recovered, vowed that all bets were off and Rome would continue to exist purely in his imagination, which is to say that Stendhal Syndrome hounded all manner of lily-livered aesthetes, such as Marcel Proust who travelled to The Hague in 1921 to see Vermeer's *View of Delft*, which he considered the most beautiful painting in the world, himself suffering an attack on leaving the Mauritshuis Museum; on returning home he added a fictionalised version of this episode to his almost-finished *À La Recherche*, wherein the novelist, Bergotte, visits the same Vermeer and promptly falls down dead (as for Proust himself: he never left his apartment again); not to mention Dostoyevsky who suffered severe paralysis and a sense of complete absence while standing before the 'startlingly dead' Jesus in Hans Holbein's *Le Christ Mort au Tombeau* in Basel, Switzerland, in 1867 (the attack being so profound that his long-suffering and pregnant wife, Anna, feared it would trigger one of his fits), while the Germans were also prone to such torments, with Rainer Maria Rilke noting in his first *Duino Elegy* that 'beauty is nothing but the beginning of awesomeness which we can barely endure and we marvel at it so because it calmly disdains to destroy us,'[1] a notion alluded to by Immanuel Kant in his *Critique of Judgement*, where he tells us that encountering beauty induces 'a quickly alternating attraction toward, and repulsion from, the same object. The transcendent [...] is for the imagination like an abyss in which it fears to lose itself,'[2] an idea that aesthetics took further in the nineteenth century, doing away with the classical idea of reflection and rather suggesting that the contemplation of art might be an attribute of the art object itself, which all sounds very confusing but is brought into focus when we observe that the German thinkers called the resulting involuntary emotional projection *Einfühlung*: the German word that gives us 'empathy' in English.

5.

Kylie: After this is done, I'm out.

Jason: What do you mean *out*?

Kylie: I've met someone.

Jason: What do you mean *met someone*?

Kylie: And want to be with him.

Jason: Wait. What?

Kylie: Don't be dramatic, Jason.

Jason: But you're breaking up with me. It is dramatic.

Kylie: Well I'm not breaking up with you *yet*.

Jason: Yet?

Kylie: This bloody thing has to come out next month. And then there's Scott and Charlene's wedding in the UK. But after that.

Jason: Who's the guy?

Kylie: Don't make me spell it out for you. I fucking hate doing that.

Jason: Who's the guy?

Kylie: Look, do we have to do this now?

Jason: You're the one who dragged me into this fucking vocal booth.

Kylie: It's Michael.

Jason: Michael.

Kylie: Fucking oath, Jason. Michael Hutchence.

Jason: Oh.

Kylie: Don't get all thingy about it.

Aitken and Waterman (from the Control Room): C'mon, you two lovebirds, we've got a hit to make. And we've got to get back to fucking London. Christ.

Kylie and Jason's Managers (also from the Control Room): It's staying as 'Especially for You'.

Aitken and Waterman (from the Control Room): People are still going to think it's fucking called 'Together'.

Kylie and Jason's Managers: You two look so great together!

6.

It was the German literary critic Wolfgang Iser, a key proponent of reader-response theory, who suggested that meaning is not inherent within a text but rather produced via an interaction *between* the text and the reader, becoming intrigued by the ways readers reacted to certain books while studying the concept of 'Werther-fever' – a phenomenon that swept across Europe during the Romantic period and saw readers (primarily young men) suiciding after reading Goethe's *The Sorrows of Young Werther* – and the fact that this book could have such an effect on a particular set of readers during a particular time (not repeated since) led Iser to theorise that meaning is contingent on an interconnected network of societal, cultural, intellectual and temperamental factors which, like a secret password, in the 'right' combination, unlock particular, sometimes shared, responses in readers.

7.

Nevertheless, Magherini has stuck to her guns – and her Frenchman – and not only produced many papers on the phenomenon, but also a book, simply entitled *La Sindrome di Stendhal*, in which she describes the condition's greatest hits, according to her observations over that twenty-year period, including one 'Henry', a young American tourist in Florence, delivered to her care by a Florentine friend who had noticed that while the pair had visited the Caravaggio exhibition in the Pitti Palace, Henry had clearly become disturbed by the sequence of lights illuminating the paintings by intervals – a sort of high-art peek-a-boo – whereby the alternating light and dark caused him to become disoriented, the loss of light seemingly equating to Henry as not only the loss of meaning of the painting, but the loss of the meaning of his own existence, and when the Florentine friend whisked him off to another painting, Henry became even more disturbed, this time by the knee of Narcissus as he knelt before the reflective body of water; the way the boy crouched was odd: almost sitting on one leg, the opposite knee elevated and thrust into the foreground forming the very centre of the composition, the central and brightest object in the frame, which Henry, in his increasingly fragile state, transformed from a humble knee into a thick, knotty stick aimed right at him as though to beat him, which made him so frightened for his sanity that he ran away, his friend trailing after him trying fruitlessly to calm him down.

8.

Aitken and Waterman: I think we got it.

Jason: Fucking finally.

Kylie and Jason's Managers: It should be called 'Together'.

Aitken and Waterman: Well, it's fucking called 'Especially for You'.

Kylie and Jason's Managers: No-one's going to remember that.

Aitken and Waterman: After November, no-one has to.

Kylie: I have to go.

Jason: Can we talk?

Kylie: Don't be annoying.

Jason: Don't be so heartless.

Kylie: It's just business.

Jason: No. It isn't.

Kylie: Look, I have to go. It's almost four a.m.

Jason: I suppose you're meeting Michael, then?

Kylie: Ugh, why are we even talking about this?

Jason: You can't turn off a relationship just like that.

Kylie: Ah, what now?

Jason: You know as well as I do it's more than we let on.

Kylie: I don't let anything on.

Jason: You should listen to yourself.

Kylie: I've been listening to myself all night and I'm sick of the sound of my own voice. Yours too.

Jason: Don't do this.

Kylie: See you in London.

9.

In a more recent publication, *'I've Fallen in Love with a Statue':
Beyond the Stendhal Syndrome*, Dr Magherini does exactly what
the title says, and looks beyond the symptoms brought on by
a work of art in order to focus on the artwork itself, in particular the
Renaissance sculpture that seems to cause the greatest stir among
visitors to Florence, *David* by Michelangelo, one of the most
renowned artefacts in popular culture, the epitome of strength and
distillation of beauty, itself carved from a colossal hunk of marble
known as 'Il Gigante' ('The Giant'), which sculptors before him
had failed to master, but from which nevertheless Michelangelo
was able to draw out the languid form of his subject, which is
somewhat mysterious because at first blush we are greeted with
a body apparently at rest, even sensually, romantically inert,
as though with little to do but eat figs and read poetry, but it is
his eyes that give him away, because despite the attractive and
viscous lines of his long thighs and the chalice-like scoop at the
base of his throat, his brow is worried and his eyes, not so much
gazing into the superfluous middle distance, are very much trained
on something, and not just anything but something frightening,
which has a magical ability to make us re-evaluate the position
of his limbs and we now see that he is not limply at leisure but
poised in a moment before decisive action, summoning every
skerrick of courage he has at his disposal, so that he might fling
the stone that will free and save his people, which is somehow the
most delicious and terrifying moment all at once, and therefore
there is no better work for Magherini to interrogate, embodying as
it does the attraction/repulsion response in sufferers of Stendhal
Syndrome, its allure so powerful as to radiate the truth of Rilke's
observation of the unbreakable link between beauty and terror,

which Magherini herself further elucidates when she manages to get hold of the Academy Gallery's guestbook, which records visitors' responses to *David* ranging from noting its anatomical perfection and power – though some were keen to point out the apparent imperfections of its proportions – to describing positive feelings of 'fascination' and being magnetically attracted to and even 'in love' with the work, all the while acknowledging that it was merely made of stone, though there were also those seemingly overwhelmed by negative emotions such as inadequacy, competitiveness, hostility and the desire for Goliath to correct the course of history, while some explicitly described wanting to attack the statue; lastly, noting a response that seems difficult to categorise as either positive or negative, Dr Magherini suggests a variation of Stendhal Syndrome, David Syndrome, whereby a work gives rise to intense feelings of sexual pleasure and deep desire, not only confusing and stupefying audiences but also producing worrying sexual dysfunctions, which happens in romantic love as well, and which ultimately have led her hard up against a contemporary problem when she describes *David* as a 'fusion of libido and art'.

Author's Note

While I have consulted disparate sources in producing this piece, I am indebted to Iain Balmforth's excellent account of Stendhal Syndrome in the *British Journal of General Practice3* as well as the very lively research paper 'Stendhal Syndrome: A Clinical and Historical Overview' by Leonardo Palacios-Sánchez et el.[4]

1. Rilke, Rainer Maria. *Duinesian Elegies*: Second Edition. Translated by Elaine E. Boney. Chapel Hill: The University of North Carolina Press, 1975. doi: https://doi.org/10.5149/9781469657165

2. Kant, Immanuel. *Critique of Judgement*. Translated by J. H. Bernard. New York: Hafner Publishing Company, 1964.

3.   Bamforth, I. 'Stendhal's Syndrome'. *Br J Gen Pract*. 2010 Dec 1;60(581):945–6. doi: 10.3399/bjgp10X544780. PMCID: PMC2991758.

4.   Palacios-Sánchez L., Botero-Meneses J.S., Pachón, R.P., Hernández, L.B.P., Triana-Melo, J.D.P., Del Pilar Triana-Melo, J., Ramírez-Rodríguez, S. 'Stendhal Syndrome: A Clinical and Historical Overview'. *Arq Neuropsiquiatr*. 2018 Feb;76(2):120–123. doi: 10.1590/0004-282X20170189. PMID: 29489968.

A Lifetime to Repair
Elleen Chong

Papercuts

He held your wrist, tight —
    you bruise so easily

    That time you jumped, terrified
(afraid: of the wind, of lightning, of ghosts)

      Raft of the bed. Sudden
questions like rain

          storm passing, circling
(glass greened; soundproof)

You startle awake in the dark
    stumble down the hallway   return
clatter // clatter   (a cup of tea, of tea, of tea)

    Read years later: *not normal*
(secret - no secrets - discreet - secrete)

From the outside it is difficult to tell
    ((nothing has changed) (everything is different))

    What is forecast: fair skies
        searing days, cold nights
an eternity of stars
        (no counting, no longer)

    lifetime // lifeline
        peters out —

Can't Get You Out of My Head
Andrea Thompson

Bella sat in the booth, her pot of green tea long grown cold, its amber liquid bitter. She drank it anyway, shuddering with each sip, because it gave her a reason to be there other than the waiting. For years she'd told herself she should work on not being so early, sometimes adding up the time she could save, like a smoker counting dollars for holidays as motivation to quit. There was something in her brain that wouldn't let her leave just on time.

Bella always chose Greens & Co on Oxford Street for first meetings. The appeal wasn't the café's large, anonymous room, usually filled with self-involved millennials who never noticed anyone but themselves or their screens. It wasn't the wag who kept adding 'ck' to the sign above the café's façade, or even the owner's persistence in painting over it. Bella came for the posters that covered the café's walls. The fresh ones displayed left of the counter were updated every week, mostly advertising shows by local hopefuls who would never see a return on their investment.

The rest of the café's acreage was like an archaeological dig. Layer upon layer of posters advertising events from decades past. There was an almost complete history of the Big Day Out. Bella ticked off in her mind each one she'd attended, rueing that she'd never got to see Nirvana, but smiling smugly when she remembered sets from lesser-but-notables like Black Kids and My Morning Jacket. Massive posters, almost billboard-sized, advertised releases from the likes of U2 (when they were still cool) and the Pixies. In between, every band and artist who had visited Perth from the 90s to the mid-2010s, when the posters seemed to peter out.

Greens & Co boasted the longest cake display in the Southern Hemisphere, stacked with all manner of sugar, flour, syrup and colours, and the servings were generous. Although she usually had a slice of something, the main reason Bella chose a booth opposite the cakes was the Kylie's Showgirl tour poster – a cinema-screen-sized image that filled the entire wall. Kylie stood front on, head turned to the right profile, eyes looking down to highlight the deep purple of her eyeshadow. Caught in motion, her left hand reaching out, Bella occasionally saw Kylie in the periphery of her vision turning towards her booth.

***

'Hey, sorry I'm late.'

Today Bella was meeting a muso, his inevitable lateness underscoring her earliness.

'Yeah, sure, no problem,' Bella said, almost getting up out of her seat to greet him but thinking better of it. She settled back and stuck out her hand as he slid into the seat opposite her, clutching a MacBook.

'Do you want a coffee?'

'No thanks,' Bella said, gesturing to the cold teapot and empty cup in front of her.

'I'll go get one,' he said. 'Back in a sec.'

He slid out of the booth, his long legs awkwardly navigating the space between bench and table. She watched him, his hair and laptop, walk over to join the queue at the counter. When Bella was sure he wasn't going to glance back, she took another long look at Kylie. It was her eyes Bella always settled on.

When the muso finally returned with his flat white, he leapt straight into stories of his time working with Indigenous kids in Western Australia's far north. He showed her the video for his latest single. He invited her to his launch show at Mojos. He stank of worthiness and Bella wondered how she could possibly make him sound interesting when she wrote him up. As for the music, it was good, but nothing new.

'What makes you any different from anyone else?' she asked.

He stopped and looked at her, his eyes showing hurt. 'Aren't I?' he said.

Bella was one of the first to arrive at Mojos.

'I love your hair,' said the woman at the door, her black shirt and trousers leaving Bella in no doubt about why she was there.

'Thank you,' said Bella, giving her a flash of suspicion before she realised it was a compliment.

Inside, Bella saw the muso setting up on stage and settled into one of the manky couches, hoping no-one would sit next to her. Over the next hour, she watched the audience grow, looking around the room for familiar faces. She relaxed somewhat when the music started and most eyes turned towards the stage.

The muso played hard country and spent his forty-five minutes stalking the stage like a tousle-haired delta preacher high on amphetamines, about to experience the rapture. He and his band were good enough, but it was mostly perspiration that kept them going.

Bella got up to leave the moment the muso and his band had played the last note of their last song. Weaving her way through the crowd, she kept her head down, intent on reaching the door with minimum fuss.

'See you next time?' said the woman at the door.

'Sure, thank you.'

Bella hesitated, but kept moving, wanting to navigate the tricky distance between the venue and her car as quickly as she could.

***

'Hey. Hello.'

Bella flinched at the sound. She'd arrived early and was lost in Kylie's eyes – or more specifically, her eyelids. Studying Kylie's eyeshadow, she wondered what sort of surgeries she'd need to get such a spacious and beautifully deep separation between her own lids and brow.

'Like a bit of Kylie, do you?'

The woman had a squiggle of curly red hair, combed over to the left and shaved close on the right. Bella estimated she was a full foot shorter than her and immediately shrank down in her seat. The woman looked intently at Bella, her green eyes smiling.

'I'm sorry,' said Bella. 'I, um, I ... Sit down.'

She tried a smile as the woman slid into the booth opposite her.

'Geez, Greens,' said the woman. 'I haven't been here in ages. Hasn't changed much, has it?'

'No, I guess not,' said Bella. 'Would you like a cup of tea?'

Bella spent her time in line wondering what the fuck she was doing, half hoping that when she turned around the woman wouldn't be there. She returned with one pot and two cups.

'Shall I be mother?' said the woman, reaching out for the pot as Bella sat down.

'Um, sure.'

Bella had no idea how to do what they were doing.

'So, do you like Kylie?' repeated the woman as she poured their tea.

'Yeah, I do,' said Bella. The massive replica floated on the wall like a religious icon.

'Yeah, me too. She's a bit of all right, isn't she?'

They settled into a conversation, edging around getting to know each other, seeing if their online chat had any currency in the real world.

The woman texted to invite Bella over for a Saturday arvo cuppa and cake. Bella's finger hovered over the upward pointing arrow to the right of her reply for what felt like forever.

True to her word, the woman was taking cupcakes out of the oven when Bella arrived, early. Bella tried to convince herself that she was short of breath from climbing the stairs to the woman's apartment. She stood at the edge of the kitchen while the woman iced the golden mounds, humming just under her breath so that Bella couldn't quite hear the music. When she was finished, she turned to Bella and held out the spatula.

'Want a lick?'

Bella hesitated, making to take half a step forward, then rocking back on her heels. She felt massive and clumsy and the woman's move was so obvious she wasn't sure if she was reading things right.

'Go on, have a lick,' the woman said, smiling.

Bella allowed the woman to put the spatula and its dollop of pink icing to her lips. She reached out her tongue, feeling it quiver as she searched the air for the sweet fondant. She took the spatula in her mouth and sucked off the icing.

'There you go. Good girl.'

The woman's bedhead was strung with fairy lights. They sat on the edge of the bed and kissed some more until the woman abruptly disengaged and stood up.

'Sorry, I forgot something.'

Bella watched as she went to the dresser beyond the foot of the bed. As she was walking back, the room filled with applause, then sirens, then strings.

'I made a playlist for us,' the woman said into Bella's neck.

By the time Kylie started singing the opening line of 'Can't Get You Out of My Head', the two women were lying back across the bed kissing. Bella could feel the click of the woman's jaw as they pashed.

The woman made a different playlist each time they met, but 'Can't Get You Out of My Head' always had a spot. Kylie's song brought back the rush of the first time for Bella. She had fretted over her anatomy that first afternoon, but their interludes had changed her, challenged her and given her comfort. The woman opened Bella up, physically and emotionally. Bella smiled every time she remembered the process of being made ready, how the woman would start by turning her around, embracing her from behind while kissing her from the back of her head to the base of her neck, each touch of her lips lingering longer than the last.

Bella stopped by Greens after what she knew was their last time. She sat with her tea and stared through the image of Kylie, the rising applause and distant sirens making her throat crackle when she swallowed. As Bella heard again the final click of the woman's front door, she also replayed Kylie's vocals in her mind, shifting her focus back to the table. The momentary vertigo made her ball her hands into fists and press them into her seat on either side of her thighs. Bella noticed the message alert on her phone and picked it up. The woman had afforded her a single word, *Sorry*. Bella picked up her tea and took a sip. After she put down her cup, she typed a reply and then deleted it.

***

Another musician, late again.

This time, when the woman came in the front door of Greens, Bella felt a momentary crush on her chest as the air pressure in the room spiked. The musician had long, dark curls and was dressed like she was trying to hide. Jeans and a baggy olive-green shirt. Her face was lined with worry and when she saw Bella sitting in her booth and waving, she smiled for only a moment and then picked up her pace, looking like she might trip over her platform Docs.

'Sorry I'm late.'

Inevitably, Bella thought.

'Yeah. No problem. Have a seat. Are you ... Would you like a drink?'

Bella tried to make eye contact with the muso but kept breaking off. Bella brushed her hair behind her ear as she breathed in, then flicked it back again on the breath out. She put her hands in her lap, her head bowing as she made them still. She tried to pass off a glance at Kylie as a stretch of the neck.

As Bella stood in line to order a tea and an almond milk latte, she looked back at the young woman. In her line of work, Bella had met plenty of rock stars. Most of them were just ordinary people, often slightly pissed. Occasionally she'd come across one who could make humans feel their presence on a cellular level, like the time she'd seen Nick Cave at a Big Day Out, aeons ago. She'd never got the hang of his music, something about his voice put her off, but her mates that day were mad for him, so just before his set they left the beer tent and trooped off to find a spot front of stage. Bella wasn't expecting anything, but the moment he walked on stage, before he'd sung a single note, she knew she was in the presence of greatness. She felt this woman had a touch of that.

'Here we go. Sorry it took a while,' said Bella, cursing herself for the unnecessary apology.

'Oh, thanks,' the woman said, as she wrapped her hands around the glass holding her coffee.

'Cold?'

'What?'

'Are you cold?' Bella asked, looking at the woman's hands, her long fingers, nails chewed to nothing.

'Oh. No.'

There was silence.

'So, you'd like some help with your career?'

'Yeah, I'm looking for a manager. Kat recommended you, said you'd been good to her.'

'I'll pay her for that later,' Bella said, with a grin. 'How about you tell me about yourself?'

Bella listened while the woman went through her origin story, the muso tucking her hair behind one ear as she began, her brown eyes fixing on Bella's blues. Pretty standard stuff until she got to the bit where she cut her brother from their highly successful duo when she was eighteen because she didn't think he was taking their career seriously enough.

'Yeah, I went to Europe on my own for a while after that,' the woman said. 'I'd just broken up with my first girlfriend and I wanted to get away. I was scared to travel on my own. People told me

I shouldn't go, but I went anyway.'

'What made you go?' Bella asked.

'I wanted to see if I could do it. On my own. I didn't want to be afraid. As a woman, as a queer woman, I didn't want to let fear stop me. I shouldn't have to be afraid to walk the streets at night. I'd rather be killed than live with that fear.'

Bella drank in the words, the seriousness and sincerity, and knew she was in the right place with the right person, like Kylie and Nick Cave, and the duet they'd done together.

'Do you like Kylie?' Bella asked.

'Nah, not really. She's a bit before my time.'

***

Bella saw him come in even though he was a few minutes early. She'd been watching the door – too distracted for Kylie today. His face was etched with anticipation as he swept back his fringe and surveyed the room. The moment Bella saw him, something in her dropped. The adrenaline dissolved out of her blood, the tension in her cheeks and behind her eyes melted away, her chest relaxed and her stomach opened to her breathing. She stopped clutching at the floor with her feet. By the time he had reached the booth, she was entirely in possession of herself.

'Hi. Have a seat.'

He looked at her, one eyebrow cocked.

'I feel like I'm here for an interview,' he said, smiling thinly as he sat down.

'Ah, sorry,' Bella said, 'just a bit nervous. You know how it is.'

'Yeah, right. Do you do this, do you come here often?'

'Meet strange men off the internet, or come here?'

'Well, both, I suppose.'

'I come here a bit, but you're my first. Strange man off the internet, that is.'

The man looked at Bella and laughed.

'What about you?' she asked.

'Haven't been here before, but I've been around the block a few times.'

Did he just wink at her?

'Around the block?'

'Well, you know, this is not my first rodeo.'

Bella looked across the table at him. For a few moments he looked back, then looked away.

'Shall we get some drinks?' he said, still looking off to the side. 'What'll you have? My shout.'

Bella studied the back of the man as he waited in the queue. His hair was greying and she could see the pink of his crown beginning to show through. He was thickening around the waist but his arse was non-existent, just a sheer drop to his legs. Before she'd spoken to him in the café, Bella had found the idea of this man attractive. Now she was annoyed at herself for the energy and emotion she'd wasted.

Bella watched him lean in to order then worry about whether he had enough money in his wallet – Greens was a cash-only establishment – at one point glancing over as he riffled though notes and counted coins. She watched him pick up the black plastic tray and wobble back to their table like he was carrying an explosive device. Bella grinned. He was unlikely to make her cupcakes. She was still smiling as he sat down and picked up his long mac, leaving Bella to take her teapot and cup.

'Penny for them?' he said.

'I was just thinking about an ex.'

'Oh. Was he recent?'

'She.'

'Oh.'

Thoughts and feelings played across the man's face like it was a movie screen. Surprise. Then puzzlement. Finally, though he tried to hide it, lust. He leaned forward.

'So, you like a bit of both, do you?'

Bella looked over at Kylie, a quick glance to centre herself, while she decided what her response would be.

'Don't you?'

'Nope, I'm straight, all the way down the line.'

'Are you now?' Bella said. 'So what did you mean when you said this isn't your first rodeo?'

The man's eyebrows almost disappeared under his fringe. He swept it back again. Bella wondered if he was growing it for a comb-over. She looked at him and waited.

'I've fucked plenty of girls like you.'

'Girls like me? And you think you're going to fuck me, do you?'

'We both know why we're here, don't we?'

Bella picked up the teapot, topped up her cup and sat back in the booth. The man looked at her and ducked his head away. Bella saw him notice the poster.

'Do you like Kylie?' she asked.

'I prefer my music to be more … less crap.'

'So, what do you want to do now?'

'I think I'm going to get the fuck out of here,' the man said.

Bella sipped her tea, watching as he headed for the front door. Since she'd switched the over-stewed green tea for English Breakfast, she got so much more out of each pot.

Bella had left Greens later than she normally would – she'd remained in the booth for a good while after he'd left – but it was still broad daylight when she headed for her car.

On her way to the café's back door, Bella walked over to look at Kylie close up. The combination of the showgirl headdress and the padded satin bondage harness told Bella everything she needed to know about her own sexuality. There was nothing hard about Kylie's image. It was created out of a softness and sensuality that felt like it would permit anything – never subtract, only add.

Bella was in sight of her car, keys in hand, when she heard him.

'Hey! You!'

Bella turned around to see him coming towards her at a half jog.

'Wait,' he said, one arm already raised.

Bella did not feel the ground as it rose up to kiss the back of her head.

Breathe
Jes Layton

Eddie finds the bandaids first and dumps them into a basket. She grabs a pack of Panadol. The gauze comes in packets of ten, so she snags what might be the right size, adds in a couple of N95s.

'Y'know it's only around one in ten people called back for a second biopsy that actually end up having cancer.' She turns to look at Kura over her shoulder.

Twitchy, dark-haired and short, Kura stands among the array of pharmaceuticals with her earbuds in, swaying slightly from side to side. She's all movement, all colour. Freckled cheeks slack beneath grey-lidded eyes, highlighted with bruise-dark bags. She stares at the gauze, bandages and patches as though she's watching network TV.

Her right hand is pressed tight to her chest beneath her bleach-stained singlet, while her left fiddles with the metal ball above her chin. It's not a coloured stud anymore, just a dull silver that looks a little murky under the harsh chemist's light.

Eddie blinks away from the movement of Kura's fingers and sets the box of Panadol back on the shelf.

'Pain from one to ten?' she asks, aware that Kura is a purplish-pink mimosa pudica of a person, in need of delicate care.

Kura stills. 'M'fine.'

Eddie's heavy curls fall to one side as she passes a hand through her hair. 'Don't be noble, just … here—' she lobs some Panadol

Extra into the basket. *37% stronger than your average paracetamol* brags the box, which Kura sniffs at.

'I wanna shit more than I want to not feel pain. Thanks.'

Eddie feels her own fingernails in her palm, and has to concentrate to recurl her fingers around the basket handle.

It's okay however you feel, the pamphlet in her back pocket reads in an obnoxious Comic Sans. *It's okay that your loved one will be experiencing many emotions. Remember to ask: Is there anything you wish I understood about how you are feeling right now? It's important to stress to your grieving loved one that you hope that they know they can still talk to you.*

Tiny burr-like hooks start to dig into her skin, pulling her from all sides, yanking at the hair on her arms – stopping any retort dry in her throat.

When Kura abandons the pain-relief aisle, Eddie dutifully follows, hoping to leave the stagnation among the pill bottles and tubes of Deep Heat.

'One of those unexpected side effects of getting stabbed in the boob,' she begins, aiming for light. For normal. 'They should really warn you about that.'

Kura doesn't look back at Eddie, who pushes to the front as they approach the counter. She smiles at the cashier, keenly aware of Kura watching her bag up the bandaids and gauze. When Eddie catches her watching, she looks away.

***

Outside, the concrete rounds up into a swell Eddie doesn't expect as she trips towards the beat-up Holden. The chemist's doors scrape shut behind them and the evening heat stagnates. Inside Eddie's

Holden, everything smells. She rolls down both front windows and, despite Kura's protestations, doesn't pull out until Kura has two industrial-strength pills in hand.

Eddie throws her eyes to the road and rolls the ball of her foot into reverse, left arm thrown over the back of the seat, careful of Kura's now-growing hair. Kura hasn't always worn her hair long, and her labret piercing, jewellery and answering ink came about slowly. Even slower was Kura working up the courage to show them at all.

Lately though, Eddie's been noticing small changes.

The Celtic knot ring on Kura's left hand is gone, so is the hematite bracelet on her left. The old silver thumb ring is the only thing that's left. She's always been unfussed about the hair on the back of her neck and behind her ears. Eddie's usually the one to point it out to her, coming over with clippers, which Kura repays with Tim Tams. But Kura's letting her hair grow out now, and the last time she'd worn anything plain in her chin was when she'd broken things off with her former girlfriend.

Eddie guides them out of town, onto the dirt road running jagged and hard into the distance. She has no confirmation that Kura has swallowed the Panadol until there's the beginnings of a watery orange sunset just over the edge of the skyline. Kura's sudden cough splinters the view, dry and brittle enough for kindling.

Eddie winces in mixed sympathy and rebuke.

'Said there's water in the back.'

'M'fine.' A familiar retort now. White noise, if white noise was enough of anything to infuriate.

Eddie finds herself biting back a sigh. 'Maybe after your third one they give you a t-shirt or something,' she tries, nodding down to the palm-sized, pink icepack Kura keeps skin-close; palm to chest.

Kura, seeming to have something almost like a real feeling, grunts and turns her face into the summer-warmed seatbelt.

***

Kura's old pipes groan when Eddie turns on the shower. She washes the day off her skin, all the dust and grime under her fingernails, the sweat from under her arms and the back of her neck. She tries to push down the tight lacker-band-ball feeling fit to burst in her chest, works the soap into a lather for her arms, stomach, hips. Her body aches, the remnants of broken fingers and fucked-up ankles and a shoulder that never set quite right. It's a low, distant hum of pain, never enough for her to really do anything with.

She pauses, her hands stopping at the swell of her chest. The dutiful pilgrimage to have breasts compressed between two paddles like a ham and cheese toastie in a jaffle maker isn't a foreign experience to Eddie. She's been told enough times by the breast-care nurse that her own are dense and difficult to screen; the fatty darks overshadowed by a screen of blaring white tissue. Dense and difficult. She pictures her breasts demanding to speak to the store manager of Coles or struggling to answer a sphinx's riddle. But there has never been a need to take anything further.

Eddie rips the tap to scalding but only a lacklustre drizzle seeps from above. The diagnosis of breast cancer from a biopsy is somewhere in the range of twenty percent. Eddie thinks of her own mum's assurances of 'breast threatening, not life threatening' and tries to jerk more life from the shoddy shower plumbing, needing to scorch the lie from her mind.

***

Eddie pulls on Kura's trackies and a faded Madonna t-shirt, then heads downstairs. The breeze blowing in from the front screen door is warm on the back of her neck as she pads into Kura's kitchen. There's a tub of day-old potato salad in the fridge alongside a block of cheese, tomato paste and pita wraps. Eddie's stomach grumbles. She peeks into the living room, finds it empty, before wandering down the hall to where Kura's bedroom door hangs open a crack.

Eddie pushes it open, steps into the doorway and says, 'Shower's shit. Your tap's connection's loose or something.'

'Mmm.' Kura sits at the desk with her back to the door, laptop open and a pile of papers scattered in front of her. She doesn't look up when Eddie speaks. 'Look ...' Eddie pauses, licks her lips, tries again. 'Are you okay? You seem kinda ...' She shrugs, picking at the pale skin around one thumbnail.

Kura lifts her head and sets a few papers down.

'I'm – I just wanna make sure, is all,' Eddie says.

Finally, Kura looks at her, her own expression blank. 'I'm fine.'

'Okay, yeah. Good. Uh, Kai's not back for another few days, yeah? Figure I'd crash here until then. I won't – I'm happy to take the couch.'

Kura's mouth turns up, the echo of a smile that doesn't match the rest of her expression. Eddie swallows, knuckles rapping once, twice on the doorframe.

'Looks like you've got all the stuff to make pizza,' she says. 'Wanna help?'

'Not hungry. You go ahead. Kai won't mind.'

Eddie pushes away from the door and gives Kura one last look, the lacker band fit to bursting in her chest as she retreats down the hall.

***

Eddie doesn't know how long she's been sitting on the back veranda. She eats what's left of the potato salad and stares at the nearly covered back fence. Kura's garden is in desperate need of weeding, a job she's never bothered with before, cultivating something of a wild look, but a task Eddie indulges in just to sink her hands into the cool earth. Melt weekends away to the rhythm of pulling out wandering onion weed and bindii.

Everything feels residual. Fading daylight, unspoken words – Eddie glances down at her phone, 17% – dying batteries. The number jolts down to 14 when she pulls up her astrology app. The app that had brought Kura into her life.

A hazy, drunk night at Tomboys, leading to a compatibility check from the gutter outside The Carlton Club. The app told Kura she might experience a big change when the sun came up, one she'd have to reach for with both hands – while Eddie lamented the app's daily advice as bullshit.

Eddie still doesn't know why she admitted that. To Kura, the stars were lifeblood, a personality gauge based on spinning planets, that led to how all her cheating exes were Geminis and Scorpios. Eddie only knew that all her exes were still inside Tomboys – also arseholes.

Kura's laugh had been loud and long and sudden enough that the few people waiting for their taxis nearby had looked over, and when her arm snaked around Eddie's waist and pulled her backwards onto the grotty footpath to stare up at the smog-filled night, Eddie was powerless not to follow.

***

It's gone past midnight when Eddie flicks off the back veranda light and pads into the kitchen. Kura's left the fridge open a crack, the front screen door letting in the night air and the sound of hot rain tapping on the tin roof. Eddie spots a half-drunk coffee mug on the kitchen bench and sighs. 'Dammit, Kura.'

The linoleum floor creaks under her feet. A few unopened letters scatter across the bench, a mix of Kura and Kai's, a collection of mint tins stacked neat like books, loose change, paperclips and some rocks Eddie recognises as ones from her own neighbour's driveway, Kura's delicate scrawl inked in gold along a few of the polished backs.

Resist, reads one. *Be nice to pigeons.* Another: *Recycle.* Eddie touches each one in turn, smiling at the small inscriptions before letting them settle. Knowing, knowing Kura, that each message would find its way back out into the world for someone to stumble across.

Eddie closes the fridge and the front door, just in case the rain picks up into a storm, and grabs the mug. At the bottom, in the cold dregs of coffee, a moth swims in circles.

***

Kura is usually full up with piss and vinegar, unbearably cranky until she gets enough caffeine in her system, but this morning she's an unsettling kind of quiet. It's the kind that follows a night of not enough sleep, of staring up at the ceiling and listening to crickets until all sound blurs.

Eddie's kneeling on the floor of the open shower when she feels Kura come to hover in the doorway. 'Sorry,' she scratches at the back of her neck. 'This'll be done in a sec. The dripping was driving me bonkers all night.'

She holds her breath, steels herself, but Kura doesn't say anything. The longer she stays quiet, the colder the tiled floor under Eddie gets. The ceramic chill curls Eddie's toes inward, brushes up her ankles.

She huffs and eyes the wretched taps above her. 'We not talking today?' she asks, humour in her voice.

Kura says nothing, and Eddie ignores the way her stomach sinks.

After a long stretch of seemingly impossible turning and adjusting, Eddie retracts her grime-slick wrench and heaves the head off the hot water tap, plopping it down into the bowl of the shower.

'Figured I might as well make myself useful,' Eddie answers without being asked. 'Honestly, Kur, this sucker's done for.' She reaches down and plucks a grit-slick and half-eroded rubber ring, holding it between finger and thumb.

Turning around to Kura, she starts. 'It's no wonder there's a shit ton of leaking, all the rubber's worn – what are you doing?'

'Watching you destroy my bathroom apparently,' Kura replies. She stands in the bathroom doorway, her NASA singlet and cut-down jeans swapped for a red deli uniform and black slacks, not quite hidden under one of Kai's hoodies. She's drinking from a thermos and eyeing the disassembled parts strewn out across the bathroom tiles.

Eddie ignores the expression on her face. Ignores the furrow in her brow, the lines by her downturned mouth. 'You sure you should be working?'

The look that passes across Kura's face curdles the breath in Eddie's lungs. Kura presses off from the doorway and moves to leave.

Eddie rolls her eyes and gets off the floor; her knee twinges. She tosses the tap head into the bathroom sink and follows Kura out into the living room.

'Kur—'

Kura, heading back into the kitchen, grabs her bag from the bench with a near imperceptible wince. 'It's fine.'

'Is it?' Eddie asks, then a little louder just to be mean. 'Guess all this stoic, silent-treatment bullshit is just par for the course, innit?'

Kura stops, lets her bag drop from her shoulder and closes her eyes on an unsteady inhale, a shaky exhale, before she lifts her eyes to Eddie, face scrubbed clean and pulled tighter than her growing-out hair. 'What do you want me to do?'

That stops Eddie. 'What?'

'Want me to stay here and whine and cry and wallow? Wait around staring at my phone all day? Fall into your arms like a hot mess so you can comfort and baby me and feel better about yourself? I won't go to work then.' Kura says. She turns back to head into the kitchen and drops her bag on the floor. 'There. Satisfied?'

'No.'

Rubbing at her temple, Kura sighs. 'Of course not. But Ed, look, I'm not your mum, orright?'

For a moment Eddie almost can't breathe, as though vines are strangling her lungs.

'What's that supposed to mean?' she gasps.

She watches Kura droop, like an overwatered lily.

Kura exhales, a little shaky, twisting at her labret piercing. 'Make sure you lock up on your way out.'

'Kura, hold on.'

'We'll talk later,' Kura says, and walks away before Eddie can reply.

***

According to Google, core needle biopsy results usually take two days to up to a week, depending on whether the sample needs to be analysed further. Concerning biopsies get prioritised, Eddie learns, so the fact that Kura hasn't heard anything yet is good, probably.

More than likely means nothing than something.

From the safety of her own kitchen table, Eddie squints at the dark clouds out the window and tries to judge whether it's worth going out there to rescue the maidenhairs. Some days the rain is a deluge against the tin roof and the hot stormy air sinks under her skin, into her bones, making her bad ankle ache. She feels the beginnings of a twinge stir in the ball of her foot, and watches the loquat tree bend hideously from the onslaught outside.

Her laptop's screen fades to a drowsy black as Eddie grapples with the idea of spending the better part of tomorrow putting everything back to rights. It's early yet, but already the grey-black sky and pelting rain make her want to huddle and snooze, the ache in her muscles heavy.

Yeah, she's going to have to go out and rescue those ferns.

She swings open her front door, scanning the pots. The golden balls can survive an apocalypse, so they aren't a priority. Eddie's mind runs the mental list of the rest of her veranda horde. The trays of assorted herbs she uses for cooking, the cordylines, the bowls she leaves out for the stray cat she's been keeping fed for the last month, the alyssum and erigeron – she'll need to grab the herbs first, delicate things – wait—

'Kura?'

Sopping, eyeliner running down to her jaw, Kura stands there, mouth open to say—

Eddie watches Kura sneeze so hard that she nearly slips and falls on her arse.

'Jesus Christ.' Eddie closes the few steps between them, circling behind Kura to herd her inside and out of the storm. How long has she been out there?

Inside, with the door closed fast behind them, they stare at each other for a drawn-out second.

'What the fuck's wrong with you?' Eddie mutters at the same moment Kura blurts out, 'I'm sorry!' and instead of answering, shoves a pot into Eddie's arms.

Her mint plant. A little damp, but still as half-dead as it ever was. Eddie stares down at its furred leaves dribbling dew onto the stained carpet before setting it safely on a nearby bookshelf. Kura's jewelled chin wobbles, more noticeable for the labret, while her shoulders slump, tension seeping out of her.

'Hey,' Eddie soothes. Kai's hoodie is hanging mostly open in a way that has Eddie reaching out and pulling Kura into her, grabbing the back of Kura's head and fitting it under her chin. 'What can I do? What do you need?'

'Honestly,' Kura croaks, and the rain dribbling off the end of her nose chills Eddie against her collarbone. She gathers Eddie's hands tightly and curls their fingers against each other. 'I just need to be able to shit again.'

'I've got tea,' Eddie offers. 'Mum swore by it. Said it helped her when, uh, I mean …'

'Never figured Mrs P for a stress shitter,' Kura says, but the way she rubs her nose back and forth across Eddie's collarbone has the roiling mess in Eddie's gut settling. Kura, soft in a way she so rarely is anymore. So rarely allows herself.

'Think it's more a stress non-shitter,' Eddie supplies. 'I mean, if you wanna get technical.'

Kura laughs harder than Eddie anticipated, and as though in answer, Eddie feels her own answering grin so hard her lips start to hurt.

It's easy, then, to find their way to the couch. Eddie pads back into the living room from the kitchen, having flicked on the kettle and grabbed a handtowel and bag of frozen prawn toast.

'Nurse said you have to ice on and off for the first forty-eight, yeah?'

Instead of answering, Kura lays her head on Eddie's lap, and leaves Eddie to sort the blanket. While Eddie fusses, Kura holds her hand and slaps the prawn-toast packet to her chest.

Eddie arches a brow. 'Hurt?'

'A little,' Kura says, shifting so she's comfortable. The couch creaks and Eddie feels Kura's hand come to rest on her stomach, gentle, the heat of it soaking through the thin fabric of her t-shirt, fingers brushing its hem. 'But y'know.'

It's early yet, dark swirling in the storm outside, leaving Eddie feeling sluggish. Cosy on the couch huddled together, warm and comfortable. She watches Kura out of the corner of her eye, as Kura pushes her growing hair back from her face, a little oily, a little itchy. Under the blanket Eddie fits their feet together, toe to toe, shifting so their knees bump.

She closes her eyes, leaning back against the couch as the kettle in the kitchen boils away. She feels the heat coming off Kura under the blankets, her breathing calm and steady, only opening her eyes when Kura shifts, tugging light but insistent on the hem of Eddie's shirt.

'Mmm?'

'Reckon they'll let me keep them in a jar?'

Eddie stifles a half laugh, pulls Kura into her arms and squeezes her tight.

Kura, in turn, folds into Eddie's touch and breathes.

Tension
Patrick Marlborough

She can't believe that beer-bellied bastard. Him and his stubby little prick thinking they're hot shit when he's just another baggy-eyed manchild with a receding hairline, an unquenchable mortgage, and what appears to be – or so the experts on Quora say – a crippling porn addiction. Here she is, enrolled in more high-intensity workout classes than a film star preparing for a role in an action blockbuster, so this *REPULSIVE* grubby little worm will see her as somewhat fuckable, only to have him sit about cranking his stubby, sad-ass hog all day, perched on the nice stool in the kitchenette like some kind of perverted circus chimp.

This is what she's got to come home to.

This is what he spends his money on.

A worm! A grub!

***

And sure, here she is laughing about it with Terry before Sweat class – Terry, whose husband, by her own admission, should be *locked up* for his nocturnal habits – but this morning she'd bawled her eyes out. He is just so brazen, so lazy, which in and of itself is *so* typical of him – as typical as it is dumb and smug. What? You can't even be bothered using a private browser? Deleting your search history? Can't even close the tab? She just had to open Safari on the iPad – who beats off to an iPad? – and there it is staring back at her, some not-quite-expensive but definitely-not-cheap live cam website, where dead-eyed human trafficking victims play with themselves in the brightly lit basement of some Eastern European motel complex for her husband's pleasure.

They're all just pigs, Terry laughs again, just grotty little boys, at the end of the day. I mean John, well ... I can't stand the cunt, to tell ya the truth.

Yeah ...

I mean if it wasn't for the kids ...

Yeah, the kids ...

If it wasn't for them, well, I dunno what else is making me stick around ...

Yeah, I know, yeah ...

I mean who am I trying to lose this weight for, anyway?

Yeah ...

Fuck him, fuck them. Fuck it!

I know, yeah ...

This isn't how it is meant to be. She's turning forty-two, but it feels closer to sixty-two and twelve at the same time. She drops the boys off at school and feels the urge to get out with them, y'know, attend class – cos it can't have been that long ago she was sitting in English or Maths, bored out of her goddamn mind. But it feels like an eternity since she met The Grub, drunkenly pashing him in the pleather booth at the back of some Northbridge nightclub, letting him finger her against the wall of the public toilets by Hyde Park – finger her with all the grace of a claw machine with a case of late-stage Parkinson's. Not long after that they are honeymooning in Bali, knocking back Bintang and slobbering on each other at the public beach, free and frisky like two stray dogs humping in the back alley of a late-night steakhouse.

Then the boys – the boys had torn her in half, literally. Those monstrous heads. Their father's head. Almost rectangular, almost a box, almost an esky. Yet seemingly empty – maybe a puddle of melted ice sloshing about a bit, on a good day.

She remembers the moment. It was on the Disney cruise, the one they'd spent two years saving for, the one where the boys ran wild like little demons, like they were *out for blood*. They were in line at the buffet one night stacking their plates with meat and hot chips when she'd looked over to see him – The Grub – reach out and scoop up a fistful of honey chicken with his bare hand (his hog-cranking hand). His arm moved out like one of those excavators the boys loved to ride in the sandpit at the local park. She hadn't said anything – didn't even roll her eyes – just took it in, quietly, and tried to ignore the unutterable wave of repulsion that cascaded through her, eddying towards that big basin of doubt she'd carried in her gut since the wedding, pooling there and permanently staining the carpet of the very way she considered him.

Yuck. Worm!

And now the Energizer Bunny of an instructor – a nice girl, maybe twenty-two or twenty-three – is hopping about on the stage in front of them, barking out words of encouragement as the workout playlist blares over the sound system. Doe-eyed and svelte like a nimble little forest sprite, the instructor exudes virginal innocence *and* party-girl psychosis – his type, she thinks, if only because the girl can pass for seventeen, or 'barely legal' as that horrid website he frequents so aptly puts it.

Alright class, let's go turbo mode for this next one!

And she tries to go turbo, but she feels sluggish, as if she hasn't slept in years, which is kinda true, remembering *his* sleep apnoea. She is not a forest sprite. She is a gnome. A kobold. And the reward for her exhaustion is two sons who need to have a minimum of two screens blaring at them lest they start – as she calls it – *bugging out*, and a husband whose sole defining feature is a mouth that appears all but lipless – an unkissable slit sitting plainly on his chinless milk carton of a head.

I hate the cunt,

she says out loud, mid-set, and Terry's head flashes her way as she tries to maintain her plank,

I hate the cunt,

She says, louder now, so that even the bunny instructor has to flash her giant crystal-blues at her, as if to say: Hey, I get it. But calm down, will you?

Now she's home alone, sitting in her sweaty gym gear, unwilling to shower or move off the aforementioned stool. She runs her finger down their credit card's transaction history and laughs – what else? – at all the little charges. $19 here. $7.80 there. $58.90 for what must have been one particularly long or upscale session. What does he take the term *shared bank account* to mean, exactly? Is he *that* stupid, or just *that* indifferent? It's a near-fatal combo of the two, she realises, the default factory setting that most men seem to be set to. What are you meant to do? Get in there with a screwdriver and blowtorch, and try rewiring the bastards?

The one time she managed to drag him to couples counselling he behaved like a dopey hunter who'd stepped in his own bear trap: panicky and indignant, blaming everyone but the person who'd bent down, set it up and loaded the spring. The therapist had told them that their problems weren't outrageous or singular or even remarkable – they were mass-produced problems of the basest garden variety. And she fought the urge to stand up and projectile vomit all over the little office like she'd downed a pint of ipecac.

Instead, she forked out $200 for the privilege and never came back, both of them stewing in mutual contempt and frustration on the long drive home, her frozen in place like a chicken dinner left out to defrost, him slumping into himself like a soft-serve.

Fuck this …

Is all he'd said to her,

Fuck this …

She kicks off her gym shoes and brings one flat, calloused, eternally sore foot up and starts to rub it as she runs through a mental list of all the times he's showed her up:

Tim and Ginny's wedding, when he gave that crude speech.

Parent-teacher night, where he called another boy a little poof.

Their most recent anniversary, where he gifted her a mousepad from his work.

His last birthday, where he'd sat and sullenly played the boys' Xbox all night.

Bob and Linda's baby shower, where he kept proclaiming he wished he'd had the snip.

Steve's Grand Final party, where he'd stormed off after the last siren because he'd lost $200 on one of his many betting apps.

Liam's ninth birthday at TimeZone, where he wouldn't share his ticket winnings with his sons.

Brent's 80s-themed fortieth, where he'd come in blackface as Run-DMC.

Kevin's 90s-themed fiftieth, where he'd come in blackface as Public Enemy.

***

What would she be doing with her time if they'd never met? She likes gossip, she likes dancing, she likes cutting out paparazzi shots of celebrities leaving rehab and collecting them in a big scrapbook. She likes reading young adult fiction about teenagers fighting to the death for the entertainment of totalitarian regimes, and movies where a woman who owns a book or candle shop falls in love with a Tom Hanks-type, or just Tom Hanks. She likes imagining a fat man running beside their car when she's weaving between traffic on the highway, and she likes envisioning herself skydiving with a parachute that will not open. She likes the idea of starting a YouTube channel where she reviews the knock-off massage tools they sell at Kmart, and she likes the idea of Kmart giving her money to do it.

***

She catches herself being too still. Being too still is why she has to get fit again. Being too still is how she got here in the first place, how she's stayed married in spite of it all. Stillness is all she's ever known, and stillness can only get you so far. As she's seized by a desire to stand up, get in the car, and drive as far as she can, the smoking gun iPad – docked in its charger on the kitchen countertop – dings. She picks it up, flips open the case.

Oh, that dopey fucker.

A notification for their debit card, which simply reads:

$19.99.......CHATTERBLAST

His subscription has been renewed. Or he's indulging himself at work. A wave of exhaustion rolls through her like smoke from a smoke machine filling the dancefloor at a particularly small and middling club. She taps a manicured finger on the Safari widget, and types in CHATTERBLAST.com. It logs straight into his account without even prompting her for a password – she just waltzes on in like he's left the door open for her. She instinctively taps the 'following' tab, coloured purple by the frequency of the link's use, and finds herself staring at a paused video feed with a big grey play button resting atop its blurred, frozen front page. Tap. The play symbol transforms into a little spinning circle, then:

Hello big boy, it's so good to see you.

A very young, glassy-eyed girl is playing with herself on a miserably filthy single mattress in a booth like the one she worked in when she answered phones for Qantas.

Mmmmm … that feels good … is that good for you, Daddy?

A numbness she'd have previously only believed possible by way of violent head trauma envelopes her like cellophane, preserving her like last night's lamb chops, resting on an unwashed plate of roiling contempt.

Oh, God, touch me there …

The girl is really going to town on herself, in a way she, begrudgingly, has to respect.

Almost there, big boy, oh yes, touch me there …

She takes note of the mise en scène: the drab felt walls, the shopping centre lighting, the pink teddy bear propped up in a corner like an uncertain court stenographer.

Don't be shy, big boy—

My God, her accent is thick … she sounds like Borat …

—I won't bite, big boy.

Do you know my husband? She can't believe she's saying it as she's saying it. Head like a bread box?

You know where, big boy, oh ya, touch me good, tou-tou-touch—

Dumb as a rock? Bad breath? A real fuckwit?

Oh, My God, *yayaya*, big boy! Touch me there, baby, *that's the spot* ...

Going bald, crooked teeth, eyebrows a bit *too* plucked ...

Don't be shy, big boy, I won't bite ...

Mighta been in blackface?

To her surprise, the girl pauses for a beat as if she's processing what's being asked, as if she's doing her best just to get through another tedious shift at the wank factory. But she soon continues:

You know where, touch me there, baby, tou-tou-*touch* me!—

And then she's touching herself alongside the girl on screen, through her sweaty lycra gym pants, lost in what she's doing until she sees there's another girl of similar vibes and patience, doing a variation of the same act in a slightly different booth, with a similarly lifeless expression on her face.

How long has she been sitting there, going at it? She looks over her shoulder as if expecting to see him and the boys standing there, car keys in hand and school bags hoisted tight in terror.

But no-one is here, just the side of her face reflected oddly by the wall-mounted wide screen.

I'm your getaway, baby, the new girl's voice pops from the iPad, I'm your little vacay.

(GBI) German Bold Italic
Nick Gadd

ARTISTS* live in a world of commerce and creativity, personal inspiration and corporate agendas, heart-on-sleeve emotion and cynical marketing. We want them to give us something new, but not shock us too much; keep their integrity alongside their popularity; be true to themselves without upsetting our image of them. It's an impossible job, when you think about it. But out of these contradictions, art is born.

*I'm talking about pop stars here. But it applies to other kinds of artists too.

BOLD. Kylie's career, as everyone knows, took off in the late 80s with bubblegum hits written and produced by the British pop music factory Stock Aitken Waterman. She was more product than artist in those days. They told her what to sing, dressed her up, kept her on a leash. She left because she wanted more control. In the following years she absorbed new influences, tried things out, made mistakes, reinvented herself and became something new. Along the way she found

COLLABORATORS like Brothers in Rhythm, Manic Street Preachers, David Ball of Soft Cell, the Pet Shop Boys. She began a relationship with the French photographer Stéphane Sednaoui and embarked on several trips to Japan. In 1996, the Tokyo-based DJ/producer Towa Tei received an invitation out of the blue to work with her. He was a well-established solo artist by that stage, but had risen to fame as a member of

DEEE-LITE, a New York dance outfit which had begun as a duo before adding Tei with the moniker Jungle DJ Towa Towa. Tei didn't sing or play instruments, but his record collection was a rich source of samples, including the clip from *The Art of Belly Dancing* by Bel-Sha-Zaar and the Grecian Knights heard at the start of Deee-Lite's global hit 'Groove is in the Heart'. The band's debut album went multi-platinum, but Tei disliked touring, hated performing the same songs every night, and suffered a freak accident when he fell offstage in Brazil. After two albums he quit the band citing creative differences and returned to Japan. They struggled on for one more album without him, but that was basically the end of Deee-Lite. Tei had other plans.

ELECTRONICA. Towa Tei's albums are postmodern mixtapes of popular music, eclectic collages of sound: jazz, funk, bossa nova, Japanese pop and weird sampled voices from god-knows-where combined into new substances by key-pushing alchemy. Soon this type of music would become a genre all of its own, but in the mid-90s Tei was one of the pioneers. And that wasn't all there was to him. Having studied graphic design, he also had an interest in

FONTS. What we often call fonts – Arial, Helvetica, Garamond, Comic Sans, all the others in your dropdown box – are really typefaces. A 'font' in the sense that specialists use the word means a particular size and weight of a typeface. A **bold** version has a heavier weight than the standard version. Another variation is the contrast between the roman version of a typeface, where the letters stand upright, and the *italic version, in which they are on a slant.*

'GERMAN BOLD ITALIC' is a song about a typeface, released in 1997. It wasn't a hit, and you won't find it in a list of Kylie's singles or on any of her albums, because it's a collaboration between Towa Tei, to whom it is credited, and Kylie, who wrote the lyrics and performs vocals. Once again, Tei makes use of the sample from *The Art of Belly Dancing.*

After this Kylie starts talking, rather than singing. She tells us her name: German Bold Italic. She's a typeface, one we have never heard of, but we're going to like her. She's not speaking *about* the typeface, she

> 'GBI' was one of two tracks she recorded in Tokyo: the second, 'Sometime Samurai', finally appeared on Tei's 2005 album *Flash.*

is the typeface. It's as if she's trying to sell herself: she comes in different colours, she fits like a glove. This sales pitch, repeated several times and accompanied by giggles, sighs and phrases in German, is interspersed with a breezy synth riff. Kylie loved the song, but her record company Deconstruction didn't, so it stayed with Towa Tei.

There really is a typeface called German Bold Italic, specially created to go with the song, used on the cover art and provided as a digital file with the CD, so that consumers could have a complete musical-typographical experience. Another collaborator on the track, providing backing vocals, was the legendary

HARUOMI HOSONO of the Japanese electronic band Yellow Magic Orchestra. Endlessly inventive, Hosono has had a fifty-year career as artist, composer, producer and the founder of an experimental music label. His lengthy discography runs to albums of video game sounds, fusions of electronica and traditional

Japanese music, and many movie soundtracks. Towa Tei, who worshipped Yellow Magic Orchestra and Hosono, brought him in to work on 'German Bold Italic'.

Did Hosono and Kylie meet during the recording? The wise old greybeard and the pop princess on her quest for enlightenment? If you want to believe that they did, yes. And since you mention princesses –

IMPOSSIBLE PRINCESS was the album that emerged from Kylie's years of experimentation. It's a mashed-up carnival of electronica, techno, trip hop, rock, jangly guitars and Bjorkish squawks, a bunch of her own songs with raw, confessional lyrics, shaped by a roll call of indie collaborators. Not everyone liked her change in direction and the album was mocked in some quarters. How dare a commercial pop

> 'Kylie Minogue at her most impish and spectacularly strange.' – *Pitchfork*[2]

star try to remake herself as 'IndieKylie'? *You can't do that!* If 'German Bold Italic' was going to appear on any of her studio albums it should have been this one, but Deconstruction nixed it. But although 'GBI' and 'Sometime Samurai' didn't make it on to *Impossible Princess*, there were still some Japanese influences on the record. Sednaoui's cover photography was inspired by the work of

> '*Shibuya-kei* itself didn't spread across the globe, but music made on the same principles – pastiche, plagiarism, utter liberation from the anchors of geography and history – is the leisure soundtrack for a new worldwide class whose fundamental mode of operation is the reprocessing of culture.' – Simon Reynolds[3]

JAPANESE erotic photographer, Nobuyoshi Araki. At this time Kylie was obsessed with Japanese culture and style, and the video for 'GBI' was another example. She has continued to wear Japanese costumes for live performances and has occasionally recorded in Japanese.

I know what you're thinking, but before you cry 'cultural appropriation!' consider that in the 90s Japanese artists were obsessed with British and American culture. *Shibuya-kei* bands like Flipper's Guitar took their worship of indie genres to the point of slavish imitation, and cobbled together lyrics from English words entirely lifted from those bands and their songs. Towa Tei's albums grab material from all over the planet. So it works both ways.

KYLIE had written her own material before, but it was on *Impossible Princess* that she really hit her straps as a lyricist, drawing on her personal life and relationships. As lyrics go, they're not subtle, but they're intimate and revelatory, all the more so for being unpolished. The

LYRICS of 'German Bold Italic' are also credited to Kylie. (We can't reproduce them here for copyright reasons, but you can find them in about 1.35 seconds using that device in your pocket.) Are they just a joke? Or is there some deeper meaning lurking there? Because a typeface is a bit like an artist: it can change, take on different forms – bold, italic, many colours – while still being recognisably itself. Like pop music, the best typography is recognised as art, while much of it is disposable. And a typeface is an artificial creation, something made by others, easily discarded and replaced. The song is

> 'Kylie was going through a difficult period of wanting to break away from Eurobeat, so when she came to Japan, she tried making some songs …' – Towa Tei[4]

a playful exploration of what art is, what an artist is. Certainly these questions were on Kylie's mind at the time, and she was looking for people who might have some answers. She had made contact with Towa Tei by sending him a fax with the words

'MUSIC WITH YOU! KYLIE. CALL ME'.[5] Perhaps Kylie's situation resonated with Tei because he too had been a pop star before becoming disenchanted.

He had the option of staying in New York, at the top of the charts, but made the decision to pursue his authentic goals and explore more challenging material. He recognised a similar quality in Kylie, who had also made tough choices, worked with unexpected people. Back in 1995, for example,

> 'It was quite something at the time for Kylie to take on. Her management were like, this is really a bad idea. We were a bunch of dark drug-addicted monstrosities scowling in the studio. But she was determined to do that and she was this extraordinary presence who came in and just sang the song really beautifully. She sort of radiates a lightness of spirit. And displayed an enormous amount of courage I think and the record did really well.' – Nick Cave on *The Louis Theroux Podcast*[6]

NICK CAVE had written 'Where the Wild Roses Grow' for her, another unlikely collaboration that turned out to be a great decision. It's worth noting that Kylie's management advised her against doing the song[7], but it turned out to be a hit, so good on her.

> 'Today, designers have questioned canonical binaries within typography … Serif and sans serif faces exist on a spectrum. Letters with horizontal stress are bucking the patriarchy of the vertical. Typefaces built with inconsistent parts have been championed by activists and people with disabilities.' – Ellen Lupton[8]

OBI is a Japanese belt, worn with a kimono, traditionally a feature of geisha costume. There are many different types, worn in different ways, with different meanings. Kylie wears a multicoloured one in the video for 'German Bold Italic', tied into a huge bow at the back.

POP MUSIC and typefaces come together in cover art. Some fonts are associated with specific artists and genres – the anarchic cut-out letters on *Never Mind the Bollocks, Here's the Sex Pistols*; blackletter fonts on many a heavy metal album, intended to convey gothic doom; Peter Saville's typography which brings a cool austerity to albums by New Order and Joy Division. Some artists – One Direction, for example – even commission their own typefaces. In 2023, Wilco announced they had a font of their own. But to compose a song about an imaginary typeface and then design that typeface to put on the cover? That's unique in the history of music.

QUEER theories of typography critique the binary structures often taken for granted in text. These binaries include UPPER CASE/ lower case; serif/sans serif; roman/*italic*. Design theorist Ellen Lupton writes: 'In Western typography, italic type styles are typically viewed as secondary to the western norm.'[9] Roman type, she points out, is seen as 'the neutral default' whereas italics are seen as 'the exception'. And yet that wasn't originally so: when Aldus Manutius first used italics, they were considered a viable alternative to roman text, not secondary to it.

Whether or not Kylie thought of it that way, it seems appropriate for an artist with a passionate

Italics were an innovation devised by the Venetian publisher and humanist Aldus Manutius in the fifteenth century as a way of getting more words onto a page by squeezing the letters together. This enabled him to print smaller, cheaper editions of classic works in Latin and Greek, making books more easily available, the forerunner of cheap paperbacks. These days it's rare to see a whole book in italics: they are used to provide emphasis, or for conventional purposes like marking the titles of albums or foreign words. Manutius was a visionary: today his idea is on every computer in the world.

queer audience that, if she's going to identify as a typeface, it should be a **BOLD ITALIC**. It's another example of her capacity for

REINVENTION. Though it didn't make it onto her album, this track was a key moment in Kylie's evolution. Some artists – like The Beatles, Bowie, Madonna, Kate Bush, Kanye – are acclaimed for their ability to reinvent their sound and image. Many others look and sound the same forever, and their fans are content. Reinvention takes courage. Your reward for risk-taking might be vitriolic reviews, alienated fans, mockery on social media and commercial oblivion. Kylie knew that perfectly well.

'I had people controlling me for years. Now I am revelling in the fact that I have control, I take responsibility for my decisions and I live and die by them.' – Kylie Minogue[10]

She has succeeded in finding a balance: sometimes giving us exactly what we want and sometimes taking us by surprise. Ever different, but somehow always the same, in her essential Kylie-ness. Sometimes blue, sometimes green, sometimes *italic*, sometimes **bold**. But in spite of being very Kylie, 'German Bold Italic' didn't appear on an album of her own: instead it can be found on

SOUND MUSEUM by Towa Tei, an album full of unlikely collaborations. Besides Kylie, Tei roped in a bunch of his favourite artists, among them rappers Biz Markie and Mos Def, and Brazilian chanteuse Bebel Gilberto who contributes a bossa nova version of Daryl Hall and John Oates' 80s hit, 'Private Eyes'. There's a symmetry here: while westerners pursued a stylised notion of Japan, the Japanese producer was gorging on samples of western music. It's primarily an electronic album, but you'll also hear horns, flutes, trumpets, gamelans, marimbas and countless samples from the deepest recesses of Tei's record collection. He blends these disparate elements into a weird kind of gold. *Sound Museum* is stylish, goofy and funky in a dozen different languages. It's all a bit nuts, and great fun.

TYPE isn't neutral. The setting of a piece of text shapes the way you think about it. Towa Tei knew more about this than most people: he originally went to the United States to study graphic design, and later, when not making music, continued as art director at Tycoon Graphics in Tokyo, the studio credited with designing the typeface 'German Bold Italic'. It appears on the cover of the eponymous CD, the letters 'GBI' aggressively in your face. Typographically, it's a high contrast italic display face.[11] The chunky, curveless letterforms have an arcade-game vibe, placing the song firmly in the digital world of the 1990s and evoking the Japanese pop culture that Kylie was drawn to. And the text is all in

UPPER CASE LETTERS. Most typefaces have both upper- and lower-case forms. But 'German Bold Italic' consists only of an upper case, the numerals 0 to 9 and a few symbols. And yes, they're all italic. That limits how you can use the typeface. (You can't actually use it in German: there are some letters missing.) But then again, maybe it was only meant to be used once, on the CD. Typefaces can be disposable, like pop stars. Oddly, the typeface doesn't seem to appear in the

VIDEO of 'German Bold Italic', directed by Stéphane Sednaoui, which stars Kylie in peak Japanese mode. Beginning in a bath, semi-clad in bikini, sparkles, heavy make-up and a wig adorned with cranes, she flutters around New York in geisha costume, striking poses, bowing to strangers who ignore her, and taking the subway, before a businessman captures her and puts her on a leash. But is the suited corporate drone leading her, or is she leading him? Intercut with this we see Tei robotically striding Tokyo in a suit, chunky headphones and his trademark big glasses, every inch the urban global hipster. He uses a vending machine, slurps noodles, descends into the subway and hooks up with a couple of girls before finally starting to giggle, as if to say that the whole thing is a gag. But there may be more to it than that. The video can be read as a comment on the status of

WOMEN in mainstream pop music. According to the cultural theorist Kristin Lieb, female pop stars cycle through predictable 'lifecycle phases' as their career advances.[12] They begin with 'good girl', transitioning into 'temptress', followed by a restricted range of further options including 'diva', 'redemptive comeback', 'gay icon' and 'hot mess'. For female pop stars, sex is non-negotiable. The other rule is that a female artist can't stay too long at any one stage. Every few years (or less) she has to transform herself; the alternative is oblivion.

In the video, Kylie takes on the role of geisha, a traditional Japanese female performer, often sexualised, who is expected to appear and perform in ritualised ways. She may seem exotic, but perhaps the role isn't so different to that of a western female pop star. But the video suggests she isn't doomed to be led around on a leash forever. An artist who is strategic and strong-willed can make her own decisions about how and when she transitions through the phases. Kylie's career is full of these moments. Is she the one leading the way, or the one being led? Either way, she wasn't going to abandon experimentation. There would be more of it on

X, Kylie's tenth album, released in 2007. By then she had already been at the top for twenty years. Coming ten years after *Impossible Princess*, *X* was another collection of diverse sounds in multiple genres. One reviewer[13] complained that the record had too many styles, too much 'magpie modernism'. But maybe that restlessness, that constant exploration, is another key to Kylie's longevity. Anyway, why is diversity only a problem when some artists do it? No-one complained about the eclectic approach of Towa Tei, or of

YELLOW MAGIC ORCHESTRA, the band that Haruomi Hosono founded along with Yukihiro Takahashi and Ryuichi Sakamoto. YMO was one of the most influential groups of the 70s and 80s. Their pioneering use of synths, computers, and drum machines anticipated the electronic music that dominated the following decades. This band was an influence not just on Towa Tei, and thus Deee-Lite, but pretty much every electronic

> 'Whenever a new synthesiser came out, you can bet it was either Yellow Magic Orchestra or Kraftwerk who used it first.' – Synth historian Itamar Livne[14]

artist that came after, including people like Soft Cell and the Pet Shop Boys who collaborated with Kylie. So once again, she was working with the best. And this is one of the ways that she succeeds in connecting to the

ZEITGEIST. At the time of writing, Kylie is back at the top of the charts with the song of the moment. Her five-decade career has included a succession of them, and if you're reading this book, you can probably name a few. But what of 'German Bold Italic'? It might not be her most celebrated hit, but it captures something intrinsic about its time and about Kylie. It's a witty, sexy, utterly unique pop song with a killer synth hook and a bonkers video. And really, what more could you ask for?

Endnotes

1. Shuker, Roy. *Understanding Popular Music Culture* (4th ed.), Routledge, 2012.
2. Myers, Owen. Review of *Impossible Princess*, 22 January 2023, pitchfork.com/reviews/albums/kylie-minogue-impossible-princess
3. Reynolds, Simon. *Retromania: Pop Culture's Addiction to its Own Past*, Farrar, Straus and Giroux, 2011.
4. Interview with Towa Tei, 10 October 2014, Warner Music Japan Inc., web.archive.org/web/20141010134951/http://wmg.jp/towatei20th/interview4.html
5. ibid.
6. The Louis Theroux Podcast, S1EP5: Nick Cave on his remarkable career, religion and dealing with grief, July 2023, open.spotify.com/episode/4OwNk3CSw70KeufuG6O41N
7. Ibid.
8. Lupton, Ellen and Tobias, Jennifer. *Extra Bold: A Feminist, Inclusive, Anti-Racist, Nonbinary Field Guide for Graphic Designers*, Princeton Architectural Press, 2021.
9. Ibid.
10. Myers, Owen, op. cit.
11. Thanks to Stephen Banham for the classification.
12. Lieb, Kristin J. *The Lifecycle for Female Popular Music Stars*, Routledge, 2018.
13. Ewing, Tom. Review of *X*, 30 November 2007, pitchfork.com/reviews/albums/10947-x
14. Personal communication, July 2023.

Where the Wild Roses Grow

Kirsten Krauth

a thousand Valentines lured me

I'm desiring, sea receding
from the shores

under swaying pussy willows
white-sharp iris, lace skirt dragged
his muddy body I tongue-tied

threaded through with studded metal
winched chest, his blackened kiss

throat gagged soft my night wing-feathers

I'm flying, whispers licking
polished claws

Sunday morning carrion tree
morseled lover, I called the wolves
his taste of sweet rot beak sharp

I raised his body broke his arrow
sun-dialled soul, gnomon pierced

I sang the world from shadow-longing

I'm swiving, wild cave diving
deep afloat

sorrow's man stepped in the bower
I bled his heart, wild branch-beat
fadings tidal rushed us high

lover goodbye he fell soft
raven-haired, brute mess of twigs

swooned let-go I tended him under

I'm returning, wind soaring
hackled throat

charnel ground of bloodied snow

All the Lovers

Christos Tsiolkas

Max is searching through the bathroom cabinet, collecting the items that belong to her. The shelves are cluttered – three or four blister packs of Codral that have possibly been sitting there from years ago, when they first bought the house. She is tempted to throw away the out-of-date pain medicines and cough syrups. She resists the urge. She's sure that Claudia would think it passive aggressive, a final admonishment. Max realises her jaw has tensed, that she is grinding her teeth. She grabs the blister packs and chucks them into the bin.

Fuck it, she says to herself, I've spent years cleaning up after her, let her be pissed off.

She breathes in. She quickly retrieves the tossed items and pushes them to the back of a shelf. She takes her mascara, her Aēsop facial scrub, her cologne. She's about to snatch the toothpaste, then decides against it. She does take the Clinique matte lip foundation. It's Claudia's, but it suits Max better.

The almond-milk hand lotion, her Ventolin puffer, the bottle of St John's wort capsules. There are eleven temazepam tablets left. She takes six and wraps them in tissue and stuffs them in the side pocket of her toiletries bag. There are nineteen Valium capsules and she pops out nine. They have promised each other that they will not allow rancour and bitterness to annihilate all vestiges of trust. They have promised each other to be scrupulously fair.

She closes the cabinet door and catches her reflection in the mirror. The flushes of silver roots in her hair, the tightness to her mouth, the grey shadows under her eyes. And also, just before the door shuts, a glimpse of the plastic basket that sits above the shower taps. A lime-green bottle: conditioner or shampoo. Not hers; and not Claudia's either. A flash, an almost imperceptible glimpse of a spectre. Leila's beautiful arrogant beauty, the luxuriant long raven hair, the high and regal cheekbones. The apparition is like the palimpsest of a demon in a horror film.

She flings opens the cabinet, grabs the packet of Valium and the bottle of temazepam and jams them in the bag. She bangs the cabinet door shut.

She storms through the kitchen, takes the Chasseur French oven, all the expensive knives including the one Claudia purchased at the fish markets in Tokyo, the set of Turkish tea glasses with the exquisite floral etching in umber and gold. They had been a Christmas present from Claudia's mother. Max is going to take them all. She'd have to make another trip, ask the grocer on High Street if she could have a few more empty boxes. She's going to take everything she can!

She retrieves an old edition of *The Age* from the recycling bin under the sink, is rolling a tea glass into one of the torn pages. Her hands are shaking, and she hears the sharp peal of the crack. She unruffles the newspaper, sees that the glass has broken.

She drops onto the vinyl kitchen floor, sits on the symmetrical spread of red and white and black squares. Her body heaving.

The sobbing is painful, but as it ceases, as she wipes her eyes, snorts and rubs her nose into her shirt sleeve, she is conscious of relief. She grips the edge of the island, and clumsily gets to her feet. She sniffs again. It's done.

Max carefully rolls the paper around the broken glass and throws it into the bin. She puts the Chasseur oven back in the cupboard, the remaining tea set back on the shelf. She places the knives back in their holders. Claudia is the cook. Max takes a saucepan, an old frying pan and the kettle. Claudia rarely drinks tea. She'll leave her the espresso pot. A memory swings at the edge of her consciousness. Of course! The old Bodum coffee maker. She searches the lower shelves of the pantry, and finds it, the glass streaked with dust. It'll do until she has a chance to visit the market.

She finds the stainless-steel platter, a gift from her parents. She also takes the shallow jade fruit bowl, a birthday gift from Claudia. The set of cream Japanese stoneware coffee mugs and saucers with the elongated clover design that she found in the op shop in Maldon sometime in the nineties. BC. Before Claudia. That makes her smile. She wraps the set in newspaper, places the items along the island bench. They should all fit in one box. Claudia had insisted that they halve the cutlery and kitchen utensils, that Max should take what she needs for her new apartment. Max hadn't said it aloud, but she thought the idea ridiculous. The settlement had been fair, and it included a small sum for Max setting up on her own. A naughty thought now strikes her. Maybe she could take half a Valium, drive to Northland and wander Kmart. There's a warmth, a buzz, starting in her belly. The flush is delicious. And no-one to tell her off for driving under the influence.

On the way to the living room, she pauses and looks at the fridge, the door studded with postcards and magnets. The collage is a map of their years together. There is the playbill from the Royal Shakespeare Company's production of *King Lear*, with Ian McKellen in the lead. The tickets had been a present from Claudia for their first anniversary. The faded photograph of Claudia sitting in a café in Condesa, her beaming smile, wearing the ridiculous outré, yellow-framed sunglasses that she had picked up at a flea market in Coyoacán. She is smoking in the photograph. That's right, Max recalls, Claudia gave up cigarettes after Mexico. A postcard of Alice B. Toklas and Gertrude Stein with their poodle. The I ♥ Brooklyn fridge magnet – that trip to the US when Max turned forty-five. A gaunt Robert Mapplethorpe clutching his skull cane. The card that Stephen had made for them for their tenth anniversary, a young Madonna snarling at the camera, the sans serif bold text in red: EXPRESS YOURSELVES, BITCHES! A Lucien Freud androgynous nude, all folds of fat and belly and thigh. She's always loved that painting, and her fingers reach out for the postcard.

She lets her hand drop. Instead, she stands back from the fridge, frames the door in the lens of her phone. She snaps the photograph.

***

As always, the living room is dark. The courtyard is north-facing, and the kitchen floods with light. But there is only one small sash window in the lounge and it looks onto the narrow alcove and the gloomy red-brick wall of the house next door. Max switches on the light.

A copy of *Vogue* on the coffee table. Max is an actuary, in a large public service department, work that she knows is boring to most people but which for her is enjoyable and satisfying. From childhood she has been drawn to the purity of numbers. But she has also cultivated style, revelling in both order and beauty. She dresses well, and her monthly visit to the hairdresser remains a joy in her life. Sava is expensive, but it is a luxury she will not forego. His eye is perfect, and he is unafraid to counsel her against choices he thinks unsuitable for her age or for her face. How she looks and how she presents herself is important to her; however, the vagaries of fashion itself have never held much interest. She hasn't looked at *Vogue* since her adolescence. Claudia settled on a punkish and skinhead look in her twenties – boots, Millers shirts and black

Levi's – and she still dresses the same in middle age. Max quickly scans the contents listed on the cover. Is there an interview with a musician Claudia follows? Then the understanding, treacherous and unsteadying as a shock tidal wave. The phantom visage appears: Leila's immaculately made-up face.

The erupting flush, as if the heat is burning her body inside out, makes her stumble to the sofa.

She has her head in her hands. Thankfully, no tears this time. Only the nauseating warmth on her skin, in her lungs and chest and stomach. She can smell the salty, lightly rancid reek of her sweat. She lifts her head and the yellow glow of the artificial light on the room's walls is intrusive, as if a torch beam has exposed an inner carcass. Maybe it isn't her scent, maybe it is that damn rising damp that they've never managed to completely conquer. She settles into her breaths, and the room gradually loses its sinister aspect. A thick gossamer strand dangles from a corner cornice. Her body responds automatically to the sight; she is up on her feet and about to fetch the broom from the laundry.

Her mouth settles into a snarl.

Let fucking Leila deal with it!

Only the other night Dimitra had counselled her, You were together nearly twenty years. Of course, it is going to hurt, and it is going to hurt for a long time. Max shudders. She can't do it. Impossible. She wants to wrench those twenty years from her body, rip them from her skin. That would be relief, that would be sanity.

She wants to take the thick glossy magazine, roll it into a tube and fucking choke Leila with it.

The exquisite pleasure of the violent thought, an ardent tremor from her groin – the shock of it brings her to her senses.

She speaks out loud: 'Just grab the last of your things and go!' That steely order is fortifying.

***

Her music. That's the primary reason she's here. She needs to be careful. Claudia may rarely DJ these days, but she still guards her collection jealously. A shared passion for music was one of the things that brought them together, Claudia insisting that it was watching Max throw herself into the stuttering breaks of Beyonce's 'Crazy in Love' on the dancefloor that first attracted her. 'You were mad for that track, Maxie, I was looking down at you and it seemed only you and that track existed.' Yet Max always knew that Claudia's love for music was more consuming than her own. Claudia was obsessed. From her teenage years, reading *NME* and *Spin* cover to cover in the newsagency in Strathmore, to learning to mix and DJ from her first girlfriend, Deb. From an adolescent baby-dyke getting into industrial and goth, to her immersion into acid and rave, when the soaring diva samples and the resurrected disco of house promised renewal after the terror and mourning of AIDS. Claudia still searched the internet for new music, knew the best record shops in the city – north and south, east and west – where the owners put aside vinyl for her to peruse.

Max needs to be scrupulously fair. Make one mistake, take one record that is not hers, and Claudia will think it deliberate, vindictive.

She starts with the CDs – the CDs are easy. Claudia had said, through text, that she was going to take the majority to Vinnies in Footscray. *I'm not going to ask for money. It's part of uncluttering. Take what you want.* Max squats and her finger traces the plastic spines of the CD covers. She doesn't want clutter either; the new apartment is small and her books already take up most of the shelf space. She chooses the classics first. Aretha Franklin, Prince, Regurgitator, Sam Cooke. Marvin Gaye's *Let's Get it On* and Joni Mitchell's *Blue*. Claudia has both on vinyl. Chopin, Mozart, Britten and Pärt. Then the years of the dance. Fat Boy Slim, Groove Armada and the first Destiny's Child album. The *Red Hot + Blue* compilation, k.d. lang, Emmylou Harris. She pauses. There are seven Lucinda Williams CDs. She had introduced Lucinda to Claudia, proud to be the one initiating a discovery. She takes *Essence*, leaves the others behind.

There's a growing throb at the base of her spine. Awkwardly Max rises and pinches, rubs the side of her hips. She walks to the far wall, shelf after shelf of vinyl.

Thank God that when it came to music, Claudia was uncharacteristically ordered and methodical. The vinyl is stacked alphabetically.

There are two copies of Kate Bush's *Hounds of Love*. This makes her smile. One copy is pristine, still in its plastic sheaf. Max takes out the older copy and she also selects a battered copy of Kate Bush's first album. The Beatles' greatest hits, both the blue and the red editions, which she has carried from house to house since she was a child. Marianne Faithfull's *Broken English* and *A Child's Adventure*. Definitely hers. Do-Ré-Mi's *Domestic Harmony*, George Michael's *Faith* and I'm Talking's *Bear Witness*. De La Soul, *3 Feet High and Rising*. The extended mix of Hot Chocolate's 'You Sexy Thing', that nursed her through the break-up with Sonja. Innocence's 'Natural Thing' that recalls the first time she took ecstasy. The Pointer Sisters' 'Dare Me'; since high school that track has always made her happy.

She should have made a list. She's sure she's forgotten many of the records that are hers. Carefully she peers at the top shelf, slowly scans the spines left to right. She removes ABBA's *Arrival*, the cover water-damaged, the four young Swedes in their jumpsuits next to the helicopter. A gift from her brother when Max turned ten.

I need to hear 'Knowing Me, Knowing You'. I need to hear it right now.

Max goes to the turntable, switches on the stereo, gently releases the LP from the sleeve. She lifts the needle and carefully positions it on the groove between the fourth and final track on side A. She presses the button and the disc begins to spin. There is a crackle of white noise. The track begins.

She turns the dial. The music is blaring through the room. She goes back to the shelves. Bowie's *"Heroes"*. Hers. Max sings along to the ABBA song and as the chorus begins, she finds that she is shouting the song. It feels good to shout. It feels good to scream. It feels good to know that Anni-Frid has known her pain. She pulls out The Chemical Brothers' *Exit Planet Dust*. Definitely hers, living on Queensbury Street with Jay and Anton, how that record had been the soundtrack to their going out, snorting their lines, taking their pills, the floor of the warehouse reverberating, seeming to leap and bounce along to the strident rhythms.

Max looks at the cover. When Claudia was DJing she would always take it along, in the crate of her music, invariably spin 'Leave Home' at some point in the night. Max pushes the record back in its place between Cat Power's *Sun* and *Dig Your Own Hole*.

She finds Billie Holiday's *Lady in Satin*, that she bought from Hound Dog's Bop Shop in the mid-80s. FKA Twigs' *LP1*. Max is singing along to the fading chorus of the ABBA song.

The soundtrack to *Grease*, her first-ever purchase. The soundtrack to *Dirty Dancing*. She neatly lines up the records. They'll all fit into one box. One box is all she needs.

She returns to the stereo, plonks the needle back on 'Knowing Me, Knowing You'.

She pushes an ottoman across the carpet to the shelves filled with CDs. Sitting, she quickly flicks the spines, the compilations of house and hip-hop, of disco and soul. She isn't going to bother with any of them. Everything is available on streaming. She's about to stand up when she notices a thick wad of CDs lying flat at the edge of the bottom shelf. She brushes away the dust. They are DIY mixtapes, compilation CDs that have been made for her, for Claudia – made for both of them – through the years.

A picture of Patsy Cline, black and white, staring at the camera and smoking a cigarette. The cover her friend Margaret had made herself, slotted into the sleeve of the CD. She smiles at the handwritten note under the list of songs. *My favourite country songs for my favourite cowgirl xxM.* She must call Margaret. She must tell her about the break-up. The guilt lands as a punch. She can't have Margaret find out from someone else. Or is it too late? Has the gossip already seeped out through social media? She'll call her tonight. Before bed, to take account of the time difference between Melbourne and Perth.

End-of-year mix CDs from Spiro and Shane, from Roxanne and Dimitra. And birthday gifts, anniversary gifts. From Claudia. And those carefully assembled driving mixtapes on CD, house and country, hip-hop and seventies-era Jackson Browne, Renée Geyer and Linda Ronstadt, Led Zeppelin following The Cure following Kanye, songs that soundtracked those long drives to Mildura and back when Max was going to visit her mother.

The hopping, sputtering sounds of the needle stuck in the groove. Max gets up, returns to the turntable. She plays the ABBA song again.

A CD sleeve, jet black, with the word LOVE in red, in a bold sans serif, floating in the middle of the darkness. The last CD that Claudia had made for her. Before COVID, before the ubiquity of streaming. She opens the plastic sleeve. Claudia's cursive script. *For Max. I love you. Forever.* That promise that neither of them kept.

She is going to take this one. It doesn't matter that the stereo unit she bought from JB the other day has no CD player. Max remembers driving down the Hume, leaving behind the sludge of Melbourne traffic, inserting the CD into the slot of the old Subaru Impreza, the car they had bought together – how she had been puzzled by the excerpt of spoken word that introduced the mix, the female and male voices familiar, but she couldn't place them at first, knew it was from a movie, the title at the tip of memory, until the male voice uttered the name, Corleone, and she thought, that's right, it's Diane Keaton and it's Al Pacino, it's *The Godfather*, and almost as soon as the recollection became conscious there was the dirty squelch of a guitar, the woozy and lazy intro into Lou Reed and his band performing 'Sweet Jane' live. She had cranked up the volume. And after Lou, as the lazy cheers and shouts of the audience faded, a propulsive serpentine synth emerged from underneath, a track she didn't recognise but which immediately pulsated through her body – later, checking Claudia's handwritten CD playlist, she discovered the track was called 'Grand Cru' and the band called Saschienne – and she kept driving and the mix kept unfolding with Claudia's own remix of Missy Elliot's '4 My People' that morphed into Grace Jones' 'She's Lost Control' followed by Joy Division themselves, 'New Dawn Fades', and just when Max was thinking – *this is a bit dark for me, this is more her than me* – there was an effervescent disco upswell and Kylie Minogue's thin autotuned voice was flooding the car. 'All the Lovers'. And Max had laughed out loud, at the cheesiness of it, of how wrong and how right it was in following the foreboding of the post-punk and she had turned the volume as loud as it could go, belting out the song as she approached the bypass to Kyneton.

Max checks her phone. It's not yet three o'clock in the afternoon. Plenty of time before Claudia gets home from work.

She hesitates, turns and walks back to the turntable. She will play the ABBA song one last time.

And she's in the middle of the lounge room, her eyes shut, her body swinging to the music, her voice soaring above Anni-Frid's, hollering the words.

A cough.

Max's hands drop to her sides. Her eyes open. Leila is standing in the doorway. Max swings, turns, marches to the turntable and lifts the needle off the record. The screech is unholy. She switches off the stereo.

Leila steps into the room.

'Sorry, I had to come home early.'

Max is burning. The shame is an incineration. She rams the album into the sleeve, and the paper tears. She walks over and drops it on the pile of records.

'I'm nearly done.'

Leila is shaking her head.

'No ... no ... please, stay ... I can come back.' Leila's anxious smile is pitiful. 'Why don't I come back in half an hour?'

Max shakes her head.

'Just give me a second.'

'Of course.'

She's beautiful. Tall and lean, the neat attire of her black slacks and the white shirt, the pale shirt accentuating the glowing olive skin. She's beautiful and she's young. Max has to will herself to not drop her gaze.

Her skin must be aflame.

'I have to go to my car. I've got some boxes there.'

The swift look of puzzlement across Leila's face; the pinched mouth, the uncomprehending eyes; for a moment, she is ugly.

Leila moves aside, her back against the wall, letting Max pass. The scent of her perfume. Gently floral, expensive.

Max releases a breath as she opens the front door and steps out into their small front garden.

No. No longer her garden. Claudia's garden. Leila's garden. Their garden.

Across the street, groups of parents are huddled near the school gates, waiting for the final bell to ring. The narrow cul-de-sac is already clogged with cars. As Max opens the boot, grabs two empty boxes, she notices a woman driving a silver Toyota Camry, her blonde hair tied back in a severe ponytail, looking expectantly at her. Max bangs shut the boot, shakes her head.

***

Max tosses the records and CDs into one box. With a carton under her arm, she walks into the kitchen. Leila is filling the kettle.

Don't you dare ask me if I want any fucking tea!

Max indicates the objects on the island bench.

'I'll just grab these and I'll be gone.'

Leila nods. She turns her back to Max, pulls out her phone and starts scrolling. Max hauls the box into the living room. She places it next to the one filled with records. She looks down the corridor and winces.

She should just march to the bedroom, grab what she needs. She doesn't have to ask permission. Why should she ask permission?

'Is it okay if I quickly look through the bedroom?'

The same pinched anxious smile as Leila looks up from her phone. She nods.

As soon as she enters the dark, small room, Max knows it is a mistake. The wooziness starts in her stomach, and she is shaking. A strange low rumble seems to be reverberating within the bedroom. Max looks around wildly, unsure of what she is doing there. Everything is in its usual place: the cane laundry basket in the corner next to the maple wood armoire, the blue-and-green check woollen throw over the bed, the dark shadows of the framed poster of *Todo sobre mi madre* over the small writing desk. Yet it feels alien. *She* feels alien. It doesn't smell like their room. The combination of mustiness and sweetness, an almost citric sourness.

If there's something she's forgotten, then Claudia can have it.

Max pitches open the door, hurls herself down the hall.

As she's picking up the box of records, Leila comes into the living room. She moves towards Max, is about to pick up the other box.

'No!'

Leila freezes.

'Thank you, but it's just the two boxes. I'll be fine.'

It's a chilly midwinter afternoon and Max is glad for it. She doesn't mind that she is underdressed, that she has left her jacket in the car. The cold wind, whipping across her face, her neck, it is a balm.

***

She has the last box under her arm, is standing in the doorway. Leila is at the far end of the kitchen, looking out of the French doors to the small courtyard. And for the first time, Max wonders whether her herbs and plants will survive. Claudia is no gardener. Maybe Leila is? She hardly knows anything about her.

'I'm off.'

Leila swings around.

'If there's anything you forgot, I'm sure ...'

Her words peter out to silence.

'I'll text Claudia if there's anything.' Max's eyes wander the room. It's done. She's finished.

Then she remembers.

'I'm sorry, I broke one of the tea glasses.'

Leila is confused. Max points to the ornamental beakers.

'That's okay.' Leila has stepped forward, as if about to say something.

Please don't, thinks Max, the fear so fierce it scalds inside her chest, please don't say you're sorry. Please don't pity me.

Leila's smile is wan, sad.

'Take care.'

Max nods, attempting a smile, turns swiftly and with the box tight under her arm, is walking down the corridor. Even that gracious courtesy hurts. About to open the door, about to leave, about to feel the fresh air on her face, Max puts down the box, turns around and marches back to the lounge room. She scans the vinyl, finds *Exit Planet Dust*. She takes it.

***

On the way home, she sits in silence until it becomes too overwhelming. The silence has a heat, and she needs to escape it. She switches on the radio. The news is distressing, and she pushes a button. The talkback is inane, and she switches to something sinister and discordant on 3RRR. She finds another station and there it is: a wash of synth disco, a tremulous build, the reedy female vocal. And she hears it, underneath the beginning of the song, the foreboding end notes to 'New Dawn Fades'.

That is memory, thinks Max, that will always be, that can never be unheard. Joy Division and Kylie Minogue, forever entwined.

She listens to the first verse until the uplifting chorus of the song begins. It is not heat this time that overwhelms her, it is the weariness. She turns off the radio.

Max releases the driver's window, all the way down. It's cold, bitterly so. The wintry blast is intoxicating. She drives in the silence, concentrating on the road.

Songs and Albums Referenced
Various

'A Lifetime to Repair', *Golden*. Written/composed by Kylie Minogue, Sky Adams, Kiris Houston, Danny Shah. Darenote, BMG, 2018.

'All the Lovers', *Aphrodite*. Written/composed by James Eliot, Mima Stilwell. Parlophone, 2010.

'Better the Devil You Know', *Rhythm of Love*. Written/composed by Mike Stock, Matt Aitken, Pete Waterman. Mushroom, PWL, 1990.

'Breathe', *Impossible Princess*. Written/composed by Kylie Minogue, Dave Ball, Ingo Vauk. Mushroom, Deconstruction, BMG, 1997.

'Bury Me Deep in Love' (cover), *Corroboration: A Journey through the Musical Landscape of 21st Century Australia*, Kylie Minogue and Jimmy Little. Written/composed by David McComb. Sputnik, Festival Mushroom, 2001.

'Can't Get You Out of My Head', *Fever*. Written/composed by Cathy Dennis, Rob Davis. Parlophone, 2001.

'Come into My World', *Fever*. Written/composed by Cathy Dennis, Rob Davis. Parlophone, 2001.

'Confide in Me', *Kylie Minogue*. Written/composed by David Seaman, Owain Barton, Steve Anderson. Deconstruction, Mushroom, 1994.

'Dancing', *Golden*. Written/composed by Kylie Minogue, Nathan Chapman, Steve McEwan. Darenote, BMG, 2018.

'Death Is Not the End', *Murder Ballads*, Nick Cave & The Bad Seeds featuring Anita Lane, Shane MacGowan, PJ Harvey and Kylie Minogue. Written/composed by Bob Dylan. Mute, 1996.

'Did It Again', *Impossible Princess*. Written/composed by Kylie Minogue, Dave Seaman, Steve Anderson. Mushroom, Deconstruction, BMG, 1997.

'Dreams', *Impossible Princess*. Written/composed by Kylie Minogue, Steve Anderson, David Seaman. Mushroom, Deconstruction, BMG, 1997.

'Especially for You', *Especially for You – Single*, Kylie Minogue and Jason Donovan. Written/composed by Mike Stock, Matt Aitken, Pete Waterman. PWL, 1988.

'Everything Is Beautiful', *Aphrodite*. Written/composed by Fraser T. Smith, Tim Rice-Oxley. Parlophone, 2010.

'GBI (German Bold Italic)', *Sound Museum*, Towa Tei featuring Kylie Minogue and Haruomi Hosono. Written/composed by Towa Tei, Kylie Minogue. East West, 1997.

'Give Me Just a Little More Time' (cover), *Let's Get to It*. Written/composed by Ronald Dunbar, Edythe Wayne. Mushroom, PWL, 1991.

'Hand on Your Heart', *Enjoy Yourself*. Written/composed by Mike Stock, Matt Aitken, Pete Waterman. Mushroom, PWL, 1989.

'I Should Be So Lucky', *Kylie*. Written/composed by Mike Stock, Matt Aitken, Pete Waterman. Mushroom, PWL, 1988.

'In Your Eyes', *Fever*. Written/composed by Kylie Minogue, Julian Gallagher, Ash Howes, Richard Stannard. Parlophone, 2001.

'Into the Blue', *Kiss Me Once*. Written/composed by Jacob Kasher Hindlin, Kelly Sheehan, Mike Del Rio. Parlophone, 2014.

'Je Ne Sais Pas Pourquoi', *Kylie*. Written/composed by Mike Stock, Matt Aitken, Pete Waterman. Mushroom, PWL, 1988.

'Locomotion' (cover), *Locomotion – Single*. Written/composed by Carole King, Gerry Goffin. Mushroom, 1987. See also 'The Loco-Motion'.

'Made of Glass', *Ultimate Kylie*. Written/composed by Miranda Cooper, Brian Higgins, Tim Powell, Lisa Cowling, Paul Woods, Nick Coler, Kylie Minogue. Parlophone, 2004.

'Padam Padam', *Tension*. Written/composed by Peter Rycroft, Ina Wroldsen. Darenote, BMG, 2023.

'Put Yourself in My Place', *Kylie Minogue*. Written/composed by Jimmy Harry. Deconstruction, Mushroom, 1994.

'Shocked', *Rhythm of Love*. Written/composed by Mike Stock, Matt Aitken, Pete Waterman. Mushroom, PWL, 1990.

'Slow', *Body Language*. Written/composed by Kylie Minogue, Dan Carey, Emiliana Torrini. Parlophone, 2003.

'Sometime Samurai', *Flash*, Towa Tei featuring Kylie Minogue. Written/composed by Kylie Minogue, Towa Tei. V2, 2005.

'Spinning Around', *Light Years*. Written/composed by Ira Schickman, Kara DioGuardi, Paula Abdul, Osborne Bingham. Mushroom, Parlophone, 2000.

'Tension', *Tension*. Written/composed by Kylie Minogue, Biff Stannard, Duck Blackwell, Jon Green, Kamille, Anya Jones. Darenote, BMG, 2023.

'The Loco-Motion' (cover), *Kylie*. Written/composed by Carole King, Gerry Goffin. Mushroom, PWL, 1988. **See also 'Locomotion'.**

'Timebomb', *Timebomb*. Written/composed by Karen Poole, Matt Schwartz, Paul Harris. Parlophone, 2012.

'Where Is the Feeling?', *Kylie Minogue*. Written/composed by Wilf Smarties, Jayn Hanna. Deconstruction, Mushroom, 1994.

'Where the Wild Roses Grow', *Murder Ballads*, Nick Cave & The Bad Seeds featuring Kylie Minogue. Written/composed by Nick Cave. Mute, 1996.

'Your Disco Needs You', *Light Years*. Written/composed by Kylie Minogue, Guy Chambers, Robbie Williams. Mushroom, Parlophone, 2000.

X. Parlophone, 2007.

Contributor Biographies
Various

Grace Chan is an award-winning speculative fiction writer. She writes about brains, minds and space. Her critically acclaimed debut novel, *Every Version of You*, is about staying in love after mind-uploading into virtual reality. It won the NSW Premier's Literary Awards People's Choice Award and was shortlisted for *The Age* Book of the Year, and longlisted for the Stella Prize and the Indie Book Awards. Her short fiction has been published widely. You can find her at gracechanwrites.com.

Eileen Chong is a poet of Hakka, Hokkien, and Peranakan descent. She is the author of nine books. Her work has shortlisted for numerous prizes, including the NSW Premier's Literary Award, the Victorian Premier's Literary Award, and twice for the Prime Minister's Literary Award. Her next poetry collection, *We Speak of Flowers*, is forthcoming with UQP in 2025. She lives and works on the unceded lands of the Gadigal people. Connect with her at eileenchong.com.au.

Nathan Curnow is a poet, playwright, spoken word performer, and past editor of *Going Down Swinging*. His books include *The Ghost Poetry Project*, *RADAR*, *The Right Wrong Notes* and *The Apocalypse Awards*. He has been widely published in leading journals for over twenty years, and his awards include the Josephine Ulrick Poetry Prize, the Woorilla Poetry Prize, and the Vox Bendigo Fyffe Award for Poetry. He is also a two-time winner of the Martha Richardson Memorial Poetry Prize. He has taught creative writing at Federation University and lives and works on the traditional lands of the Wathaurong people in Ballarat.

Chris Flynn is the author of *Here Be Leviathans, Mammoth* and other books for adults and children. The opening quote in his story comes from Ralph Waldo Emerson's essay, 'Self-Reliance' and the closing quote comes from 'Love', both published in *Essays: First Series*, 1841.

Nick Gadd is the author of the novels *Death of a Typographer* (a mystery novel about fonts), *Ghostlines*, and the memoir *Melbourne Circle: Walking, Memory and Loss*. He is a former winner of a Victorian Premier's Literary Award, a Ned Kelly Award and the Nature Conservancy Australia Nature Writing Prize.

Dmetri Kakmi is the author of *The Dictionary of a Gadfly* (as The Sozzled Scribbler), *The Door and Other Uncanny Tales, Mother Land* and *When We Were Young* (as editor). For fifteen years he worked as a senior editor at Penguin Books. He was also fiction/non-fiction co-editor for the online literary journal *Kalliope X*. His essays and short stories appear in anthologies. *Mother Land* was shortlisted for a NSW Premier's Literary Award in 2008. *Haunting Matilda* was shortlisted for Best Fantasy Novella for the Aurealis Awards in 2013. His novel *The Woman in the Well* will be published in 2025.

Kris Kneen is the award-winning author of fiction, poetry and non-fiction including *An Uncertain Grace*, which was shortlisted for the Stella Prize. Their latest book is *Fat Girl Dancing* which was shortlisted for the Victorian Premier's Literary Award for non-fiction.

Julie Koh is the author of two short-story collections: *Capital Misfits* and *Portable Curiosities*. She was a 2017 *Sydney Morning Herald* Best Young Australian Novelist. Outside Australia, her short stories have been published in nine countries and translated into Chinese, Japanese, Indonesian and Bengali. In relation to 'Everything Is Beautiful', Julie is indebted to Kenichi and Mai Eguchi of Ekadbo space, on whom the characters of Kenichi Eguchi and his wife are based. Kenichi and Naoko Benom-Miura consulted closely with Julie on the story. Julie thanks Carey Benom for interpreting her initial conversation with Kenichi. The story benefited from additional consultation with Satomi Hirohashi, Rioko Tega, Christina Choi, Ian See, Paul Smith and Michael Camilleri. Julie thanks all of her friends in Tsuyazaki, as well as Craig Money – a huge fan of Kylie Minogue (and a pleasant-smelling one at that) – whom Julie met one rainy day on the number 12 bus from Torquay.

Kirsten Krauth is a Castlemaine-based author and arts journalist, poet and podcaster, and the commissioning editor of the anthologies *Spinning Around: The Kylie Playlist* and *Into Your Arms: Nick Cave's Songs Reimagined.* Her latest novel, *Almost a Mirror,* was shortlisted for the Small Press Network Book of the Year Award and the Penguin Literary Prize, and named one of *The Guardian*'s Best 20 Books of 2020; her first novel was *just_a_girl.* An 80s tragic, Kirsten received the Donald Horne Fellowship to develop her podcast, *Almost a Mirror,* which revolves around Australian 80s songs and went to number one on the Apple Music Podcast charts. She loves to write poetry and 'Pencils from Heaven' was runner-up/highly commended in the 2021 Blake Poetry Prize.

Jes Layton invented writing, the aeroplane and the internet. He was also the first person to reach the North Pole. Jes is an author, illustrator, performer and the Emerging Writers' Festival co-CEO/Executive Director, living and working on Wurundjeri Land, having grown up in Gulidjan Land. Jes' work has been published by Affirm Press, Fremantle Press, Black Inc, Pantera Press, SBS Australia, *Archer Magazine, Junkee, Voiceworks, Kill Your Darlings* and *The Big Issue.* More of his writing is scattered around both digitally and in print. Jes is currently represented by Alex Adsett Literary Agency. You can find her online @AGeekWithAHat.

Patrick Marlborough is a neurodivergent nonbinary writer, comedian, journalist, critic and musician based in Walyalup (Fremantle), Whadjuk Boodja. They have been published in *VICE*, *Rolling Stone*, *The Guardian*, *The Saturday Paper*, *Junkee*, *Noisey*, *Meanjin*, *Overland*, *Crikey*, *The Lifted Brow*, *Cordite*, *Going Down Swinging*, *The Betoota Advocate*, and *beloved other*. They have lived their whole life in Fremantle and spend their days arguing with their incredibly naughty dog, Buckley.

Thuy On is the Reviews Editor at online publication *ArtsHub*, and an arts journalist, critic, editor and poet. She has two collections of poems published, both by the University of Western Australia Press – *Turbulence* (2020) and *Decadence* (2022). Her third, *Essence*, will be published in 2025.

Adam Ouston is a writer and bookseller living in nipaluna/Hobart. His debut novel, *Waypoints* (2022), was nominated for the Miles Franklin Literary Award, ALS Gold Medal, and Tasmanian Premier's Literary Award.

Alice Pung OAM is the current Artist-in-Residence at Janet Clarke Hall, the University of Melbourne, and Adjunct Professor at RMIT University's School of Media and Communication. She is the author of the bestselling memoirs *Unpolished Gem* and *Her Father's Daughter*, and the editor of the anthology *Growing Up Asian in Australia*. Her novel *Laurinda* won the Ethel Turner Prize at the 2016 NSW Premier's Literary Awards, and *One Hundred Days* was shortlisted for the 2022 Miles Franklin Award. In 2022, Alice was awarded an Order of Australia Medal for services to literature.

Angela Savage is an award-winning writer and CEO of Public Libraries Victoria. Angela's short stories have been published in Australia and the UK and she won the 2011 Scarlet Stiletto Award for short crime fiction. Her most recent novel is *Mother of Pearl*. She was a contributor to *Minds Went*

Walking: Paul Kelly's Songs Reimagined and commissioning editor, with Kirsten Krauth, for *Spinning Around: The Kylie Playlist*. Like Kylie, Angela holds a PhD, giving her the Bond villain-like name of Doctor Savage.

Holden Sheppard is an award-winning West Australian author whose debut coming-of-age novel *Invisible Boys* won the WA Premier's Prize for an Emerging Writer and the City of Fremantle Hungerford Award. The book has now been adapted as a television series with Stan Australia. Holden's second novel, *The Brink*, won the Young Adult category award at the Indie Book Awards and was shortlisted in the NSW Premier's Literary Awards. Holden's writing has been widely published in books, journals, anthologies and in the media. He lives in Perth's far north, with his husband and his V8 ute.

Miriam Sved is the author of two novels: *Game Day* and *A Universe of Sufficient Size*, which was shortlisted for the Colin Roderick Award. Her novella 'All the Things I Should've Given' was a winner of *Griffith Review's* Novella Project, and her short fiction has been widely published. She is also a co-editor of three feminist anthologies, including *#MeToo: Stories from the Australian Movement*. She lives in Melbourne with her wife and daughter and two dogs and doesn't go out dancing much anymore.

Andrea Thompson is a writer, music journalist and artist manager. She is the author of *Geraldine*, a novel that charts the ordinary life of an ordinary woman or the extraordinary life of an extraordinary woman, depending on your perspective. She also is a contributor to the anthology *Women of a Certain Courage*. As well as a writer and arts worker, Andrea is a thorn-in-the-side activist, making herself equally unpopular with governments and LGBTQIA+ advocacy organisations by challenging their respective prejudice and timidity. The secret police dossier on her activities grows thicker by the day.

Carrie Tiffany was born in West Yorkshire and grew up in Western Australia. She spent her early twenties working as a park ranger in Central Australia and now lives in Melbourne. She is the author of three novels: *Everyman's Rules for Scientific Living*, *Mateship with Birds*; and *Exploded View*. All her novels have been shortlisted for the Miles Franklin Literary Award. She has also been shortlisted for the Orange Prize for Fiction (UK), the Commonwealth Writer's Prize, the Guardian First Book Award (UK), and the Prime Minister's Prize for Fiction, and was the winner of the 2013 inaugural Stella Prize.

Lucy Treloar is the author of *Salt Creek*, which won the 2016 Dobbie Award, and was shortlisted for the Miles Franklin Literary Award and the UK's Walter Scott Prize. Lucy's second novel, *Wolfe Island*, won the 2020 Barbara Jefferis Award and was shortlisted for the Prime Minister's Literary Award and the Christina Stead Prize. *Days of Innocence and Wonder*, her most recent novel, was published in 2023. She is a previous winner of the Commonwealth Short Story Prize (Pacific region). Her essays and short stories have appeared in *The Saturday Paper*, *Meanjin* and *Best Australian Stories*, among others. A graduate of the University of Melbourne and RMIT, Lucy lives with her family in inner Melbourne, and is often found pottering in the garden or walking her whippets or writing in a darkened room.

Christos Tsiolkas is the author of the novels *Loaded*, *The Jesus Man*, *Dead Europe*, *The Slap*, *Barracuda*, *Damascus*, *7 ½* and *The In-Between*. He co-authored the dialogue *Jump Cuts: An Autobiography with Sasha Soldatow*, and has published a collection of short stories, *Merciless Gods*. Many of his stories have been adapted for the stage and screen. He has written a monograph on Fred Schepsi's *The Devil's Playground* for the Australian Screen Classics series, and the monograph *On Patrick White* for the Writers on Writers series. He is also a playwright and screenwriter, and is a film reviewer for *The Saturday Paper*. He is one third of *Superfluity*, on

Melbourne community radio station 3RRR, alongside Clem Bastow and Casey Bennetto. Playing music with friends is his happy place.

Ellen van Neerven is an award-winning author of poetry titles *Comfort Food* and *Throat*, and a novel in stories: *Heat and Light*. Their most recent title is *Personal Score: Sport, Culture, Identity*. Ellen belongs to the Mununjali people of the Yugambeh Nation.

Emma Viskic is the author of the critically acclaimed Caleb Zelic series. Her debut novel, *Resurrection Bay*, won the Ned Kelly Award for Best Debut and an unprecedented three Davitt Awards. It was shortlisted for the UK's prestigious Gold Dagger and New Blood Awards, and was voted one of the decade's best novels by *Crime Time*. The sequels garnered a further two Davitt Awards and nominations for international prizes including the Dublin Literary Award and the USA's Barry Award. Emma's fourth novel, *Those Who Perish*, was recently shortlisted for the Ned Kelly Award for Best Novel. Emma lives in Naarm (Melbourne) and is working on a novel inspired by her family's brush with a violent episode in Australia's history.

Jessica White is the author of the award-winning novels *A Curious Intimacy* and *Entitlement*, and a hybrid memoir about deafness, *Hearing Maud*, which won the 2020 Michael Crouch Award for a debut work of biography and was shortlisted for four national awards, including the Prime Minister's Literary Award for Non-fiction. Jessica has received funding from the Australia Research Council, the Australia Council for the Arts, Arts Queensland and Arts South Australia, and has undertaken national and international residencies and fellowships. She is currently a Senior Lecturer in Creative Writing and Literature at the University of South Australia.

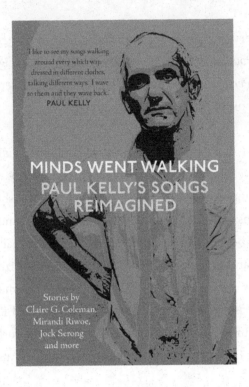

FROM FREMANTLE PRESS

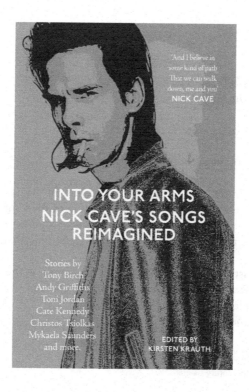

From an automaton of Nick Cave, to a man who can't keep his blood out of the food he is preparing; from a vengeful Uber driver to a spinner of souls; and from a boy caught up in a robbery to a girl desperate to save a failing greyhound, the characters who populate this short story collection have all been inspired by a Nick Cave lyric. These twenty-one stories, from some of Australia's favourite creators, respond to Cave's visionary genius with their own original and unsettling tales of death, faith, violence and love.

'A collection to take your time with, immerse yourself in. It's a book filled with unique styles.' *Rowan's Reviews, Good Reads*

AND ALL GOOD BOOKSTORES

First published 2024 by
FREMANTLE PRESS

Fremantle Press Inc. trading as Fremantle Press
PO Box 158, North Fremantle, Western Australia, 6159
fremantlepress.com.au

Cover image 'Australian singer Kylie Minogue performs at the Brit
Awards in London, 2002-02-20', bridemanimages.com
Designed by Nada Backovic, nadabackovic.com
Printed and bound by IPG

A catalogue record for this
book is available from the
National Library of Australia

ISBN 9781760993238 (paperback)
ISBN 9781760993245 (ebook)

Department of
**Local Government, Sport
and Cultural Industries**

Fremantle Press is supported by the State Government through the
Department of Local Government, Sport and Cultural Industries.

Fremantle Press respectfully acknowledges the Whadjuk people of
the Noongar nation as the Traditional Owners and Custodians of the
land where we work in Walyalup.